MODERN JEWISH STORIES

MODERN JEWISH STORIES

edited by
GERDA CHARLES

PRENTICE-HALL, INC.,
ENGLEWOOD CLIFFS, N.J.

Second printing . . . . . . March, 1966

First American Edition, 1965

Library of Congress Catalog Card Number: 65-22196
T 59502

PRENTICE-HALL INTERNATIONAL, INC., *London*
PRENTICE-HALL OF AUSTRALIA, PTY., LTD., *Sydney*
PRENTICE-HALL OF CANADA, LTD., *Toronto*
PRENTICE-HALL OF INDIA (PRIVATE) LTD., *New Delhi*
PRENTICE-HALL OF JAPAN, INC., *Tokyo*

Contents

Introduction

The first short stories ever written were of course Jewish short stories. Joseph's encounter with Potiphar's wife is a short story. *The Book of Ruth* is a long short story; so is *Esther*. And as we come down through the centuries we find that the Jewish way of Talmudic teaching always used the short story as a method of instruction. The earlier Jewish sages may have employed it with a feeling that they were sugaring the pill, the hard core of what they wished to impart, by doing so. But with their usual good sense and marvellous understanding of human psychology, they did it. Since "art" was only to be employed as an aid to holiness, they used stories "to teach" (the necessary moral sanction is typically Jewish) and they went on using them though their attitude was a slightly condescending one. Apart from the moral stance, the Jewish mind in essence was never, in the remoter past, really in accord with the creative faculty. Philosophical, exegetical, it was constructive of laws rather than fancies.

This being so, when the "baba buch" and the "maase buch", two enormously popular collections of tales, were published in the 16th century they were printed not in Hebrew, the language of education and culture, but in Yiddish, the "kitchen language" used mostly by women who—then as now—preferred a good story to a philosophical essay. The rather charming irony about this state of affairs is that it was partly through the popularity of these stories with women that the Yiddish language was preserved and lived to be used in the creation of one of our greatest literary glories, the 19th-century golden age of Yiddish writing when Mendele Moshe, Peretz, Sholom Aleichem and others produced their great, classic works.

Modern Jewish readers, caught up like everybody else in the cold, sterile complexities of contemporary life, tend to create a kind of Merrie England myth about these authors and their period. The lives they portrayed in the little *shtetls* (small towns or villages) of Russia, Poland, Lithuania, however narrow, perilous, constantly menaced as we know them to have been, are now looked back on as dreams of pastoral simplicity and warmth—though stranded, unlike other peasant societies, always with an adoration for learning. So that when we read these stories today something in us responds with passionate nostalgia to this vision of ourselves and we long for it to be true of us even now. When Sholom Aleichem, for instance, says: "Look at these boys who haven't got a pair of trousers to their name and still they want to study. Ask them: 'What are you studying? Why are you studying?' They can't tell you. It's their nature . . ."—when he says this, though we know very well that study for its own sake is no longer a salient feature of our Jewish lives yet we long to believe it is so.

Yet Sholom Aleichem and his peers were they alive today would not be so sentimental. Their stories were very often tough, bitter in flavour, self-torturing and questioning. These terms apply also, though perhaps more mildly, to the stories of the Anglo-Jew, Israel Zangwill, the first and still perhaps the greatest writer on Jewish themes we have yet seen in Britain. Zangwill was not a romantic writer either but a poetic realist, compassionate but clear-eyed.

Although Yiddish writers, some of them very good, were continuing to pour out, simultaneously with and after Zangwill, stories of Jewish life during the 19th and the first half of this century, not much else in this field was being done in either Europe or America. Jewish creative writers there were of course in numbers; but their connection with Jewish life was on the whole minimal. They did not, generally speaking, even begin to approach the huge, almost virgin territory of middle- or lower-class Jewish Diaspora experience for their material. In Britain only a few of our writers dabbled about on the fringes. In the United States the position was slightly better, but even there the interest wasn't all that great. *Curiosity* was missing. And so—more importantly—was love. The raw, blatant life of the immigrant masses was so horrifying—and worse, constricting—to live that the Jewish artist's first thought on lifting his head was to escape from it.

What has come to be known as "the breakthrough" into the position as it is today, where we have a large group—increasing every day—of magnificently gifted Jewish writers all engaged in presenting with wonderful variety the contemporary Jewish scene, has come about for a number of reasons. Popular explanations range from the felt impact of the Nazi horror, forcing upon the creative imaginations of our writers a re-thinking of their Jewish positions . . . to the prideful creation of the State of Israel and a strengthening patriotism; from the fact that Western civilisation has now become so urban and industrialised that it suits and feeds the natural Jewish bent to the fact that most of our younger writers are now two or three generations removed from the old, forcibly transplanted stock and so feel rooted enough to flower. But whatever the ultimate cause, stories by Jewish writers *with Jewish content* have at last leaped the barriers which for so long separated them both from the non-Jewish reading world and from "literature".

"With Jewish content." This is the criterion (together with contemporaneity—roughly what has been made accessible over the last thirty years) which I have borne in mind throughout while making my selection for this volume. And it is a measure

of how far we have advanced in this sphere that had I attempted even twenty years ago to apply the same rule I would have been obliged—so far as Western experience is concerned—to break it since not enough stories of quality would have been available. Today there is so much choice that my chief anxiety has been over certain unavoidable injustices of exclusion. Many superb writers whom I should like to have seen represented here have, for one reason or another, had to be left out.

One of the most difficult of the many problems of choice which I had to face was how to prevent the Americans from overweighting the whole book. For, though the position has vastly improved, it must be said that the creatively gifted European Jews are still not turning with anything like the power and originality of the Americans to either the present or the immediate past of their racial experience. The contribution—though I have searched far and wide—from Central and Eastern Europe is, with the exception of Babel, not great; or, if great, remains largely untranslated and extremely difficult to get at. The German-writing authors seem to be—understandably and for the historical reasons we all know—almost silent. What we call *churban* literature, that is, the literature of the holocaust, though it has produced one or two very fine novels, does not seem as yet to have forced out from our writers a large body of short stories of comparable power. In general, outside Israel (where some very remarkable short stories are being written) the great, splendid achievement is with the English-speaking countries: England, the Commonwealth and, above all, America.

In Britain the last few years have seen an unprecedented rise in the number and quality of Anglo-Jewish creative writers. The group is still not a very large one comparatively speaking. No genius has yet appeared; or if he has we remain unastounded. But there is undeniable ferment, talent, work going on at a great pace . . . though the best of it is perhaps going into the drama and the novel rather than the short story. While a number of promising Jewish Canadian writers have lately appeared on the scene the palm among the overseas, English-speaking countries must in this connection go to the South Africans, whose work I find particularly attractive; strong, delicate, full of feeling and luminously truthful.

A strong delicacy of feeling is perhaps the nearest one can get to defining in a phrase the particular "Jewishness" of Jewish writing. It is inadequate, but then so is every other attempt I have ever come across. There is also, it has been suggested, a "particular rhythm"; or a recognisable "angle of vision". But whatever it is, certain components can always be felt to be there. The first is a kind of courtesy towards, a respect for, suffering. The second is a regard for "good". We still, in spite of everything that has happened to us, believe in it. There is therefore nearly always to be found the third quality of optimism—again in spite of everything. And this in turn gives rise to our fourth and perhaps most easily noticeable characteristic of all: humour.

The humorous story is something at which our writers have always excelled. I have singled out for this collection one of the marvellous Hyman Kaplan stories, but there are many others. Another element, very often running side by side with comedy, is fantasy; seen at some of its contemporary best in the beautiful, sadly-comic, heart-rending stories of Bernard Malamud and Isaac Bashevis Singer. And yet another is the struggle, sometimes cruel and powerful as in the remarkable work of Isaac Babel, between aesthetics and morality. What endows Babel with his enormous, present-day meaning is his attempted flight from moral purpose to beauty. But this is the kind of escape—or contest—which in the Jewish soul cannot be allowed since it is against not our will but our destiny. What, in the end, gives even Babel his strength is the struggle of his characters with their individual acts. Like all Jewish writers, Babel is ultimately concerned with the *personal.* This is a very important element in us. We hardly ever make great, vague, fancy statements of the "Man is . . . such and such", or "Man must . . .

this or that" kind. Jewish stories are always about the *particular;* the absurdities, the trials, the humiliations, the decisions, the sometimes wretched expediencies we must all face in day-to-day living.

Again, we do not glorify war. Even in the story I have included by Yizhar dealing with the recent Israeli war, the tone is humanistic, anti-heroic. In general the Jewish temper is sweet rather than militant. There has always been in us a certain contempt for the military mind, a questioning of "heroic" values. Far, far more important to us than any battlefield is the home; though battles rage there too! Jewish family life is compounded equally of warmly protective love and a bitten-in obstinacy which almost if never quite wrecks it.

But perhaps the most important of all the qualities to be found in our best contemporary writers is one which I might define as a kind of tender sophistication. It is an emphasis on feeling . . . but feeling rendered with high intelligence. It is not sentimental, not in any way flamboyant. It is quiet, it is sober . . . but it is at the same time complex and subtle, radiant with imaginative sympathy and—above all—forgiving. There is, in the greatest Jewish short stories, a kind of wise, patient, accepting forgiveness for all our faults. And with it goes equally an unashamed emphasis on the necessity of goodness.

To finish with a word more of explanation about the selection. . . . The criticism may well be levelled that some of these stories are already well-known and that I should have tried to break new ground. This, as I have already indicated, I attempted but with little result. And since famous stories are on the whole famous *because* they are so good, to exclude excellence from what is meant to be a representative, modern collection on the grounds that we have met it before seemed to me not sensible.

Finally, may I say that I include a story of my own only because of a firm request from my publishers that I do so.

Gerda Charles

The Conversion of the Jews

PHILIP ROTH

Philip Roth was born in New Jersey in 1933. He received his education at Bucknell University and the University of Chicago. In 1960 his collection of short fiction, *Goodbye Columbus,* won the National Book Award. He has contributed to many periodicals, including *The New Yorker, Esquire* and *Paris Review*. His novel, *Letting Go,* won much critical acclaim. Roth has been awarded many prizes, among them the Houghton Mifflin Literary Fellowship, a Guggenheim Grant, the Aga Khan Prize for Fiction and the Daroff Award of the Jewish Book Council of America. He is married and lives in New York City.

"You're a real one for opening your mouth in the first place," Itzie said. "What do you open your mouth all the time for?"

"I didn't bring it up, Itz, I didn't," Ozzie said.

"What do you care about Jesus Christ for anyway?"

"I didn't bring up Jesus Christ. He did. I didn't even know what he was talking about. Jesus is historical, he kept saying. Jesus is historical." Ozzie mimicked the monumental voice of Rabbi Binder.

"Jesus was a person that lived like you and me," Ozzie continued. "That's what Binder said——"

"Yeah? . . . So what! What do I give two cents whether he lived or not. And what do you gotta open your mouth!" Itzie Lieberman favoured closed-mouthedness, especially when it came to Ozzie Freedman's questions. Mrs. Freedman had to see Rabbi Binder twice before about Ozzie's questions and this Wednesday at four-thirty would be the third time. Itzie preferred to keep *his* mother in the kitchen; he settled for behind-the-back subtleties such as gestures, faces, snarls and other less delicate barnyard noises.

"He was a real person, Jesus, but he wasn't like God, and we don't believe he is God." Slowly, Ozzie was explaining Rabbi Binder's position to Itzie, who had been absent from Hebrew School the previous afternoon.

"The Catholics," Itzie said helpfully, "they believe in Jesus Christ, that he's God." Itzie Lieberman used "the Catholics" in its broadest sense—to include the Protestants.

Ozzie received Itzie's remark with a tiny head bob, as though it were a footnote, and went on. "His mother was Mary, and his father probably was Joseph," Ozzie said. "But the New Testament says his real father was God."

"His *real* father?"

"Yeah," Ozzie said, "that's the big thing, his father's supposed to be God."

"Bull."

"That's what Rabbi Binder says, that it's impossible——"

"Sure it's impossible. That stuff's all bull. To have a baby you gotta get laid," Itzie theologized. "Mary hadda get laid."

"That's what Binder says: 'The only way a woman can have a baby is to have intercourse with a man.' "

"He said *that*, Ozz?" For a moment it appeared that Itzie had put the theological question aside. "He said that, intercourse?" A little curled smile shaped itself in the lower half of Itzie's face like a pink moustache. "What you guys do, Ozz, you laugh or something?"

"I raised my hand."

"Yeah? Whatja say?"

"That's when I asked the question."

Itzie's face lit up. "Whatja ask about—intercourse?"

"No, I asked the question about God, how if He could create the heaven and earth in six days, and make all the animals and the fish, and the light in six days—the light especially, that's what always gets me, that He could make the light. Making fish and animals, that's pretty good——"

"That's damn good." Itzie's appreciation was honest but unimaginative: it was as though God had just pitched a one-hitter.

"But making light . . . I mean when you think about it, it's really something," Ozzie said. "Anyway, I asked Binder if He could make all that in six days, and He could *pick* the six days he wanted right out of nowhere, why couldn't He let a woman have a baby without having intercourse."

"You said intercourse, Ozz, to Binder?"

"Yeah."

"Right in class?"

"Yeah."

Itzie smacked the side of his head.

"I mean, no kidding around," Ozzie said, "that'd really be nothing. After all that other stuff, that'd practically be nothing."

Itzie considered a moment. "What'd Binder say?"

"He started all over again explaining how Jesus was historical and how he lived like you and me but he wasn't God. So I said I under*stood* that. What I wanted to know was different."

What Ozzie wanted to know was always different. The first time he had wanted to know how Rabbi Binder could call the Jews "The Chosen People" if the Declaration of Independence claimed all men to be created equal. Rabbi Binder tried to distinguish for him between political equality and spiritual legitimacy, but what Ozzie wanted to know, he insisted vehemently, was different. That was the first time his mother had to come.

Then there was the plane crash. Fifty-eight people had been killed in a plane crash at La Guardia. In studying a casualty list in the newspaper his mother had discovered among the list of those dead eight Jewish names (his grandmother had nine but she counted Miller as a Jewish name); because of the eight she said the plane crash was "a tragedy." During free-discussion time on Wednesday Ozzie had brought to Rabbi Binder's attention this matter of "some of his relations" always picking out the Jewish names. Rabbi Binder had begun to explain cultural unity and some other things when Ozzie stood up at his seat and said that what he wanted to know was different. Rabbi Binder insisted that he sit down and it was then that Ozzie shouted that he wished all fifty-eight were Jews. That was the second time his mother came.

"And he kept explaining about Jesus being historical, and so I kept asking him. No kidding, Itz, he was trying to make me look stupid."

"So what he finally do?"

"Finally he starts screaming that I was deliberately simple-minded and a wise guy, and that my mother had to come, and this was the last time. And that I'd never get bar-mitzvahed if he could help it. Then, Itz, then he starts talking in that voice like a statue, real slow and deep, and he says that I better think over what I said about the Lord. He told me to go to his office and think it over." Ozzie leaned his body towards Itzie. "Itz, I thought it over for a solid hour, and now I'm convinced God could do it."

Ozzie had planned to confess his latest transgression to his mother as soon as she came home from work. But it was a Friday night in November and already dark, and when Mrs. Freedman came through the door she tossed off her coat, kissed Ozzie quickly on the face, and went to the kitchen table to light the three yellow candles, two for the Sabbath and one for Ozzie's father.

When his mother lit the candles she would move her two arms slowly towards her, dragging them through the air, as though persuading people whose minds were half made up. And her eyes would get glassy with tears. Even when his father was alive Ozzie remembered that her eyes had gotten glassy, so it didn't have anything to do with his dying. It had something to do with lighting the candles.

As she touched the flaming match to the unlit wick of a Sabbath candle, the phone rang, and Ozzie, standing only a foot from it, plucked it off the receiver and held it muffled to his chest. When his mother lit candles Ozzie felt there should be no noise; even breathing, if you could manage it, should be softened. Ozzie pressed the phone to his breast and watched his mother dragging whatever she was dragging, and he felt his own eyes get glassy. His mother was a round, tired, grey-haired penguin of a woman whose grey skin had begun to feel the tug of gravity and the weight of her own history. Even when she was dressed up she didn't look like a chosen person. But when she lit candles she looked like something better; like a woman who knew momentarily that God could do anything.

After a few mysterious minutes she was finished. Ozzie hung up the phone and walked to the kitchen table where she was beginning to lay the two places for the four-course Sabbath meal. He told her that she would have to see Rabbi Binder next Wednesday at four-thirty, and then he told her why. For the first time in their life together she hit Ozzie across the face with her hand.

All through the chopped liver and chicken soup part of the dinner Ozzie cried; he didn't have any appetite for the rest.

On Wednesday, in the largest of the three basement classrooms of the synagogue, Rabbi Marvin Binder, a tall, handsome, broad-shouldered man of thirty with thick strong-fibred black hair, removed his watch from his pocket and saw that it was four o'clock. At the rear of the room Yakov Blotnik, the seventy-one-year-old custodian, slowly polished the large window, mumbling to himself, unaware that it was four o'clock or six o'clock, Monday or Wednesday. To most of the students Yakov Blotnik's mumbling, along with his brown curly beard, scythe nose, and two heel-trailing black cats, made of him an object of wonder, a foreigner, a relic, towards whom they were alternately fearful and disrespectful. To Ozzie the mumbling had always seemed a monotonous, curious prayer; what made it curious was that old Blotnik had been mumbling so steadily for so many years, Ozzie suspected he had memorized the prayers and forgotten all about God.

"It is now free-discussion time," Rabbi Binder said. "Feel free to talk about any Jewish matter at all—religion, family, politics, sports——"

There was silence. It was a gusty, clouded November afternoon and it did not seem as though there ever was or could be a thing called baseball. So nobody this week said a word about that hero from the past, Hank Greenberg—which limited free discussion considerably.

And the soul-battering Ozzie Freedman had just received from Rabbi Binder had imposed its limitation. When it was Ozzie's turn to read aloud from the Hebrew book the rabbi had asked him petulantly why he didn't read more rapidly. He was showing no progress. Ozzie said he could read faster but that if he did he was sure not to understand what he was reading. Nevertheless, at the rabbi's repeated suggestion Ozzie tried, and showed a great talent, but in the midst of a long passage he stopped short and said he didn't understand a word he was reading, and started in again at a drag-footed pace. Then came the soul-battering.

Consequently when free-discussion time rolled around none of the students felt too free. The rabbi's invitation was answered only by the mumbling of feeble old Blotnik.

"Isn't there anything at all you would like to discuss?" Rabbi Binder asked again, looking at his watch. "No questions or comments?"

There was a small grumble from the third row. The rabbi requested that Ozzie rise and give the rest of the class the advantage of his thought.

Ozzie rose. "I forget it now," he said, and sat down in his place.

Rabbi Binder advanced a seat towards Ozzie and poised himself on the edge of the desk. It was Itzie's desk and the rabbi's frame only a dagger's-length away from his face snapped him to sitting attention.

"Stand up again, Oscar," Rabbi Binder said calmly, "and try to assemble your thoughts."

Ozzie stood up. All his classmates turned in their seats and watched as he gave an unconvincing scratch to his forehead.

"I can't assemble any," he announced, and plunked himself down.

"Stand up!" Rabbi Binder advanced from Itzie's desk to the one directly in front of Ozzie; when the rabbinical back was turned Itzie gave it five-fingers off the tip of his nose, causing a small titter in the room. Rabbi Binder was too absorbed in squelching Ozzie's nonsense once and for all to bother with titters. "Stand up, Oscar. What's your question about?"

Ozzie pulled a word out of the air. It was the handiest word. "Religion."

"Oh, now you remember?"

"Yes."

"What is it?"

Trapped, Ozzie blurted the first thing that came to him. "Why can't He make anything He wants to make!"

As Rabbi Binder prepared an answer, a final answer, Itzie, ten feet behind him, raised one finger on his left hand, gestured it meaningfully towards the rabbi's back, and brought the house down.

Binder twisted quickly to see what had happened and in the midst of the commotion Ozzie shouted into the rabbi's back what he couldn't have shouted to his face. It was a loud, toneless sound that had the timbre of something stored inside for about six days.

"You don't know! You don't know anything about God!"

The rabbi spun back towards Ozzie. "What?"

"You don't know—you don't——"

"Apologize, Oscar, apologize!" It was a threat.

"You don't——"

Rabbi Binder's hand flicked out at Ozzie's cheek. Perhaps it had only been meant to clamp the boy's mouth shut, but Ozzie ducked and the palm caught him squarely on the nose.

The blood came in a short, red spurt on to Ozzie's shirt front.

The next moment was all confusion. Ozzie screamed, "You

bastard, you bastard!" and broke for the classroom door. Rabbi Binder lurched a step backwards, as though his own blood had started flowing violently in the opposite direction, then gave a clumsy lurch forward and bolted out of the door after Ozzie. The class followed after the rabbi's huge blue-suited back, and before old Blotnik could turn from his window, the room was empty and everyone was headed full speed up the three flights leading to the roof.

If one should compare the light of day to the life of man: sunrise to birth; sunset—the dropping down over the edge—to death; then as Ozzie Freedman wiggled through the trapdoor of the synagogue roof, his feet kicking backwards bronco-style at Rabbi Binder's outstretched arms—at that moment the day was fifty years old. As a rule, fifty or fifty-five reflects accurately the age of late afternoons in November, for it is in that month, during those hours, that one's awareness of light seems no longer a matter of seeing, but of hearing: light begins clicking away. In fact, as Ozzie locked shut the trapdoor in the rabbi's face, the sharp click of the bolt into the lock might momentarily have been mistaken for the sound of the heavier grey that had just throbbed through the sky.

With all his weight Ozzie kneeled on the locked door; any instant he was certain that Rabbi Binder's shoulder would fling it open, splintering the wood into shrapnel and catapulting his body into the sky. But the door did not move and below him he heard only the rumble of feet, first loud then dim, like thunder rolling away.

A question shot through his brain. "Can this be *me?*" For a thirteen-year-old who had just labelled his religious leader a bastard, twice, it was not an improper question. Louder and louder the question came to him—"Is it me? Is it me?"—until he discovered himself no longer kneeling, but racing crazily towards the edge of the roof, his eyes crying, his throat screaming, and his arms flying every which way as though not his own.

"Is it me? Is it me Me ME ME ME? It has to be me—but is it?"

It is the question a thief must ask himself the night he jimmies open his first window, and it is said to be the question with which bridegrooms quiz themselves before the altar.

In the few wild seconds it took Ozzie's body to propel him to the edge of the roof, his self-examination began to grow fuzzy. Gazing down at the street, he became confused as to the problem beneath the question: was it, is-it-me-who-called-Binder-a-bastard? or, is-it-me-prancing-around-on-the-roof? However, the scene below settled all, for there is an instant in any action when whether it is you or somebody else is academic. The thief crams the money in his pockets and scoots out the window. The bridegroom signs the hotel register for two. And the boy on the roof finds a streetful of people gaping at him, necks stretched backwards, faces up, as though he were the ceiling of the Hayden Planetarium. Suddenly you know it's you.

"Oscar! Oscar Freedman!" A voice rose from the centre of the crowd, a voice that, could it have been seen, would have looked like the writing on scroll. "Oscar Freedman, get down from there. Immediately!" Rabbi Binder was pointing one arm stiffly up at him; and at the end of that arm, one finger aimed menacingly. It was the attitude of a dictator, but one—the eyes confessed all—whose personal valet had spat neatly in his face.

Ozzie didn't answer. Only for a blink's length did he look towards Rabbi Binder. Instead his eyes began to fit together the world beneath him, to sort out people from places, friends from enemies, participants from spectators. In little jagged starlike clusters, his friends stood around Rabbi Binder, who was still pointing. The topmost point on a star compounded not of angels but of five adolescent boys was Itzie. What a world it was, with those stars below, Rabbi Binder below . . . Ozzie, who a moment earlier hadn't been able to control his own body, started to feel the meaning of the word control: he felt Peace and he felt Power.

"Oscar Freedman, I'll give you three to come down."

Few dictators give their subjects three to do anything; but, as always, Rabbi Binder only looked dictatorial.

"Are you ready, Oscar?"

Ozzie nodded his head yes, although he had no intention in the world—the lower one or the celestial one he'd just entered—of coming down even if Rabbi Binder should give him a million.

"All right then," said Rabbi Binder. He ran a hand through his black Samson hair as though it were the gesture prescribed for uttering the first digit. Then, with his other hand cutting a circle out of the small piece of sky around him, he spoke. "One!"

There was no thunder. On the contrary, at that moment, as though "one" was the cue for which he had been waiting, the world's least thunderous person appeared on the synagogue steps. He did not so much come out the synagogue door as lean out, onto the darkening air. He clutched at the doorknob with one hand and looked up at the roof.

"Oy!"

Yakov Blotnik's old mind hobbled slowly, as if on crutches, and though he couldn't decide precisely what the boy was doing on the roof, he knew it wasn't good—that is, it wasn't-good-for-the-Jews. For Yakov Blotnik life had fractionated itself simply: things were either good-for-the-Jews or no-good-for-the-Jews.

He smacked his free hand to his in-sucked cheek, gently. "Oy, Gut!" And then quickly as he was able, he jacked down his head and surveyed the street. There was Rabbi Binder (like a man at an auction with only three dollars in his pocket, he had just delivered a shaky "Two!"); there were the students, and that was all. So far it wasn't-so-bad-for-the-Jews. But the boy had to come down immediately, before anybody saw. The problem: how to get the boy off the roof?

Anybody who has ever had a cat on the roof knows how to get him down. You call the fire department. Or first you call the operator and you ask her for the fire department. And the next thing there is great jamming of brakes and clanging of bells and shouting of instructions. And then the cat is off the roof. You do the same thing to get a boy off the roof.

That is, you do the same thing if you are Yakov Blotnik and you once had a cat on the roof.

When the engines, all four of them, arrived, Rabbi Binder had four times given Ozzie the count of three. The big hook-and-ladder swung around the corner and one of the firemen leaped from it, plunging headlong towards the yellow fire hydrant in front of the synagogue. With a huge wrench he began to unscrew the top nozzle. Rabbi Binder raced over to him and pulled at his shoulder.

"There's no fire . . ."

The fireman mumbled back over his shoulder and, heatedly, continued working at the nozzle.

"But there's no fire, there's no fire . . ." Binder shouted. When the fireman mumbled again, the rabbi grasped his face with both his hands and pointed it up at the roof.

To Ozzie it looked as though Rabbi Binder was trying to tug the fireman's head out of his body, like a cork from a bottle. He had to giggle at the picture they made: it was a family portrait—rabbi in black skullcap, fireman in red fire hat, and the little yellow hydrant squatting beside like a kid brother, bareheaded. From the edge of the roof Ozzie waved at the portrait, a one-handed, flapping, mocking wave; in doing it his right foot slipped from under him. Rabbi Binder covered his eyes with his hands.

Firemen work fast. Before Ozzie had even regained his balance, a big round, yellowed net was being held on the synagogue lawn. The firemen who held it looked up at Ozzie with stern, feelingless faces.

One of the firemen turned his head towards Rabbi Binder. "What, is the kid nuts or something?"

Rabbi Binder unpeeled his hands from his eyes, slowly,

painfully, as if they were tape. Then he checked: nothing on the sidewalk, no dents in the net.

"Is he gonna jump, or what?" the fireman shouted.

In a voice not at all like a statue, Rabbi Binder finally answered. "Yes, yes, I think so . . . He's been threatening to . . ."

Threatening to? Why, the reason he was on the roof, Ozzie remembered, was to get away; he hadn't even thought about jumping. He had just run to get away, and the truth was that he hadn't really headed for the roof as much as he'd been chased there.

"What's his name, the kid?"

"Freedman," Rabbi Binder answered. "Oscar Freedman."

The fireman looked up at Ozzie. "What is it with you, Oscar? You gonna jump, or what?"

Ozzie did not answer. Frankly, the question had just arisen.

"Look, Oscar, if you're gonna jump, jump—and if you're not gonna jump, don't jump. But don't waste our time, willya?"

Ozzie looked at the fireman and then at Rabbi Binder. He wanted to see Rabbi Binder cover his eyes one more time.

"I'm going to jump."

And then he scampered around the edge of the roof to the corner, where there was no net below, and he flapped his arms at his sides, swishing the air and smacking his palms to his trousers on the downbeat. He began screaming like some kind of engine, "Wheeeee . . . wheeeeee," and leaning way out over the edge with the upper half of his body. The firemen whipped around to cover the ground with the net. Rabbi Binder mumbled a few words to somebody and covered his eyes. Everything happened quickly, jerkily, as in a silent movie. The crowd, which had arrived with the fire engines, gave out a long, Fourth-of-July fireworks oooh-aahhh. In the excitement no one had paid the crowd much heed, except, of course, Yakov Blotnik, who swung from the doorknob counting heads. "Fier und tsvantsik . . . finf und tsvantsik . . . Oy, Gut!" It wasn't like this with the cat.

Rabbi Binder peeked through his fingers, checked the sidewalk and net. Empty. But there was Ozzie racing to the other corner. The firemen raced with him but were unable to keep up. Whenever Ozzie wanted to he might jump and splatter himself upon the sidewalk, and by the time the firemen scooted to the spot all they could do with their net would be to cover the mess.

"Wheeeee . . . wheeeee . . ."

"Hey, Oscar," the winded fireman yelled. "What the hell is this, a game or something?"

"Wheeeee . . . wheeeee . . ."

"Hey, Oscar——"

But he was off now to the other corner, flapping his wings fiercely. Rabbi Binder couldn't take it any longer—the fire engines from nowhere, the screaming suicidal boy, the net. He fell to his knees, exhausted, and with his hands curled together in front of his chest like a little dome, he pleaded, "Oscar, stop it, Oscar. Don't jump, Oscar. Please come down . . . Please don't jump."

And further back in the crowd a single voice, a single young voice, shouted a lone word to the boy on the roof.

"Jump!"

It was Itzie. Ozzie momentarily stopped flapping.

"Go ahead, Ozz—jump!" Itzie broke off his point of the star and courageously, with the inspiration not of a wise-guy but of a disciple, stood alone. "Jump, Ozz, jump!"

Still on his knees, his hands still curled, Rabbi Binder twisted his body back. He looked at Itzie, then, agonizingly, back to Ozzie.

"OSCAR, DON'T JUMP! PLEASE, DON'T JUMP . . . please please . . ."

"Jump!" This time it wasn't Itzie but another point of the

star. By the time Mrs. Freedman arrived to keep her four-thirty appointment with Rabbi Binder, the whole little upside-down heaven was shouting and pleading for Ozzie to jump, and Rabbi Binder no longer was pleading with him not to jump, but was crying into the dome of his hands.

Understandably Mrs. Freedman couldn't figure out what her son was doing on the roof. So she asked.

"Ozzie, my Ozzie, what are you doing? My Ozzie, what is it?"

Ozzie stopped wheeeeeing and slowed his arms down to a cruising flap, the kind birds use in soft winds, but he did not answer. He stood against the low, clouded, darkening sky—light clicked down swiftly now, as on a small gear—flapping softly and gazing down at the small bundle of a woman who was his mother.

"What are you doing, Ozzie?" She turned towards the kneeling Rabbi Binder and rushed so close that only a paper-thickness of dusk lay between her stomach and his shoulders.

"What is my baby doing?"

Rabbi Binder gaped up at her but he too was mute. All that moved was the dome of his hands; it shook back and forth like a weak pulse.

"Rabbi, get him down! He'll kill himself. Get him down, my only baby . . ."

"I can't," Rabbi Binder said, "I can't . . ." and he turned his handsome head towards the crowd of boys behind him. "It's them. Listen to them."

And for the first time Mrs. Freedman saw the crowd of boys, and she heard what they were yelling.

"He's doing it for them. He won't listen to me. It's them." Rabbi Binder spoke like one in a trance.

"For them?"

"Yes."

"Why for them?"

"They want him to . . ."

Mrs. Freedman raised her two arms upward as though she were conducting the sky. "For them he's doing it!" And then in a gesture older than pyramids, older than prophets and floods, her arms came slapping down to her sides. "A martyr I have. Look!" She tilted her head to the roof. Ozzie was still flapping softly. "My martyr."

"Oscar, come down, *please,*" Rabbi Binder groaned.

In a startlingly even voice Mrs. Freedman called to the boy on the roof. "Ozzie, come down, Ozzie. Don't be a martyr, my baby."

As though it were a litany, Rabbi Binder repeated her words. "Don't be a martyr, my baby. Don't be a martyr."

"Gawhead, Ozz—*be* a Martin!" It was Itzie. "Be a Martin, be a Martin," and all the voices joined in singing for Martindom, whatever *it* was. "Be a Martin, be a Martin . . ."

Somehow when you're on a roof the darker it gets the less you can hear. All Ozzie knew was that two groups wanted two new things: his friends were spirited and musical about what they wanted; his mother and the rabbi were even-toned, chanting, about what they didn't want. The rabbi's voice was without tears now and so was his mother's.

The big net stared up at Ozzie like a sightless eye. The big, clouded sky pushed down. From beneath it looked like a grey corrugated board. Suddenly, looking up into that unsympathetic sky, Ozzie realized all the strangeness of what these people, his friends, were asking: they wanted him to jump, to kill himself; they were singing about it now—it made them that happy. And there was an even greater strangeness: Rabbi Binder was on his knees, trembling. If there was a question to be asked now it was not "Is it me?" but rather "Is it us? . . . Is it us?"

Being on the roof, it turned out, was a serious thing. If he jumped would the singing become dancing? Would it? What would jumping stop? Yearningly, Ozzie wished he could rip open the sky, plunge his hands through, and pull out the sun; and on the sun, like a coin, would be stamped JUMP or DON'T JUMP.

Ozzie's knees rocked and sagged a little under him as though they were setting him for a dive. His arms tightened, stiffened, froze, from shoulders to fingernails. He felt as if each part of his body were going to vote as to whether he should kill himself or not—and each part as though it were independent of *him.*

The light took an unexpected click down and the new darkness, like a gag, hushed the friends singing for this and the mother and rabbi chanting for that.

Ozzie stopped counting votes, and in a curiously high voice, like one who wasn't prepared for speech, he spoke.

"Mamma?"

"Yes, Oscar."

"Mamma, get down on your knees, like Rabbi Binder."

"Oscar——"

"Get down on your knees," he said, "or I'll jump."

Ozzie heard a whimper, then a quick rustling, and when he looked down where his mother had stood he saw the top of a head and beneath that a circle of dress. She was kneeling beside Rabbi Binder.

He spoke again. "Everybody kneel." There was the sound of everybody kneeling.

Ozzie looked around. With one hand he pointed towards the synagogue entrance. "Make *him* kneel."

There was a noise, not of kneeling, but of body-and-cloth stretching. Ozzie could hear Rabbi Binder saying in a gruff whisper, ". . . or he'll *kill* himself," and when next he looked there was Yakov Blotnik off the doorknob and for the first time in his life upon his knees in the Gentile posture of prayer.

As for the firemen—it is not as difficult as one might imagine to hold a net taut while you are kneeling.

Ozzie looked around again; and then he called to Rabbi Binder.

"Rabbi?"

"Yes, Oscar."

"Rabbi Binder, do you believe in God?"

"Yes."

"Do you believe God can do Anything?" Ozzie leaned his head out into the darkness. "Anything?"

"Oscar, I think——"

"Tell me you believe God can do Anything."

There was a second's hesitation. Then: "God can do Anything."

"Tell me you believe God can make a child without intercourse."

"He can."

"Tell me!"

"God," Rabbi Binder admitted, "can make a child without intercourse."

"Mamma, you tell me."

"God can make a child without intercourse," his mother said.

"Make *him* tell me." There was no doubt who *him* was.

In a few moments Ozzie heard an old comical voice say something to the increasing darkness about God.

Next, Ozzie made everybody say it. And then he made them all say they believed in Jesus Christ—first one at a time, then all together.

When the catechizing was through it was the beginning of evening. From the street it sounded as if the boy on the roof might have sighed.

"Ozzie?" A woman's voice dared to speak. "You'll come down now?"

There was no answer, but the woman waited, and when a voice finally did speak it was thin and crying, and exhausted as that of an old man who has just finished pulling the bells.

"Mamma, don't you see—you shouldn't hit me. He shouldn't hit me. You shouldn't hit me about God, Mamma. You should never hit anybody about God——"

"Ozzie, please come down now."

"Promise me, promise me you'll never hit anybody about God."

He had asked only his mother, but for some reason everyone kneeling in the street promised he would never hit anybody about God.

Once again there was silence.

"I can come down now, Mamma," the boy on the roof finally said. He turned his head both ways as though checking the traffic lights. "Now I can come down . . ."

And he did, right into the centre of the yellow net that glowed in the evening's edge like an overgrown halo.

The Judgment of Solomon

YEHUDA YAARI

Yehuda Yaari was born in Poland in 1900. He spent a portion of his youth in the United States and then in 1920 moved to Palestine. After working in a kibbutz and as a librarian, he moved on again, this time to Canada. His books include *Prisoners of Hope, When the Candle Was Burning,* as well as plays and short stories. In 1951 he was awarded the Ussishkin Prize. Yaari presently works for the Karen Hayesod and makes his home in Israel.

I

Excuse ME for bothering you. I know, you are busy, but I simply must speak . . . No! No! Please don't put me off for some other time. I have to talk about it now, otherwise my very heart will break . . . What? No! I wouldn't like to talk about it to a woman. If a woman were to hear me, all kinds of instincts would stir inside her; and where instincts are in charge there can be no fair judgment, and all the boundaries between truth and falsehood simply fade away. Can you understand me? Yes, only a man can listen to me without being biased or prejudiced . . . Oh no! I'm not asking you to pass judgment. I know that even King Solomon, the wisest of all men, would find this case a hard one. The important thing is that you should listen to me with understanding. Well then, I shall begin at the beginning. I shall try to tell it all without any unfairness. I shan't hide anything and I shan't add anything; just as though it were another woman I were talking about.

It began three years ago, in Germany, at the time of the November riots. There was terror and murder everywhere, and the flames from the burning synagogues seemed to be taking a hold of each of us. We were a small family—my husband, I myself, and the boy of five. This is his photo. This is what he looked like then, when he was five years old. A lovely boy, isn't he? . . . Anyway, by that time it was clear to us that we had to get away. It was impossible for us to stay any longer in that accursed country. Yes, you may well stare at me in astonishment. What queer people! you must be thinking to yourself. Had it been such a Paradise in Germany before that? Hadn't they realised earlier that they would have to run for it? . . . Yes, I know. But I must tell you: We were doctors, my husband and I, and when the Nazis came to power we decided we must stay on in Germany as long as possible. We felt it was our duty. Most of the Jewish physicians simply fled all over the world, and the Aryans were forbidden to treat Jewish patients. Now you know as well as I do that the entire Jewish community couldn't get away. What was to happen to them? Who was to look after them and attend to them when they were ill? We couldn't leave our suffering and tormented folk without any medical help.

Yes, it was our Jewish conscience more than anything else that told us we must stay. Of course, we didn't find it a Garden of Eden. We went through really terrible times, and if I were to tell you the whole story I would never be done. But we thought we were doing our duty, and we bore our fate courageously and proudly. Until November, 1938.

When that dreadful time came we suddenly saw how weak and helpless we were, and we forgot all our brave resolutions. The burning, the murdered, the tortured, the fear—no, it was impossible to put up any longer with it all. We had to get away! To get out of that inferno as quickly as possible! But where could we go? Of course we wanted to go to Eretz Israel—my husband and I had always been Zionists—but we couldn't go there. We were simply idiotic, we never bothered about getting a certificate while we had a chance. Now it was too late. Other countries also slammed the door in our face. We cabled to relations in America and to acquaintances in Eretz Israel, and every day that passed without a reply seemed like a year. We dashed about as if we were mad, helpless and hopeless, without the slightest idea what we should do. And the boy, the boy! We worried about him most of all. If only we could save the child! If only we could get him away while he was still innocent and undefiled.

And then, just when it seemed to us that there was no more hope, people came to us with a proposal about him. A family we knew had been lucky, and received a permit to enter Eretz Israel. They came and suggested to us that they should take our child with them. They had received a permit for three children, but were taking only two. The third had left meanwhile to train in Holland with a youth group, before going to Eretz Israel. They could add our boy's name to their passport, they said. The matter could be arranged. They were good folk, old friends, and they wanted to help us.

And so, you might say, it was a miracle right out of Heaven! But I didn't feel like that. It's interesting. As long as I never saw a ray of hope, I thought that I would send my son over to any pack of thieves or robbers, as long as I could get him out of that pestilential atmosphere. But now I had an opportunity to save him, I didn't want to. I knew I could safely and confidently entrust the child to these people, and they would look after him as though he were one of their own. But in spite of it I did not have the heart to take this step and part from him at such a time. I simply couldn't . . . Yes, it was strange. I know it. But that's what a woman's heart is like . . . What can I tell you? I wrestled bitterly with myself. I thought I would go crazy. You understand, there was shame and horror all around; and here were people who wanted to deliver my only child from all this; yet I couldn't find the strength to agree.

My husband entreated me day after day. Sometimes gently and sometimes sternly. "Look," said he. "They will soon be leaving, and I know that afterwards you'll very much regret your stupid, completely inexplicable obstinacy." Yet at heart I still prayed that the time of their departure would pass and I would be done with all this mental and spiritual suffering.

One day, though, my husband came home as pale as a ghost, trembling all over. "Listen," said he as he came in, his voice trembling. "If you don't want him to go now he'll finish by going as an orphan. Remember my words."

When I heard this I gave in at once. He stood looking at me with such frightened eyes I was sure he must have heard news outside about some approaching danger. Maybe he had heard that they were about to arrest him and send him to a concentration camp, or something like that. After all, that kind of thing was taking place every hour. So how could I keep on refusing? "All right," I said, "I agree." Before my eyes I could see all those children whose fathers had died in concentration camps, and who were then going to Eretz Israel in groups. Those of us who were sending them off used to call them "the Kaddish Aliya," because all of them had to say the Memorial Prayer for the dead. So I told myself: Yes, better have my son torn from me now, rather than have him going with sad hopeless eyes, like those Kaddish reciters whom I have seen leaving . . .

Next day my husband took the child and led him to the home of our friends, to stay with them until they left. I asked him to do it so that I could be able to part from him little by little, and not all of a sudden at a single blow. A few days still had to pass before their departure so I went to visit him every day. The first day I spent a few hours with him; the second day, only one hour; and less on the third day. And so I parted from him little by little, gradually. I don't need to tell you that when they left I didn't go to see him off at the station. How would I have been able to? How could I have stood watching the train moving off and taking my only child away from me? Particularly as I was certain I would never see him again . . . My husband went alone, while I stayed at home weeping and grieving.

In short, the child went; and as far as I know our friends kept their promise. They looked after him properly, and treated him with as much affection and devotion as though he was their own child; maybe even more. The first letter they wrote to us was filled with happiness and wonder. The sea-trip, they wrote, had been wonderful. The whole country was bathed in pleasant sunshine, and the whole atmosphere was one of freedom. Here a man could breathe deep, here he could feel at home. Above all, the children were healthy and happy. You can imagine how glad we were, my husband and I, when we read that letter. The miracle had happened, and the child had been saved.

II

But the letters which followed were written in a mood of depression and bitterness. The good sun, the air of liberty, and the sense of being at home were not even mentioned. Instead came rain that pierced to the very bones, the feeling that they were strangers, and worries about tomorrow. They had already been so long in the country, yet they had not been able to buy a proper home or find a source of income. They were full of complaints and dissatisfaction. You know, just the kind of letters usually written by greenhorns of that type who have not yet settled down in the country, or grown used to its conditions. In spite of that, they wrote, there was nothing to worry about. They would make every effort possible to provide for the children at least, to provide for their board and enable them to get their schooling. And naturally whatever they did for their children they would do for ours. So there was nothing to worry about.

Time passed. We got another letter from them in which they joyfully told us that at last they had succeeded in making arrangements for the children. Now they were on their own—halutzim, and as befitted pioneers they were going off that week to look for a place where they could live and work, in one of the villages of Sharon or Galilee. And what arrangements had they made for their children? They had sent the children to an educational institution in the Emek for children from Germany. But our boy they had entrusted to a certain very-well-thought-of woman in Jerusalem. This was a Mrs. G.—please excuse me, if I don't tell you her name—who was well known for her generosity and high-mindedness. She also was from Germany, but she had gone to Eretz Israel many years before and had a fine house in one of the lovely quarters of Jerusalem. A well-to-do widow without children, she had gladly responded to the request of the committee which handled such matters when they asked her to take a refugee child from Germany into her home. It was our duty to praise and thank God at this piece of good fortune for the child. It would be impossible to find a better house or a kinder-hearted woman in the whole of the country. They were sure that she would look after him lovingly, and bring him up and educate him with the devotion of a real mother . . .

What can I tell you? I read that letter and then went back and read it again and again. I wept all over it. That my gentle child should have to be kept by others, that my only son should need the charity of the kind-hearted . . . But still, at heart I thanked God that he was not with us but was far far away, in a place full of sunshine, in a safe home, in a place where the air was not full of venomous hatred. For I don't need to tell you that our situation in Germany was growing worse from day to day.

Before long we got a letter from the worthy woman as well. It was a long letter that was really touching in its simplicity, deep understanding, and delicate spirit. She told us about Jerusalem, and all that she had gone through in that city ever since she arrived there. She described her house in detail and her style of life, so that we might know the environment in which our son would grow up. Finally she wrote about the boy, the state in which he entered her home, and about his qualities and character in general. During the few days he had been with her, she had already grown used to him and had learned to love him, so much so that she could not even imagine that there had ever been a time when he had not been there. She was sure he would lack for nothing there, and that she and the child would understand one another well . . . At the end of the letter my boy added a few words in his own hand. She must have helped him, because he had not yet learned to write at the time. He was very happy, he wrote, to be with Auntie G., because he loved her very very much . . .

Why should I deny it? When I read those innocent words my heart fell. I began to feel jealous. Yes, lunacy, don't you think so? But I can't hide it. For the first time in my life I felt this emotion of jealousy, a painful, forbidden emotion. They want to take my son from me, I thought. I did not feel any fear or apprehension for his fate, I really want that to be quite clear to you. I knew that he was in perfectly safe and reliable hands. And yet that knowledge made my jealousy worse. I would have felt better if I had known he was in hands that were not quite so safe or reliable. Can you understand it? It went as far as that! I felt ashamed of myself. Yes, I tried to hide it from my husband, and to bury my feeling deep inside me; but it came floating up again, even stronger than before, like a kind of horrible recurrent disease, with every fresh letter we received. For from this time on we used to receive a letter from her almost every week regularly. Each letter added something to the others. In one the boy began to go to school, in another he began to learn music. Yet each one resembled the other in its fine style and fine feeling. Sometimes that innocent line or two added by the child would be there, sometimes it wouldn't. In either case I tormented myself. If the line was there, I became all the more jealous; and if it wasn't, I would think that he had already forgotten me and didn't even send his love . . .

III

Almost a whole year passed like that. Meanwhile the war began. All this while my husband had managed to evade the murderers, but now the Gestapo caught him at last and took him off to a concentration camp. What was the reason? Who knows? I never saw him again, nor heard from him. They murdered him there, those degraded criminals; then some time later they told me to come and receive his ashes. I was left all alone in the world, a forlorn widow. I no longer received letters from Eretz Israel. Naturally they stopped at the outbreak of the war. Oh, I would have given my very soul to receive just another such letter, with or without a line or two by the child, as long as I might see that I still had something to hold on to in life, that I had not been forgotten, that I was not left alone in this lions' den. But no letters came. I took the old letters out of their hiding-place. (When the war began I hid them, because it was dangerous to keep such things.) At night I read them in bed again and again, scores of times, from beginning to end. Now they no longer made me feel jealous. No! No! Believe me, you know I was just like somebody in some Godforsaken spot, who suddenly meets a person there from his native city. Back in his native city he had disliked the man, yet here, in this place of exile, he is as happy to meet him as though they had always been the best friends . . . No, the comparison doesn't really fit. Can I say I ever hated those letters? If I had hated them, I would never have kept them so carefully, really risking my life to do so. Do you understand? But let that be, for the time being.

The days that followed after my husband's death were chaotic and hopeless. The whole world seemed to turn black, and those letters were not bright enough any longer to do more than emit faint, dead sparks. I was in a state of absolute despair, simply consumed by my terrible longing for my son. It was like the yearning of a mother on her deathbed, longing to see her beloved child for the last time before she died. And then, then I had the idea, the crazy idea: I decided I must really do something! I made up my mind to get away from Germany at once, and to try and reach Eretz Israel any way I could.

Once this idea entered my head, I decided to act on it. I would get away to my boy, to my boy! No power, no consideration whatever could have made me change my mind. Danger? Was there any danger that could frighten me any longer? In any case I no longer had any kind of life worth living. So what did I have to lose?

I'm not going to tell you all that happened to me before I got here. To tell you the truth, I myself cannot realise yet how I managed it. How I managed to steal out of Germany in the middle of the war, without an exit permit; how I succeeded in slipping through Yugoslavia after the Occupation; and all kinds of things like that. On my journey, I was in a kind of daze, physically and mentally. That seems to be what a human being is like: when he does something which is absolutely foolish and should not be done by all the laws of logic, when he has to tread a dangerous path, then he seems to fortify himself, as you might say, with a kind of armour of dazed senses and consciousness. Otherwise he would be unable to perform the action and would not take even a single step along that road. If I were to tell you some of the things that happened to me on the way which I remember clearly (I have already forgotten a great deal), you would certainly not believe me. It is hard for me myself to believe that these things really happened; it seems as though I merely dreamed them. Anyway, you see I succeeded in doing it, for here I am, sitting with you.

And now I come to the real story.

IV

One summer day I reached Jerusalem. What I felt you can imagine for yourself. As soon as I left the bus I went into a nearby drugstore, to phone Mrs. G. Trembling I took the instrument in my hand. In just another moment, I would hear my child's voice. It was hard for me to keep my feet. The moment that passed between the first ringing in the instrument and the reply seemed to last forever. At last I heard a voice. It was the maid speaking. Mrs. G. was not at home just then. I told the woman my name, and that I had just reached Jerusalem. "And what do you want?" she asked. I asked her whether she could tell me where I could stay. Naturally I had hoped that Mrs. G. would invite me to stay with her, but it seems this woman had never heard my name, and had no idea who I was. All it meant to her was that a new arrival in the country had just reached Jerusalem, and wanted to know where to stay; and that did not surprise her at all. She was quite used to it. Her mistress had a name in town and elsewhere for being an active social worker, so dozens of newcomers probably came to her with similar requests. Her answer sounded as though it was a regular standby. If I went to such and such a street, said she, I would find the special hostel for newcomers, and I would be able to stay there.

I thanked her politely and put the telephone back on its hook. And why, you may ask me, did I do that? If I felt that the woman had never heard my name and did not have the slightest idea who I was, why didn't I tell her? Why didn't I tell her that I was the mother of the child in their house, and spare myself an hour of unhappiness? But I shall tell you. Ever since I saw how people bring suffering on one another of set purpose and just in order to hurt, I prefer the suffering that people cause accidentally and by mistake so to speak. I know that sooner or later they will realise their mistake and regret the pain they caused me. And knowing this gives me what I can only describe as satisfaction. Actually, it was with a sense of deep satisfaction that I collected my belongings (they were not so many) and went to that hostel.

Before I had had time to wash and take off my dusty clothes, Mrs. G. appeared. She came alone, without the child. When I saw her, my breath simply stopped. She was so beautiful, I was enchanted. I could see she was a bit excited, but this excitement improved her looks. I am sure that you must know her. And who doesn't know her in Jerusalem? She is so nobly tall, with her healthy young face set in its grey hair, and her soft wise eyes, and her expression, motherly and strong at the same time. Yes, she is remarkably beautiful. Even now, after all that has happened, I sometimes stand enchanted at her looks.

She pressed my hand for a long moment and looked at me with eyes full of kindness. The maid had told her I had phoned and she had come at once. She was exceedingly upset at what had happened. It was true that she had received my letter from Turkey, but she had never imagined that I would be able to get here so fast. Naturally she was not going to permit me to stay here, God forbid. Not in any circumstances! She had already arranged a room for me in a pleasant hotel not far from her home. It was all right, I did not need to worry about expense. She would arrange everything. "So take your things," said she, "and come with me at once. We have to hurry in order to get home before Michael goes to sleep. He always rests and sleeps for an hour in the afternoon."

After a few polite words I took my hat and went with her. I did not want to take my belongings, in spite of her insistence. I told her I would fetch them afterwards. But at that moment my thoughts were far from hotels, my heart and soul being set on the child I was about to see in just another few minutes. There was a taxi waiting for us at the gate, but I asked Mrs. G. to send it away. I wanted to walk to her house, in order to have time to prepare myself for the meeting with the child.

It was noon. The sun was blazing cruelly. We walked slowly and silently, or more correctly: I was silent while she talked. What did she say? I don't know, I paid no attention. I was all confused. My head was full of all kinds of questions I could not answer. What should I do if the child asks me this? And if he said that, what could I answer? And suppose he asked me about his father, what could I tell him?

After about half an hour, we reached the house. As soon as Mrs. G. opened the door, she called out in a loud and excited voice, which sounded very strange: "Michael, Michael! Please come here. I have a great surprise for you!" You understand? A surprise . . . She had not told the child at all that I was about to come. A surprise . . . The child came running from the other room, and Mrs. G. pointed her finger. "Here is your surprise," said she quietly. "Do you recognise her?"

The child turned quite pale. To this day I can't explain to myself why I stood as though I were paralysed, why I did not fall on his neck and embrace him and hug him and kiss him as I had intended to do, and as any other mother would have done in my place. Why not? Was I so astounded at the change which had taken place in him during these years? When he left me he had been a delicate little boy with milk teeth that gleamed at a distance, and now I saw before me a growing lad, big for his age, with two teeth missing in his mouth. Was I frightened by the resemblance I suddenly saw between him and his father? Or was it because of the strange surroundings and the presence of that woman? Or maybe I already felt at that moment that there was a kind of hidden barrier between us? Anyway, I stood as though turned to stone, unable to move, as though it were a strange child before me instead of my own son whom I had not seen for three years. And he, the boy, stood for a long moment, staring at me with open mouth but not saying a word. Then he dropped his eyes and whispered as though there were no breath left in him: "My mother . . . from over there . . . from Germany . . ." And after a brief pause he went on in a more assured voice: "Yes, Mother. I recognise her." Maybe he said something else, maybe he asked about his father. I did not hear any more. I managed to see the face of Mrs. G. as she stood to one side twisting her fingers nervously. Her lips trembled, but in her eyes I saw a look of victory. And I fainted.

V

When I came to, she took me not to the hostel nor to the good hotel nearby, but to a hospital out of town. All the weariness of my wandering, all the mishaps and misery which I had undergone during those years, now set their mark on me all at once. I reeled and simply collapsed. The doctors were afraid my heart was affected, that my lungs were out of order. They put me in the hospital for about a month. During the first fortnight, I lay in bed, lonely and suffering, aching from head to foot as though I were all wounds and bruises, my soul weary almost to death. Mrs. G. came to visit me from time to time and brought me all kinds of good things. She never mentioned what had taken place in the house—just as though it had never happened at all. But the child did not come to see me even once. He had been forbidden to come, lest I grow too excited and it slow down my cure. The truth was, I did not regret it. I didn't want him to see me ill, so that he shouldn't feel sorry for me. I didn't want any pity from him. I didn't think of him in the way a mother thinks of a cherished child, but as a woman thinks of her lover and of how to win his heart. Do you understand?

Well, two weeks passed in bed and I was not getting better. I saw that unless I bestirred myself, unless I overcame the twilight mood into which I was sinking, I might gradually just go out like a candle. So I gathered the rest of my strength and got up. The doctors did not know why I got up, just as they did not know why I had collapsed. In spite of this they kept me in the hospital another fortnight for observation and study. It is just as well they did. It was a good thing they gave me a chance to walk about the hospital corridors. In that way they enabled me to get to know them, and so I even managed to find myself a job. One physician, a specialist in eye diseases, asked me to be his assistant, for that used to be my field of specialization abroad.

I left the hospital next morning, that is the morning after I had spoken to the eye specialist and he had asked me to be his assistant. It was a pleasant day at the end of summer. Lonely clouds were floating up above, like guests strolling about the sky. They shed something melancholy on the earth. But that shadow never penetrated my heart at all. That morning I felt newly illuminated, a great sense of ease; it was as though all that heavy load of weariness and depression which had been weighing on me so much during those last years had vanished. I felt renewed—prepared to begin again, to open a new leaf in the book of my life. With a light and trusting heart I went to town, and the same day I took a little apartment near the dispensary of my chief, arranged it as best I could, and began working a few days later. I was anxious to begin working at once, for I knew that nothing but work would enable me to preserve the tranquillity which had come to me in so mysterious a fashion.

In brief—I worked and found my place. Now there was nothing to prevent me from taking my son to my home, and I decided to do it as soon as possible. My salary is not particularly high, it is true, but it is enough for both of us. So what did I do? First I decided to break down the wall of estrangement between us, to get close to him and bring him back to me. Every evening after finishing my work at the dispensary I visited him and spent an hour or two talking, playing, and reading. Mrs. G. did not intervene at all, and never interfered. The boy and I sat in his room while she sat in the next one, in a large armchair, reading or knitting. Sometimes we got excited while playing and made a lot of noise. But she did not protest or show any sign of dissatisfaction. Sometimes we were so interested in what we were reading that we did not notice how the time was passing, but she never came to interrupt us or to remind us by word or sign that it was already late and time for him to go to bed. Yes, Mrs. G. behaved very well indeed towards me. Whenever I came to her home, she always welcomed me with a friendly smile and a hearty "How do you do"; and when I left she would accompany me to the door and take leave of me with a pleasant smile and a warm handclasp.

She did not say much and asked no questions. Only once, when the boy wept during my visit, did she ask me as I left why he had cried. When I told her that he had cried because I had told him of his father's death, she asked, "And how did he receive the news?" "Very bravely," I answered. To this the woman responded with a strange kind of praise: "Yes, I always knew this lad was a brave one."

But in general, it can't be denied—she treated me very well indeed. Yet I must say that this kind behaviour was just what annoyed me so much. She did not behave as though she were doing me any favour, but as though I were doing her a favour; as though she were very grateful to me for coming every evening to look after the child and play with him. You understand? It was as though she would never find a better person, or a more devoted governess in the whole of the country to look after her child . . .

Yes, those were good times for me, before winter came. All day long I was doing interesting work and extending my knowledge, and in the evening there were the hours with the child to put heart into me and strengthen me. Every evening our meetings became more free and natural. I felt that the invisible barrier between us was gradually being destroyed, day after day, and that he was coming closer and closer to me.

VI

One Sabbath day, I came in the early afternoon, not at all as usual, and suggested that we take a walk together for a few hours. Mrs. G. willingly agreed, and the boy came along very happily. It was a wonderful day. The streets were thronged with children and parents, who had come out to enjoy their Sabbath in the open air. For a long time we walked about together. We jumped about, we played at hide and seek among the rocks, we picked flowers in the fields. Then I took him to see my little dwelling, for he had never been there before. I cannot say that he felt like a stranger, but it seemed to me that he was rather nervous. He moved from one room to another quite freely, taking everything in his hands and wanting to know what it was for. But when I told him to sit down for a while and drink tea and eat some of the cakes, he refused because it was getting late. It was getting dark outside and he had to go home. He left me a few of the flowers he had picked, in a vase, and I gave him one piece of pastry to eat in the street, and we went out.

That evening I spent more time with him than usual. I washed him, I brought him his supper, I put him to bed, and then I went in to Mrs. G.'s room to talk to her. I had made up my mind to approach her that evening, to thank her for all the kindness and more than kindness she had shown, and to tell her that now I wanted to take the boy; for if not now, when then? As soon as she saw me she rose, intending to see me to the door as usual. I told her I wanted to talk to her. Naturally she understood at once what I wanted to talk about, and I saw that she was afraid of the conversation. She began playing nervously with the white necklace she wore, and without a word went back and sat down again. I sat on the couch facing her and at once came to the point.

"I shan't waste words trying to describe my gratitude," said

I to her. "Are there any words which could tell you how thankful and grateful I am for all you have done for me and my son? . . . If I were to say that you have been just a mother to him, I would not be saying too much . . . But now, I am here, I am working steadily, I have a dwelling of my own, and I see no reason why the boy should continue to stay with you, or why he shouldn't come to live with his mother . . ."

Oh, how hard it was for me to say it! I don't know why. She sat there facing me like a statue, and her face was as white as chalk. I tried to read from it what must be going on inside her, but I couldn't. Her face was smooth and expressionless, like a kind of white mask. To rouse her from her stony silence I added:

"Surely you understand me, don't you?"

To this she answered quietly, with a kind of smile:

"Yes, of course, I understand you quite well. You want to take Michael away from me. Please do. Why not? But don't you think it might be better to ask the boy first? Maybe he doesn't want to go to you . . ."

Those words absolutely stupefied me, just as if she had hit me over the head with a hammer. To go and ask the boy first . . . At that moment I knew for certain I would never dare to ask him. No! No! For what would I do if he refused? Why, it would simply kill me. And then I also understood why I had been so careful not to tell the boy of my intention while he had been at the apartment with me. After all, I had really taken him there just for that, in order to show him his new home. But I had been afraid. Yes, I had simply been afraid that he might say: I don't want to come. That was the reason I let him go without even hinting what I intended to do. Mrs. G. must have sensed it, I suppose, and that was why she came out with what she said. She knew that those words had simply disarmed me. I waited for her to say something more, but she did not add a word. She sat twisting the white necklace between her fingers very nervously. I was afraid that the string would snap any moment and the beads would scatter all over the floor. I couldn't stand it. I stood up and went away.

VII

What can I tell you? That night I hardly closed my eyes. I tossed from side to side all night long on my bed, mad with jealousy and rage and pity. Yes, pity as well. I was jealous of the woman and of her confidence. "Go and ask the boy . . ." She was not in the least apprehensive about asking him. She was sure that if he were asked he would want to stay. Why? Or maybe she was not at all so certain, but she knew my weakness and exploited it against me. And that was not at all kind. That was what made me angry. You understand: to suggest to a forlorn mother that her only child would not want to go with her! That was an act of cruelty. Yes. I almost hated her for it.

Yet on the other hand, when I pictured the fate of the woman to myself, I felt very sorry for her. For really she was just as forlorn as I was, and maybe even more so than I. Oh yes, it is quite true: she is well off and goodlooking and quite famous for her deeds of charity, yet what does she get out of it all? She is alone and childless. No child's eyes have ever brightened the gloom of her widowhood, she has never known what it is to be a real mother. Now she is growing old and a child has come her way, a really lovely child. She did not kidnap him or try to attract him by any trickery. Good, decent people brought him to her home so that she should bring him up and educate him, since he was as good as an orphan and his father and his mother were far far away. So she treated him just as any woman with a heart would have done—she was a mother to him. Is there any sin in that? She loved the child, and he loved her and called her "Mother." A short and affectionate word, Mother, which she had never heard in all her life until this child came to her home. Wasn't that worth as much as all her money and looks and good name? Of course she loves him! How could she do anything else? Is there any crime in it? And now, after they have been living together for a long time as mother and son, comes his real mother whom they had thought dead for a long time; and she wants to take him away from her. Why, if she takes him from her now, her home will be far more desolate than before, and she will be truly bereft. Is that a reward for her good deed? . . . Yes, I pitied her, in all truth. The more I thought about her the more I pitied her. I decided I must ask her pardon for going away without taking leave, and be exceedingly nice to her thereafter. For, when all is said and done, she's a really unfortunate woman.

But when I came to visit my boy next evening I did not find her at home. Nor did I find her on the evening after or on the one following. The boy told me she had gone to Tel-Aviv. On the fourth evening I found her, but she received me very coldly. She didn't open the door, she didn't stand up to meet me and didn't ask how I was. She merely said a languid good day from her armchair, as much as to say: Are you here again? And who told you to come? . . . She did this for several evenings. I suffered dreadfully from it. I simply didn't know any longer where I was in the world. So I decided to put a stop to it. No matter what happened I had to do something. It was impossible to go on any longer like that!

VIII

Well, this very morning, when the boy was at school, I took some time off from my work and went to her house to talk to her. To clear the matter up at last, and try to find a way out together with her. That was what I thought when I went there, to find a way out together with her . . . But I no longer think so. Now, after the talk we had this morning, I know that there's no solution. I can't tell you exactly what we said. I was excited and she was excited. She sat all the time, twisting her white necklace. If it didn't snap today, then the string must be made of iron. And things were said between us that I would be ashamed to repeat. Neither of us put a bridle over her mouth. But I'll tell you in brief.

After I confusedly stammered about pardon and understanding and so on, I told her there was no reason for strained relations between us, and I wanted to take the child without any delay. She had to understand. To this she answered impatiently, almost roughly: "Yes, yes, I know. I have already heard it all, once before." Here my patience began to give way. I reminded her I was the child's mother, and it seemed as though she were forgetting the fact.

To this she answered: "I have never denied it. I know you are his physical mother. But in a sense I am also his mother. It seems to me you don't want to recognise that fact."

Then I grew angry. I shouted, I wept and I entreated: "Give me the boy! Give my child back to me!"

But as for her, the more excited I grew, the calmer she became. "I didn't take him from you," said she with quiet assurance, "and I don't have to give him back to you. If you want to take him away from me, you have a choice between two courses: either you ask him—but it seems that you don't dare to do that, you are not so certain he'll want to go with you—or else you have another alternative: you can take him by force, by going to law."

I was stunned. "A new Judgment of Solomon?" said I bitterly.

"Yes, a new Judgment of Solomon," she answered firmly.

I stared into her eyes and in them I again saw that look of triumph. Oh, how I hated her then! I know it is wicked, I know one mustn't hate like that. But what can I do? I can't get rid of the feeling of animosity that awoke in me then. You understand: I felt she thought that if we were both standing in front of Solomon's throne, *she* would be the one to say: "Give her the living child," while I would say: "Cut him in two." It's a dreadful thought. Why did she think that of me? Good, I understand she thinks she's the child's mother also, but why does she think I am his mother no longer? Why? Why . . . ?

So now my position is this—a mother whose child is alive, but who is bereft. He, the child that is, has two mothers, but I no longer have a child. He is lost to me, and who knows whether I shall find him again . . . What? He is in safe hands . . . ? You also say that? Have you ever seen a person who has lost something precious and then consoles himself because what he lost is in good hands?

And please don't remind me of all the children who were left back in Europe. If only I could forget them. They stand before me all the time, every moment, they and their suffering mothers. Oh those dark faces, those wizened, shrunken bodies, those staring eyes—will it ever be possible to forget them? But, believe me, I find no consolation in that thought either.

Face from Atlantis

NADINE GORDIMER

Nadine Gordimer was born in South Africa in 1923. She had a convent education. Her published works include *The Soft Voice of the Serpent, The Lying Days, Six Feet of the Country, A World of Strangers* and *Friday's Footprint*; and she has contributed to many well-known periodicals, among them, *The Atlantic Monthly, The New Yorker* and *Harpers*. In 1961 she won the W. H. Smith £1,000 Award for fiction. She lives in Johannesburg with her husband, son and daughter.

Somehow it wasn't altogether a surprise when Waldeck Brand and his wife bumped into Carlitta at a theatre in New York in 1953. The Brands were six thousand miles away from their home in South Africa, and everywhere they had visited in England and Europe before they came to America, they had met Waldeck's contemporaries from Heidelberg whom he hadn't seen for twenty years, and never had expected to see ever again. It had seemed a miracle to Waldeck that all these people, who had had to leave Germany because they were liberals (like himself), or Jews, or both, not only had thrived, but managed to do so each in the manner and custom of the country which had given him sanctuary.

Of course, Waldeck Brand did not think it a miracle that *he* had survived and conformed to a pattern of life lived at the other end of the world to which he had belonged. (Perhaps it is true, after all, that no man can believe in the possibility of his own failure or death.) It seemed quite natural that the gay young man destined primarily for a good time, and secondly for the inheritance of his wealthy father's publishing house in Berlin, should have become a director of an important group of gold-mines in southernmost Africa, a world away from the medieval German university town where he had marched at the head of the student socialist group, and the Swiss alps where he had ski-ed and shared his log cabin with a different free-thinking girl every winter, and the Kurfürstendam where he had strolled with his friends, wearing elegant clothes specially ordered from England. Yet to him—and to his South African wife, who had been born and had spent the twenty-seven years of her life in Cape Town, looking out, often and often, over the sea which she had now crossed for the first time—it was a small miracle that his Heidelberg friend, Siggie Bentheim, was to be found at the foreign editor's desk of a famous right-of-centre newspaper in London, and another university friend, Stefan Rosovsky, now become Stefan Raines, was the managing director of a public utility company in New York, and had a finger or two dipped comfortably in oil, too. To Waldeck, Siggie was the leader of a Communist cell, an ugly little chap, best student in the Institut für Sozialwissenschaften, whose tiny hands were dry-skinned and shrunken, as if political fervour had used up his blood like fuel. Stefan was the Russian boy with the soft voice and the calm delivery of dry wit, who tutored economics and obviously was fitted for nothing but an academic career as an economist.

And to Eileen, Waldeck Brand's wife, both were people who lived, changeless, young, enviable, in a world that existed only in Waldeck's three green leather photograph albums. Siggie was the one who sat reading the *Arbeiterpolitik,* oblivious of the fact that a picture was being taken, in the photograph where the whole dim, underexposed room (Waldeck's at Heidelberg) was full of students. Eileen had been to a university in South Africa, but she had never seen students like these: such good-looking, happy, bold-eyed boys, such beautiful girls smoking cigarettes in long holders and stretching out their legs in pointed-toed shoes beneath their short skirts. Someone was playing a guitar, in that picture. But Siggie Bentheim (you could notice those hands, round the edges of the pages) read a paper.

Stefan was not in that picture, but in dozens of others. In

particular, there was one taken in Budapest. A flashlight picture, taken in a nightclub, Stefan holds up a glass of champagne, resigned in his dinner-suit, dignified in a silly paper cap. New Year in Budapest, before Hitler, before the war. Can you imagine it? Eileen was fascinated by those photograph albums, and those faces. Since she had met and married Waldeck in 1952, she had spent many hours looking at the albums. When she did so, a great yawning envy opened through her whole body. She was young, and the people pictured in those albums all, even if they were alive, over forty by now. But that did not matter; that did not count. That world of the photograph albums was lost not only by those who had outgrown it into middle-age. It was *lost.* Gone. It did not belong to a new youth. It was not hers although she was young. It was *no use* being young, now, in the forties and fifties. She thought of the green albums as the record of an Atlantis.

Waldeck had never been back to Europe since he came as a refugee to South Africa twenty years before. He had not kept up a regular correspondence with his scattered student friends, though one or two had written, at intervals of four or five years, and so, for some, when Waldeck took his wife to Europe and America, he had the address-before-the-last, and for others the vaguest ideas of their whereabouts. Yet he found them all, or they found him. It was astonishing. The letters he wrote to old addresses were forwarded; the friends whom he saw knew where other friends lived, or at least what jobs they were doing, so that they could be traced that way, simply by a telephone call. In London there were dinner-parties and plain drinking-parties, and there they were—the faces from Atlantis, gathered together in a Strand pub. One of the women was a grandmother; most of the men were no longer married to women Waldeck remembered them marrying, and had shed their old political faiths with their hair. But all were alive, and living variously, and in them was still the peculiar vigour that showed vividly in those faces, caught in the act of their life long ago, in the photograph albums.

Once or twice in London, Waldeck had asked one old friend or another, "What happened to Carlitta? Does anyone know where Carlitta is?" Siggie Bentheim, eating Scotch salmon at Rules', like any other English journalist who can afford to, couldn't remember Carlitta. Who was she? Then Waldeck remembered that the year when everyone got to know Carlitta was the year that Siggie spent in Lausanne. Another old friend remembered her, very well. "Carlitta! Not in England, at any rate. Carlitta!" Someone else caught the name, and called across the table, "Carlitta was in London, oh, before the war. She went to America thirteen or fourteen years ago." "Did she ever marry poor old Klaus Schultz—my God, he was mad about that girl?" "Marry him! No-o-o! Carlitta wouldn't marry him."

"Carlitta was a collector of scalps, all right," said Waldeck, laughing. "Well, do you wonder?" said a friend.

Eileen knew Carlitta well, in picture and anecdote. Eileen had a favourite among the photographs of her, too, just as she had the one of Stefan in Budapest on New Year's eve. The photograph was taken in Austria, on one of Waldeck's ski-ing holidays. It was a clear print and the snow was blindingly white. In the middle of the whiteness stood a young girl, laughing away from the camera in the direction of something or someone outside the picture. Her little face shone dark against the snow, burnished by the sun. There was a highlight on each firm, round cheekbone, accentuated in laughter. She was beautiful in the pictures of groups, too; in boats on the Neckar, in the gardens of the schloss, in cafés and at student dances; even, once, at Deauville, even in the unbecoming bathing-dress of the time. In none of the pictures did she face the camera. If, as in the ski picture, she was smiling, it was at someone in the group; and if she was not, her black pensive eyes, her beautiful little firm-fleshed face with the short chin, stared at the toes of her shoes, or at the smoke of her cigarette, arrested in its climbing arabesque by the click of the camera. The total impression of all these photographs of the young German girl was one of arrogance. She did not participate in the taking of the photograph, she was simply there, a thing of beauty, which you could attempt to record if you wished.

One of the anecdotes about the girl was something that happened on that ski-ing holiday. Carlitta and Klaus Schultz, Waldeck and one of his girls, had gone together to the mountains. "Oh, the luck of it!" Eileen had said to Waldeck at this point in his story, the first time he related it. "You were eighteen? Nineteen? And you were allowed to go off on your first love affair to the mountains. Can you imagine what would have happened if I had announced to my parents that I was going on a holiday with a young lover? And in Austria, and ski-ing . . ." (Poor Eileen, who had gone, every year, on a five-day cruise along the coast to stay at a "family hotel" in Durban, accompanied by her parents and younger brother and sister, or had been sent, in the winter vacation, with an uncle and cousins to hear the lions roar outside a dusty camp in the Kruger Park. She did not know which to envy Waldeck, Carlitta and Klaus most —the sexual freedom or the steep mountain snows.) Anyway, it was on the one really long and arduous climb of that delightful holiday that Carlitta, who for some hours had been less talkative than usual, and had fallen back a little, sat down in the snow and refused to move. Waldeck had lagged behind the rest of the party to mend a broken strap on his rucksack, and so it was he noticed her. When he asked her why she did not hurry on with him to catch up with the other members of the party, she said, perfectly calmly, "I want to sit here in the shade and rest. I'll wait here till you all come back."

There was no shade. The party intended to sleep in a rest hut up the mountain, and would not pass that way again till the next day. At first Waldeck laughed; Carlitta was famous for her caprice. Then he saw that, in addition to being perfectly calm, Carlitta was also perfectly serious. She was not joking, but suffering from some kind of peculiar hysteria. He begged and begged her to get up, but she would not. "I am going to rest in the shade," was all she would answer. The others of the party were out of sight and he began to feel nervous. There was only one thing he could try. He went up kindly to the beautiful little girl and struck her sharply, twice, in the face. The small head swung violently, this way, then that. Carlitta got up, dusted the snow from her trousers, and said to Waldeck, "For God's sake, what are we waiting for? The others must be miles ahead."

"And when Klaus heard what had happened," Waldeck's story always ended, "he could scarcely keep himself from crying, he was so angry that *he* had not been the one to revive Carlitta, and Carlitta saw his nose pinken and swell with the effort of keeping back the tears, and noted how very much he must be in love with her and how easy it would be to torment him." Wretched Klaus! He was the blond boy with the square jaw who always frowned and smiled directly into the camera. Eileen had a theory that young people didn't even fall in love like that any more. That, too, had gone down under the waves.

Waldeck and his young wife arrived in New York on a Tuesday. Stefan Raines came to take them out to dinner that very first night. Eileen, who had never seen him before in her life, was even more overjoyed than Waldeck to find that he had not changed. As soon as they came out of the elevator and saw him standing in the hotel lobby with a muffler hanging down untied on the lapels of his dark coat, they knew he had not changed. He wore the presidency of the public utility company, the wealth and the Fifth Avenue apartment just as he had worn the paper cap in the Budapest nightclub on New Year's eve long ago. Stefan's American wife was not able to accompany them that night, so the three dined alone. After dinner Stefan wanted to know if he should drive them to Times Square and along Broadway or anywhere else they'd read about, but they told him he was the only sight they wanted to see so soon after their arrival. They talked for two hours over dinner, Stefan asking and Waldeck answering eager questions about the old Heidelberg friends whom Waldeck and Eileen had seen in London. Stefan went to London sometimes, and he had seen one or two, but many whom he hadn't been able to find for years seemed to have appeared out of their hiding-places for Waldeck. In fact, there were several old Berlin and Heidelberg friends whom Stefan had seen once, or not at all, but who, on the Brands' first day in New York, had already telephoned their hotel. "We love Waldeck. Better than we love each other," said Stefan to his friend's wife, his black eyes looking quietly out over the room, the corners of his mouth indenting in his serious smile that took a long time to open out, brightening his eyes as it did until they shone like the dark water beneath the lamplight on a Venetian canal where Eileen had stood with her husband a few weeks before.

Eileen seemed to feel her blood warm in the palms of her hands, as if some balm had been poured over them. No man in South Africa could say a thing like that! The right thing, the thing from the heart. You had to have the assurance of Europe, of an old world of civilised human relationships behind you before you could say, simply and truthfully, a thing like that.

It was the moment for the mood of the conversation to take a turn. Waldeck said curiously, suddenly remembering, "And what ever became of Carlitta? Did you ever see Carlitta? Peter told me, in London, that she had come to live in America."

"Now that's interesting that you should ask," said Stefan. "I've wondered about her, too. I saw her once, twelve—more, thirteen years back. When she first arrived in America. She was staying quite near the hotel where you're living now. I took her out to lunch, not very sumptuous, I was rather poor at the time—and I never saw her again. She was beautiful. You remember? She was always beautiful"—he crinkled his eyes to dark slits, as if to narrow down the aperture of memory upon her—"even in a bad restaurant in New York, she was—well, the word my son would use is the best for her—she was terrific. Minute and terrific."

"That's it. That's it." Waldeck spoke round the cigar he held between his teeth, trying to draw up a light.

"We adored her," said Stefan, shaking his head slowly at the wonder of it.

"So you too, Stefan, you too?" said Eileen, with a laugh.

"Oh, none of us was in love with Carlitta. Only Klaus, and he was too stupid, he doesn't count. We only adored. We knew it was useless to fall in love with her. Neither she nor we believed any one of us was good enough for her."

"So you don't think she's in New York?" asked Waldeck.

Stefan shook his head. "I did hear, from someone who knew her sister, that she had married an American and gone to live in Ohio." He stopped and chuckled congestedly. "Carlitta in Ohio. I don't believe it. Well, we should move along from here now, you know. Sure there isn't *anywhere* you'd like to go before bedtime?"

The girl from South Africa remembered that one of the things she'd always wanted to do if she ever came to New York was to hear a really fat negro woman singing torch songs, so Stefan took them to a place where the air-conditioning apparatus kept the fog of smoke and perfume and liquor fumes moving round the tables while an enormous yellow blubber of a woman accompanied her own voice, quakingly with her flesh and thunderously on the piano.

It was only two nights later when Eileen came out of the ladies' room to join her husband in a theatre foyer during the interval, and found him embracing a woman in a brown coat. As Waldeck held the woman away from him, by the shoulders, as if to take a good look at her after he had kissed her, Eileen saw a small face with a wide grin and really enormous eyes. As

Eileen approached, she noticed a tall, sandy-haired man standing by indulgently. When she reached the three, Waldeck turned to her with the pent-up excited air he always had when he had secretly bought her a present, and he held out his hand to draw her into the company. In the moment before he spoke, Eileen felt a stir of recognition at the sight of the woman's hair, smooth brown hair in which here and there a grey filament of a coarser texture showed, refusing to conform to the classic style, centre-parted and drawn back in a bun, in which the hair was worn. "Do you know who this is?" said Waldeck, almost weakly. "It's Carlitta." Eileen was entitled to a second or two in which to be taken aback, to be speechless in the face of coincidence. In that moment, however, the coincidence did not even occur to her; she simply took in, in an intense perception of time, the woman before her; the brown coat open to show the collar of some nondescript silk caught together with a little brooch round the prominent tendons of the thin, creased neck, the flat, taut chest, the dowdy shoes with brown, punched-leather bows coming too high on the instep of what might have been elegant feet. And the head. Oh that was the head she had seen before, all right, that was the head that, hair so sleek it looked like a satin turban, inclined, with a mixture of coquetry, invitation, amusement and disdain, toward a ridiculously long cigarette holder. That hair was brown, after all, and not the Spanish black of the photographs and imagination. And the face. Well, there is a stage in a woman's life when her face gets too thin or too fat. This face had reached that stage and become too thin. It was a prettily-enough shaped face, with a drab, faded skin, as if it was exposed to but no longer joyously took colour from the sun. Toward the back of the jaw-line, near the ears, the skin sagged sallowly. Under the rather thick attractive brows, the twin caves of the eyes were finely puckered and mauvish. In this faded, fading face (it was like an old painting of which you are conscious that it is being faded away by the very light by which you are enabled to look at it) the eyes had lost nothing, they shone on, greedy and tremendous, just as they had always been, in the snow, reflecting the Neckar, watching the smoke unfurl to the music of the guitar. They were round eyes with scarcely any white in them, like the beautiful eyes of negro children, and the lashes, lower as well as upper, were black and thick. Their assertion in that face was rather awful.

The woman who Waldeck said was Carlitta took Eileen's hand. "Isn't it fantastic? We're only up from Ohio this morning," she said, smiling broadly. Her teeth were small, square and still good. On her neglected face the lipstick was obviously a last-minute adornment. "And this is Edgar," Waldeck was saying, "Edgar Hicks. Carlitta's husband." The tall, sandy-haired man shook Eileen's hand with as much flourish as a stage comedian. "Glad to know you," he said. Eileen saw that he wore sexagonal rimless glasses and a clip across his tie spelled in pinkish synthetic gold E.J.H. "Carlitta Hicks"—Waldeck put out a hand and squeezed Carlitta's elbow—"I can't believe it." "Sure is extraordinary," said Mr. Hicks. "Carlitta and I here haven't been up to New York for more than three years." "Ach, no, darling," said Carlitta, frowning and smiling quickly. She used her face so much no wonder she had worn it out. "Four at least. You remember, that last time was at Christmas?" She added to Waldeck, "Once in a blue moon is enough for me. Our life . . ." She half-lifted a worn hand, gave a little sudden intake of breath through her fine nostrils, as if to suggest that their life, whatever it was, was such that the pleasures of New York or anywhere else offered no rival enticement. She had still a slight German accent to soften her American speech.

Everyone was incoherent. Waldeck kept saying excitedly, "I haven't been out of South Africa since I arrived, that's twenty years. I'm in New York two days and I find Carlitta!"

There was time only to exchange the names of hotels and to promise to telephone tomorrow. Then the theatre bell interrupted. As they parted, Waldeck called back, "Keep Sunday lunch free. Stefan's coming. We'll all be together. . . ."

Carlitta's mouth pursed, her eyes opened wide in a pantomime "lovely" across the crowd.

"And yet I'm not really entirely surprised," whispered Waldeck to his wife in the darkening theatre. "It's been happening to us in one way or another, all the time. What do you think of the husband, what about Mr. Edgar Hicks from Ohio?" he added with a nudge.

In the dark, as the curtain rose, Eileen followed it with her eyes for a moment and then said, "I shouldn't have known her. I don't think I should ever have known her."

"But Carlitta hasn't changed at all!" said Waldeck.

Waldeck was on the telephone, talking to Stefan, immediately after breakfast next morning. Passing to and fro between the bedroom and the bathroom, Eileen could see him, his body hitched up on to the corner of the small desk, smiling excitedly at what must have been Stefan's quiet incredulity. "But I tell you he actually is some sort of a farmer in Ohio. Yes. Well, that's what I wanted to know. I can't really say—very tall and fairish and thin. Very American. Well, you know what I mean, a certain type of American, then. Slow, drawling way of speaking. Shakes your hand a long time. A weekend farmer, really. He's got some job with a firm that makes agricultural implements, in the nearby town. She said she runs pigs and chickens. Can you believe it? So is it all right about Sunday? I can imagine you are. . . . Ach, the same old Carlitta. . . ."

Sunday was a clear, sharp spring day in New York, exactly the temperature and brightness of a winter day in Johannesburg. Stefan rang up to say he would call for the Brands at about eleven, so that they could drive around a little before meeting Carlitta and her husband for luncheon. "Will it be all right if I wear slacks?" asked Eileen. She always wore slacks on Sundays in Johannesburg. "Certainly not," said Stefan gravely. "You cannot lunch in a restaurant in New York in slacks." Eileen put on a suit she had bought in London. She was filled with a childlike love and respect for Stefan; she would not have done the smallest thing to displease him, or to prejudice his opinion of her. When he arrived to fetch the Brands he said, equally gravely, "You look very well in that suit," and led them to his car, where his wife, whom they had met in the course of the week, sat waiting. His wife was perhaps an odd choice for Stefan; and then again perhaps she was not, she went along with the presidency, the wealth and the Fifth Avenue apartment, and left his inner balance unchanged. She was not so young as Eileen, but young, and a beauty. An American beauty, probably of Swedish or Norwegian stock. Hers was the style of blond beauty in which the face is darker than the hair, which was not dyed, but real. It was clean and shiny and almost silvery-fair, and she wore it as such women do, straight and loose. She wore black, and when she stood up you noticed that hers was the kind of tall figure that, although the shoulders are broad and the breasts full, tapers to too-narrow hips and too thin legs. Her eyes were green and brilliant, and crinkled up, friendly, and on the wrist of one beautiful ungloved hand she wore a magnificent antique bracelet of emeralds and diamonds. Otherwise she was unadorned, without even a wedding ring. As she shifted along the seat of the car, a pleasant fragrance stirred from her, the sort of fragrance the expensive Fifth Avenue stores were then releasing into the foyers of their shops, to convince their customers of the arrival of time to buy spring clothes. When she smiled and spoke, in a soft American voice without much to say, her teeth showed fresh as the milk-teeth of a child.

Eileen thought how different were this woman and herself (with her large, Colonial, blue-eyed, suburban prettiness) from the sort of girls with whom Waldeck and Stefan had belonged in the world that was lost to them—girls of the Twenties, restlessly independent, sensual and intellectual, citizens of the world with dramatic faces— girls such as Carlitta, inclining her dark Oriental head, had been.

The four drove through Central Park, rather threadbare after the snow and before the blossom. Then they went down to the East River, where the bridges hung like rainbows, glittering, soaring, rejoicing the heart in the sky above the water, where men have always expected to find their visions. They stopped the car at the United Nations building, and first walked along on the opposite side of the road, alongside the shabby, seedy shops, the better to see the great molten-looking façade of glass, like a river flowing upward, on the administrative block. The glass calmly reflected the skyline, as a river reflects, murky green and metallic, the reeds. Then they crossed the road and wandered about a bit along the line of the flagstaffs, with the building hanging above them. The Brands resolved to come back another day and see the interior. "So far, there's nothing to beat your bridges," said Eileen. "Nothing."

They drove now uptown to an elegant, half-empty restaurant which had about it the air of recovering from Saturday night. There they sat drinking whisky while they waited. "I don't know what we can do with the husband," said Waldeck, shrugging and giggling. "That's all right," said Stefan. "Alice will talk to him. Alice can get along with anybody." His wife laughed good-naturedly. "You know, he's *worthy* . . ." said Waldeck. "I know," said Stefan, comforting. "Same old Carlitta, though," said Waldeck, smiling reminiscently. "You'll see."

His wife Eileen looked at him. "Oh she's not," she said distressed. "She's not. Oh how can you say that to Stefan?" The girl from South Africa looked at the two men and the woman who sat with her, and round the panelled and flower-decorated room, and suddenly she felt a very long way from home.

Just at that moment, Carlitta and Mr. Edgar Hicks came across the room toward them. Stefan got up and went forward with palms upturned to meet them, Waldeck rose from his seat, a confusion of greetings and introductions followed. Stefan kissed Carlitta on both cheeks, gently. Edgar Hicks pumped his hand. In Edgar Hicks's other hand was the Palm Beach panama with the paisley band which he had removed from his head as he entered. The hovering attendant took it from him, and took Carlitta's brown coat. Carlitta wore the niggly-patterned silk dress that had shown its collar under the coat the night at the theatre, the same shoes, the same cracked beige kid gloves. But above the bun and level with the faded hairline, she had on what was obviously a brand-new hat, a hat bought from the thousands of "spring" hats displayed that week before Easter, a perky, mass-produced American hat of the kind which makes an American middle-class woman recognisable anywhere in the world. Its newness, its frivolous sense of its own ephemerality (it was so much in fashion that it would be old-fashioned once Easter was over) positively jeered at everything else Carlitta wore. Whether it was because she fancied the sun still painted her face the extraordinary rich glow that showed against the snow in the picture of herself laughing in Austria years ago, or whether there was some other reason, her face was again without make-up except for a rub of lipstick. Under the mixture of artificial light and daylight, faint darkening blotches, not freckles but something more akin to those liver-marks elderly people get on the backs of their hands, showed on her temples and her jaw-line. But her eyes, of course, her eyes were large, dark, quick. She and her husband consulted together over what they should eat, he suggesting slowly, she deciding quickly, and from then on she never stopped talking. She talked chiefly to her two friends Waldeck and Stefan, who sat on either side of her. Edgar Hicks, after a few trying minutes with Eileen, who found it difficult to respond to any of his conversational gambits, discovered that Alice Raines rode horses, and, like a swamp sucking in fast all round its victim, involved her in a long, one-sided argument about the merits of two different types of saddle. Edgar preferred the one type, and simply assumed that Alice must be equally adamant about the superiority of the other.

Eileen did not mind the fact that she was not engaged in conversation. She was free to listen to and to watch Carlitta with Stefan and Waldeck. And now and then Carlitta, forking up her cole slaw expertly as any born American, looked over to Eileen with a remark or query—"That's what *I* say, anyway" or "Wouldn't you think so?" Carlitta first told briefly about her stay in London when she left Germany, then about her coming to the United States, and her short time in New York. "In the beginning, we stayed in that hotel near Grand Central. We behaved like tourists, not like people who have come to stay. We used to go to Coney Island and rowing on the lake in Central Park, and walking up and down Fifth Avenue—just as if we were going to go back to Germany in a few weeks."

"Who's we?" asked Stefan. "Your sister?"

"No, my sister was living in a small apartment near the river. Klaus," she said, shrugging her worn shoulders with the careless, culpable gesture of an adolescent. Stefan nodded his head in confirmation towards Waldeck; of course, he remembered, Klaus had followed her or come with her to America. Poor Klaus. "What happened to him?" asked Stefan. "I don't know," she said. "He went to Mexico." Her audience of three could guess very well how it had been. When she had tired of Coney Island and the outside of Fifth Avenue shops and the rowing in Central Park, Klaus found out once again that in the new world, as in the old, he had nothing more than amusement value for her. "After three months," Carlitta had not paused in her narrative, "I went to stay with my sister and brother-in-law—she had been here some years already. But he got a job with a real estate scheme, and they went to live on one of the firm's housing projects—you know, a little house, another little house next door, a swing for the kids, the same swing next door. I came back to New York on my own and I found a place in Greenwich Village."

Ah, now, there was a setting in which one would imagine the Carlitta of the photographs, the beautiful, Oriental-looking German girl from Heidelberg, with the bold, promising eyes. And at the moment at which Eileen thought this, her ear caught the drawl of Edgar Hicks, ". . . now our boy's the real independent type. Now only the other day . . ." Edgar Hicks! Where had Edgar Hicks come in? She looked at him, carefully separating the flesh from the fine fringe of bone in his boiled trout, the knife held deliberately in his freckled hand. "Did you live in Greenwich Village?" Eileen said to him suddenly. He interrupted his description of his boy's seat in the saddle to turn and say, surprised, "No, ma'am, I certainly didn't. I've never spent more than two consecutive weeks in New York in my life." He thought Eileen's question merely a piece of tourist curiosity and returned to Alice Raines, his boy and the saddle. Carlitta had digressed into some reminiscence about Heidelberg days, but when she paused, laughing from Stefan to Waldeck, with a faltering coquettishness that rose in her like a half-forgotten mannerism, Eileen said, "Where did you and your husband meet?"

"In a train," Carlitta smiled and said loudly, directed at her husband. He took it up across the table. "Baltimore and Ohio line," he said, well-rehearsed. There was the feeling that all the few things he had to say had been slowly thought out and slowly spoken many times before. "I was sittin' in the diner havin' a beer with my dinner, and in comes this little person looking mighty proud and cute as you can make 'em . . ." So it went on, the usual story, and Edgar Hicks spared them no detail of the romantic convention. "Took Carlitta down to see my folks the following month and we were married two weeks after that," he concluded at last. He had expected to marry one of the local girls he'd been to school with; it was clear that Carlitta was the one, and the ever-present, adventure of his life. Now they had a boy who rode as naturally as an Indian, and didn't watch television; he liked to raise his own chickens and have independent pocket money from the sale of the eggs.

"Carlitta," Stefan said, aside, "how long were you in Greenwich Village?" "Four years," she said shortly, replying from some other part of her mind; her attention and animation were given to the comments with which she amplified her husband's description of their child's remarkable knowledge of country lore, his superiority over town-bred children.

Eileen overheard the low, flat reply. Four years! Four years about which Carlitta had said not a word, four years which somehow or other had brought her from the arrogant, beautiful, "advanced" girl with whom Waldeck and Stefan could not fall in love because they and she agreed they were not good enough for her, to the girl who would accept Edgar Hicks a few weeks after a meeting on a train.

Carlitta felt the gaze of the girl from South Africa. A small patch of bright colour appeared on each of the woman's thin cheekbones. Perhaps it was the wine. Perhaps it was the wine, too, that made her voice rise, so that she began to talk of her life on the Ohio farm with a zest and insistence which made the whole table her audience. She told how she never went to town unless she had to; *never* more than once a month. How country people, like herself, discovered a new rhythm of life, something people who lived in towns had forgotten. How country people slept differently; tasted their food differently; had no nerves. "I haven't a nerve in my body, any more. Absolutely placid," she said, her little, sharp gestures, her black eyes in the pinched face challenging a denial. "Nothing ever happens but a change of season," she said arrogantly, to people for whom there were stock market crashes, traffic jams, crowded exhibitions and cocktail parties. "Birth and growth among the animals and the plants. Life. Not a cement substitute." No one defended the city, but she went on, as if someone had, "I live as instinctively as one of our own animals, so does my child. I mean, for one thing, we don't have to worry about clothes."

Eileen said rather foolishly, as if in reflex, "Stefan said I couldn't wear slacks to a New York restaurant to-day."

"Stefan was always a snob," Carlitta's little head struck like a snake.

Eileen was taken aback; she laughed nervously, looking very young. Carlitta grinned wickedly under the hat whose straw caught the light concentrically, like a gramophone record. Stefan's wife smiled serenely and politely, as if this were a joke against her husband. She had taken off the jacket of her suit and beneath it wore a fine lavender-coloured sweater with a low, round neck. She had been resting her firm neck against her left hand, and now she took the hand away; hers was the kind of wonderful blood-mottled fair skin that dented white with the slightest pressure, filled up pink again the way the sea seeps up instantly through footprints in wet sand. She looked so healthy, so well cared-for, that she created a moment of repose around herself; everyone paused, resting their gaze upon her. Then Carlitta's thin little sun-sallow neck twisted restlessly, "I don't know how you stand it," she said, "I don't know how you can live in New York, year after year."

"We go away," said Stefan soothingly. "We go to Europe most summers, to Switzerland to my mother, or to Italy. Alice loves Italy."

"Italy," said Carlitta, suddenly turning over a piece of lobster on her plate, as if she suspected that there must be something bad beneath it. "Spain."

"You remember how you went off to the Pyrenees?" Waldeck said to her. From his tone it was clear that this was quite a story, if Carlitta cared to tell it.

"You can't imagine how time flies, on the farm," said Carlitta. "The years . . . just go. Sometimes, in summer, I simply walk out of the house and leave my work and go and lie down in the long grass. Then you can hear nothing, nothing at all."

"Maybe the old cow chewing away under the pear tree," said Edgar, tenderly. Then with a chuckle that brought a change of tone, "Carlitta takes a big part in community affairs, too, you know. She doesn't tell you that she's on the library committee in the village, and last year she was lady president of the Parent Teacher Association. Ran a bazaar, made around three thousand dollars." There was a pause. Nobody spoke. "I'm an Elk myself," he added. "That's why we're going on to Philadelphia, Thursday. There's a convention on over there."

Carlitta suddenly put down her fork with a gesture that impatiently terminated any current subject of conversation. (Eileen thought: she must always have managed conversation like that, long ago in smoky, noisy student rooms, jerking the talk determinedly the way she wanted it.) Her mind seemed to hark back to the subject of dress.

"Last year," she said, "we invited some city friends who were passing through the village, to a supper-party. Now it just so happened that that afternoon I could see a storm banking up. I knew that if the storm came in the night, it was good-bye to our hay. So I decided to make a hay-making party out of the supper. When those women came with their high-heeled fancy sandals and their gauzy frocks I put pitchforks into their hands and sent them out into the field to help get that hay in under cover. Of course I'd forgotten that they'd be bound to be rigged out in something ridiculous. You should have seen their faces!" Carlitta laughed gleefully. "Should have seen their shoes!"

The young girl from South Africa felt suddenly angry. Amid the laughter, she said quietly, "I think it was an awful thing to do. If I'd been a guest, I should flatly have refused."

"Eileen!" said Waldeck, mildly. But Carlitta pointedly excluded from her notice the girl from South Africa, whom Waldeck was apparently dragging around the world and giving a good time. Carlitta was sitting stiffly, her thin hands caught together, and she never took her eyes off Alice Raines' luxuriantly-fleshed neck, as if it were some object of curiosity, quite independent of a human whole. "If only they'd seen how idiotic they looked, stumbling about," she said fiercely. Her eyes were extraordinarily dark, brimming with brightness; if her expression had not been one of malicious glee, Eileen would have said there were tears in them.

After lunch, the Brands and the Raines parted from the Hicks. Carlitta left the restaurant with Waldeck and Stefan on either arm, and that way she walked with them to the taxi-stand at the end of the block, turning her small head from one to the other, tiny between them. "I just couldn't keep her away from her two boy-friends today," said Edgar, indulgently walking between Eileen and Alice. At this point the thin, middle-aged woman between the two men dropped their arms, bowed down, apparently with laughter at some joke, in the extravagant fashion of a young girl, and then caught them to her again.

Edgar and Carlitta got into a taxi, and the others went in Stefan's car back to his apartment. It was three o'clock in the afternoon, but Stefan brought in a bottle of champagne. The weak sunlight coming in the windows matched the wine. "Carlitta," said Stefan, before he drank. "Still 'terrific.' Beautiful." Eileen Brand, sitting on a yellow sofa, felt vaguely unhappy, as if she had wandered into the wrong room, the wrong year. She even shook her head sadly, so slowly no one noticed.

"I told you, same old Carlitta," said Waldeck. There was a silence. "And that husband," Waldeck went on. "The life they lead. So unlike Carlitta."

"And because of that, so like her," said Stefan. "She always chose the perverse, the impossible. She obviously adores him. Just like Carlitta."

Eileen Brand wanted to stand up and beg of the two men, for their own sake—no, to save her, Eileen, from shame (oh how could she know her reasons!)—*see* she is changed, see Carlitta is old, faded, exists, as Carlitta, no more!

She had risen, without knowing it. "What's the matter, Eileen?" Waldeck looked up. As she opened her mouth to tell him, to tell them both, a strange thing happened. It seemed that her whole mind turned over and showed her the truth. And the truth was much worse than she had wanted to tell them. For they were right. Carlitta had not changed. They were right, but not in the way they thought. Carlitta had not changed. Under that faded face, in that worn body, was the little German girl of the Twenties, arrogant in a youth that did not exist, confidently disdainful in the possession of a beauty that was no longer there.

And what did *she* think of Ohio? Of good Edgar Hicks? Even of the boy who raised chickens and didn't look at television?

"Nothing's the matter," said Eileen. "I'd like a little more wine."

It so happened that a day or two later, Stefan's business took him to Philadelphia. "Don't forget Carlitta and her husband are staying at the Grand Park," Waldeck said. "Oh I'll find them," said Stefan.

But when he came back to New York, and dined with his wife, Waldeck and Eileen the same night, he seemed entirely to have forgotten his expressed intention.

"I had a hell of a job dodging Edgar Hicks," he said, by the way. "Wherever I went I seemed to bump into that Elk convention. They were everywhere. Every time I saw a panama hat with a paisley band I had to double on my tracks and go the other way. Once he nearly saw me. I just managed to squeeze into an elevator in time."

And they all laughed, as if they had just managed it, too.

First Love

ISAAC BABEL

Isaac Babel was born in Odessa in 1894. Later, when he lived in St. Petersburg, he was helped by Maxim Gorki, who published Babel's first stories. Babel fought with the cavalry during the Russian revolution and civil war, which is the setting of many of his stories. He became known for his writing in 1923 and published his short stories successfully until about 1934. In 1937 he was arrested and sent to a concentration camp. He died there around 1940. His collected stories have appeared in many countries in various editions.

When I was ten years old I fell in love with a woman called Galina. Her surname was Rubtsov. Her husband, an officer, went off to the Russo-Japanese War and returned in October, 1905. He brought a great many trunks back with him. These trunks, which weighed nearly half a ton, contained Chinese souvenirs such as screens and costly weapons. Kuzma the yardman used to tell us that Rubtsov had bought all these things with money he had embezzled while serving in the engineer corps of the Manchurian Army. Other people said so too. The Rubtsovs were happy, so it was hard for people not to gossip about them. Their house adjoined our place, and their glass veranda jutted out over our premises, but father didn't make a fuss about it. The elder Rubtsov, who was a tax-inspector, had a reputation in our town for being a fair-minded man: he was friendly with Jews. When the officer, the old man's son, returned from the war, we could see how well he and his wife got on together.

Galina would hold her husband's hand all day long. She stared at him incessantly; she had not seen him for a year and a half. But her gaze frightened me, and I would turn away and shiver, glimpsing that obscure and shameful side of human existence. I longed to fall into a strange sleep, to forget about this life that surpassed all my fancies. Galina would glide through the rooms with her braid hanging down her back, wearing elegant red shoes and a Chinese robe. Under the lace of her deep-cut slip one could see the swelling of her white breasts squeezed downward, and the depression between them. On her robe were embroidered pink silk dragons, birds, trees with hollows in their trunks.

The whole day long she sauntered about with a meaningless smile on her moist lips, brushing against the trunks that had not yet been unpacked and the ladders for doing physical exercises strewn about the floor. Galina would bruise herself, pull her robe above her knee, and say to her husband: "Kiss baby better." The officer would bend his long legs in their narrow dragoon's trousers, in their smooth, taut leather boots with spurs, and crawling across the littered floor on his knees, smile and kiss the bruised flesh, just where a little bulge rose above the garter.

I saw those kisses from my window, and they caused me agony. Unbounded fantasies tormented me—but what's the use of talking about it? The love and the jealousy of a ten-year-old boy are in every way the same as the love and jealousy of a grown-up. I stopped going near the window and avoided Galina for two weeks, and then an event brought us together.

It was the pogrom against the Jews that broke out in 1905 in Nikolayev and other towns where Jews were permitted to live. A mob of hired murderers plundered my father's shop and killed Grandfather Shoyl. All this happened when I was out. That sad morning I had bought some pigeons from Ivan Nikodimych the fancier. For five of my ten years I had dreamed with my whole soul about pigeons. But when I finally bought them, Makarenko the cripple smashed them against my temples. Then Kuzma found me and took me to the Rubtsovs'. On their gate a cross had been chalked. Nobody molested them, and they hid my parents in their house.

Kuzma led me to the glass veranda. My mother and Galina were there in the green rotunda.

"Now we must wash," Galina said. "We must wash, my little rabbi. Our face is covered with feathers, and the feathers are bloody."

She put her arms around me and led me along a hallway full of pungent odours. My head leaned against her hip, her hip that moved and breathed. We went into the kitchen, and Galina put my head under the tap. A goose was frying on the tiled stove, glowing pots and pans hung on the wall, and next to them, in the cook's corner, was Tsar Nicholas decorated with paper flowers. Galina washed off the last smear of pigeon sticking to my cheek. "You'll look like a bridegroom now, my sweet boy," she said, kissing my mouth with her full lips and turning away.

"Your dad has troubles, you see," she suddenly whispered. "He roams the streets all day long with nothing to do. Fetch your dad home."

I saw through the window the empty street under the vast sky, and my redheaded father walking along in the roadway. He walked bareheaded, his soft red hair fluttering, his paper dickey askew and fastened to the wrong button. Vlasov, a drunken workman dressed in a soldier's wadded rags, was stubbornly pursuing him.

"Babel," Vlasov was saying, in a hoarse emotional voice, "we don't need freedom so that the Jews can corner all the business. Shine a light in the working-man's life, for his toil, for his great burdens. That's what you should do, my friend. D'you hear?"

The workman was begging my father for something, grabbing at his arm. Flashes of pure drunken inspiration and a gloomy sleepiness appeared in his face interchangeably. "We should live like the Molokan Sect," he mumbled, swaying on his weak legs. "We should live like the Molokans, but without that old God of the Old Believers. Only Jews get anything from him, nobody else."

Vlasov yelled in wild desperation against the God of the Old Believers who took pity only on the Jews. Vlasov wailed, stumbled, and tried to catch up with his Unknown God, but at that moment a Cossack patrol rode by, barring his way. An officer with stripes on his trousers and a parade belt of silver rode in front of the patrol, a tall peaked cap set stiffly on his head. The officer rode slowly, not looking right or left. He rode as though through a mountain pass, where one can only look ahead.

"Captain," my father mumbled when the Cossacks came abreast of him; "captain," my father said, grasping his head in his hands and kneeling in the mud.

"Do what I can," the officer answered, still looking straight ahead, and raising his hand in its lemon-coloured chamois glove to the peak of his cap.

Right in front of them, at the corner of Fish Street, the mob was looting and smashing up our shop, throwing out into the street boxes filled with nails, machines, and my new photo in school uniform.

"Look," my father said, still on his knees, "they are destroying everything dear to me. Captain, why is it?"

The officer murmured something, and again put the lemon glove to his cap. He touched the reins, but his horse did not move. My father crawled in front of the horse on his knees, rubbing up against its short, kindly, tousled legs.

"At your service," the officer said, tugged at the reins, and rode off, the Cossacks following. They sat passionless on their high saddles, riding through their imaginary mountain pass and disappearing into Cathedral Street.

Galina again gently pushed me to the window.

"Fetch father home," she said. "He hasn't had anything to eat since morning."

I leaned out of the window.

My father turned when he heard my voice.

"My little son," he stuttered with immeasurable tenderness.

He and I went on to the Rubtsovs' veranda where my mother

was lying in the green rotunda. Near her couch dumbbells and gymnastic apparatus were scattered.

"That cursed money," my mother cried at us. "You gave up everything for it. Human life, the children, our wretched little bit of happiness. Cursed money!" she cried out in a hoarse voice quite unlike her real voice. She jerked on the couch and fell silent.

And then in the stillness my hiccups were heard. I was standing by the wall with my cap pulled down over my forehead, and I couldn't stop hiccuping.

"You shouldn't do that, my sweet boy," Galina said with her disdainful smile, flipping me with her stiff robe. She went to the window in her red shoes and began to hang Chinese curtains on the weird cornice. Her bare arms were drowned in silk, and her braid was alive, swinging down over her hip. Enchanted, I stared at her.

I was a bookish boy, and I looked at her as at a distant scene glaringly limelighted. Then I imagined that I was Miron, son of the coalman who had his shop on our corner. I imagined myself to be a member of the Jewish Defence Corps. Like Miron, I am wearing torn shoes tied together with string, and on my shoulder a useless rifle hangs by a green cord. I am kneeling by a wooden fence shooting at the murderers. Behind the fence an empty lot stretches, heaps of dusty coal lie there. The antiquated rifle shoots badly. The murderers have beards and white teeth, they approach stealthily. I have a proud feeling of imminent death, and in the skies, in the world's blueness, I see Galina. I see a loophole cut in the wall of a gigantic house built of myriads of bricks. This purple house weighs heavily on the valley where the grey earth is loosely stamped. In the highest loophole stands Galina. From the loophole, out of reach, she smiles mockingly. Her husband, the officer, half-dressed, stands behind her kissing her neck.

Trying to halt my hiccups, I imagined all this so that I might love Galina with a bitterer, warmer, more hopeless love, or perhaps because for a ten-year-old boy the measure of sorrow was too great. O foolish fancies that helped me forget the death of the pigeons, and Shoyl's death!

Maybe I would have forgotten those murderers if Kuzma had not come to the veranda with Aba, the repulsive Jew.

It was dusk when they came. On the veranda a poor bent lamp was burning. Its flame blinked, flickering companion of unhappiness.

"I put the shroud on Grandfather," Kuzma said as he entered. "He's a treat to look at now, lying there. And I've brought the sexton along. Let him gab a bit over the dead."

Kuzma pointed to Aba the shammes.

"Let him whine awhile," the yardman said amiably. "If the sexton gets his belly filled, he'll pester God all night long."

Kuzma was standing on the threshold, his friendly broken nose twisted in all directions, and he wanted to tell us with as much feeling as he could how he had bound the dead man's chin. But my father interrupted old Kuzma.

"Please, Red Aba," my father said, "pray for the deceased. I will pay you."

"But I'm scared you won't pay," answered Aba in his tedious voice, and he placed his bearded, squeamish face on the tablecloth. "I'm afraid you'll take my rouble and go off with it to the Argentine, to Buenos Aires. You'll start a wholesale business with my rouble . . . a wholesale business," said Aba, champing his disdainful lips and dragging the newspaper across the table to him. In the paper a story was printed about the Tsar's manifesto of October 17, about the proclamation of freedom.

"Citizens of free Russia," Aba read syllable by syllable, chewing a mouthful of his beard, "citizens of free Russia, greetings on this blessed Sunday. . . ."

The old shammes held the swaying paper sideways. He read drowsily in his singsong voice, strangely accentuating the unfamiliar Russian words. Aba's accent resembled the confused mumblings of a Negro who has just come to a Russian port from his native land. It made even my mother laugh.

"I am committing a sin," she exclaimed, leaning forward from her rotunda. "I am laughing, Aba. You'd better tell me how you're getting on, you and your family."

"Ask me something else," growled Aba, not easing the grip of his teeth on his beard, and he went on reading the paper.

"Ask him something else," said my father, echoing Aba's words, and he stepped to the centre of the room. His eyes, smiling at us through his tears, suddenly turned in their sockets and focused on a point we could not see.

"*Oy*, Shoyl," my father said in a level, lying voice that was on the verge of bursting, "*oy*, Shoyl, you dear man. . . ."

We saw that he would be shouting any moment, but mother forestalled us.

"Manus," she cried, her hair dishevelled in an instant; and she started tearing at her husband's breast. "See how sick our boy is! Can't you hear how he's hiccuping? Why can't you, Manus?"

My father stopped.

"Rachel," he said timidly, "I can't tell you how sad I am for Shoyl."

He went to the kitchen and came back with a glass of water.

"Drink, little play-actor," said Aba, coming over to me. "Drink the water. It will help you as a censer helps a dead man."

He was right: the water did not help me. My hiccups increased. A howl escaped from my breast. A swelling, pleasant to touch, rose on my throat. It breathed, expanded, spread on my throat and bulged over my collar. Inside the swelling bubbled my torn and gasping breath, bubbling like water on the boil. And when toward night I was no longer the lop-eared lad I had been all my life, but a writhing mass, my mother covered herself with a shawl and, grown taller and shapelier, approached the paralysed Galina.

"Dear Galina," said my mother in a strong, ringing voice, "how we are disturbing you and your whole family! I am so ashamed, dear Galina."

Her cheeks burning, mother pushed Galina toward the door. Then she hurried back to me and stuffed my mouth with her shawl to muffle my groans.

"Try to stand it," she whispered. "Try to stand it for mother's sake."

But even had it been possible to stand I should not have tried to do so, for I no longer felt any shame.

So began my illness. I was then ten years old. Next morning they took me to the doctor's. The pogrom continued, but we were not interfered with. The doctor, a fat man, diagnosed nervous trouble.

He told us to go to Odessa as soon as possible to consult experts, and to wait there for the warm weather and the sea-bathing.

And so we did. A few days later I went with mother to Odessa, to Grandfather Leivi-Itzkhok's and Uncle Simon's. We went by the morning steamer, and already by noon the brown waters of the Bug had given place to the heavy green swell of the sea. Life at crazy Grandfather Leivi-Itzkhok's opened out before me, and I said good-bye for ever to Nikolayev, where ten years of my childhood had passed. And now, remembering those sorrowful years, I find in them the beginning of the ills that torment me, the cause of my early fading.

Translated by Esther and Joseph Riwkin

Gimpel the Fool

ISAAC BASHEVIS SINGER

Isaac Bashevis Singer was born in Poland in 1904. He attended a rabbinical seminary in Warsaw and at that time began to write fiction, first in Hebrew and then in Yiddish. He emigrated to the United States and worked as a journalist for the *Jewish Daily Forward* in New York City. His works include *The Family Moskat, Satan in Goray, The Slave* and volumes of short stories. Singer has contributed to various journals in Yiddish and English. He has won the Louis Lamed Prize and in 1964 was a candidate for the National Book Award. He lives in New York City.

I

I am Gimpel the Fool. I don't think myself a fool. On the contrary. But that's what folks call me. They gave me the name while I was still in school. I had seven names in all: imbecile, donkey, flax-head, dope, glump, ninny, and fool. The last name stuck. What did my foolishness consist of? I was easy to take in. They said, "Gimpel, you know the rabbi's wife has been brought to childbed?" So I skipped school. Well, it turned out to be a lie. How was I supposed to know? She hadn't had a big belly. But I never looked at her belly. Was that really so foolish? The gang laughed and hee-hawed, stomped and danced and chanted a good-night prayer. And instead of the raisins they give when a woman's lying in, they stuffed my hand full of goat turds. I was no weakling. If I slapped someone he'd see all the way to Cracow. But I'm really not a slugger by nature. I think to myself: Let it pass. So they take advantage of me.

I was coming home from school and heard a dog barking. I'm not afraid of dogs, but of course I never want to start up with them. One of them may be mad, and if he bites there's not a Tartar in the world who can help you. So I made tracks. Then I looked around and saw the whole market-place wild with laughter. It was no dog at all but Wolf-Leib the Thief. How was I supposed to know it was he? It sounded like a howling bitch.

When the pranksters and leg-pullers found that I was easy to fool, every one of them tried his luck with me. "Gimpel, the Czar is coming to Frampol; Gimpel, the moon fell down in Turbeen; Gimpel, little Hodel Furpiece found a treasure behind the bathhouse." And I like a golem believed everyone. In the first place, everything is possible, as it is written in the Wisdom of the Fathers, I've forgotten just how. Second, I had to believe when the whole town came down on me! If I ever dared to say, "Ah, you're kidding!" there was trouble. People got angry. "What do you mean! You want to call everyone a liar?" What was I to do? I believed them, and I hope at least that did them some good.

I was an orphan. My grandfather who brought me up was already bent toward the grave. So they turned me over to a baker, and what a time they gave me there! Every woman or girl who came to bake a batch of noodles had to fool me at least once. "Gimpel, there's a fair in heaven; Gimpel, the rabbi gave birth to a calf in the seventh month; Gimpel, a cow flew over the roof and laid brass eggs." A student from the yeshiva came once to buy a roll, and he said, "You, Gimpel, while you stand here scraping with your baker's shovel the Messiah has come. The dead have arisen." "What do you mean?" I said. "I heard no one blowing the ram's horn!" He said, "Are you deaf?" And all began to cry, "We heard it, we heard!" Then in came Rietze the Candle-dipper and called out in her hoarse voice, "Gimpel, your father and mother have stood up from the grave. They're looking for you."

To tell the truth, I knew very well that nothing of the sort had happened, but all the same, as folks were talking, I threw on my wool vest and went out. Maybe something had happened. What did I stand to lose by looking? Well, what a cat music went up! And then I took a vow to believe nothing more. But that was no go either. They confused me so that I didn't know the big end from the small.

I went to the rabbi to get some advice. He said, "It is written, better to be a fool all your days than for one hour to be evil. You are not a fool. They are the fools. For he who causes his neighbour to feel shame loses Paradise himself." Nevertheless the rabbi's daughter took me in. As I left the rabbinical court she said, "Have you kissed the wall yet?" I said, "No; what for?" She answered, "It's the law; you've got to do it after every visit." Well, there didn't seem to be any harm in it. And she burst out laughing. It was a fine trick. She put one over on me, all right.

I wanted to go off to another town, but then everyone got busy matchmaking, and they were after me so they nearly tore my coat tails off. They talked at me and talked until I got water on the ear. She was no chaste maiden, but they told me she was virgin pure. She had a limp, and they said it was deliberate, from coyness. She had a bastard, and they told me the child was her little brother. I cried, "You're wasting your time. I'll never marry that whore." But they said indignantly, "What a way to talk! Aren't you ashamed of yourself? We can take you to the rabbi and have you fined for giving her a bad name." I saw then that I wouldn't escape them so easily and I thought: They're set on making me their butt. But when you're married the husband's the master, and if that's all right with her it's agreeable to me too. Besides, you can't pass through life unscathed, nor expect to.

I went to her clay house, which was built on the sand, and the whole gang, hollering and chorusing, came after me. They acted like bear-baiters. When we came to the well they stopped all the same. They were afraid to start anything with Elka. Her mouth would open as if it were on a hinge, and she had a fierce tongue. I entered the house. Lines were strung from wall to wall and clothes were drying. Barefoot she stood by the tub, doing the wash. She was dressed in a worn hand-me-down gown of plush. She had her hair put up in braids and pinned across her head. It took my breath away, almost, the reek of it all.

Evidently she knew who I was. She took a look at me and said, "Look who's here! He's come, the drip. Grab a seat."

I told her all; I denied nothing. "Tell me the truth," I said, "are you really a virgin, and is that mischievous Yechiel actually your little brother? Don't be deceitful with me, for I'm an orphan."

"I'm an orphan myself," she answered, "and whoever tries to twist you up, may the end of his nose take a twist. But don't let them think they can take advantage of me. I want a dowry of fifty guilders, and let them take up a collection besides. Otherwise they can kiss my you-know-what." She was very plainspoken. I said, "It's the bride and not the groom who gives a dowry." Then she said, "Don't bargain with me. Either a flat 'yes' or a flat 'no'—Go back where you came from."

I thought: No bread will ever be baked from *this* dough. But ours is not a poor town. They consented to everything and proceeded with the wedding. It so happened that there was a dysentery epidemic at the time. The ceremony was held at the cemetery gates, near the little corpse-washing hut. The fellows got drunk. While the marriage contract was being drawn up I heard the most pious high rabbi ask, "Is the bride a widow or a divorced woman?" And the sexton's wife answered for her, "Both a widow and divorced." It was a black moment for me. But what was I to do, run away from under the marriage canopy?

There was singing and dancing. An old granny danced opposite me, hugging a braided white *chalah*. The master of revels made a "God 'a mercy" in memory of the bride's parents. The schoolboys threw burrs, as on Tishe b'Av fast day. There were a lot of gifts after the sermon: a noodle board, a kneading trough, a bucket, brooms, ladles, household articles galore. Then I took a look and saw two strapping young men carrying a crib. "What do we need this for?" I asked. So they said, "Don't rack your brains about it. It's all right, it'll come in handy." I realized I was going to be rooked. Take it another way though, what did I stand to lose? I reflected: I'll see what comes of it. A whole town can't go altogether crazy.

II

At night I came to where my wife lay, but she wouldn't let me in. "Say, look here, is this what they married us for?" I said. And she said, "My monthly has come." "But yesterday they took you to the ritual bath, and that's afterward, isn't it supposed to be?" "Today isn't yesterday," said she, "and yesterday's not today. You can beat it if you don't like it." In short, I waited.

Not four months later she was in childbed. The townsfolk hid their laughter with their knuckles. But what could I do? She suffered intolerable pains and clawed at the walls. "Gimpel," she cried, "I'm going. Forgive me!" The house filled with women. They were boiling pans of water. The screams rose to the welkin.

The thing to do was to go to the House of Prayer to repeat Psalms, and that was what I did.

The townsfolk liked that, all right. I stood in a corner saying Psalms and prayers, and they shook their heads at me. "Pray, pray!" they told me. "Prayer never made any woman pregnant." One of the congregation put a straw to my mouth and said, "Hay for the cows." There was something to that too, by God!

She gave birth to a boy. Friday at the synagogue the sexton stood up before the Ark, pounded on the reading table, and announced, "The wealthy Reb Gimpel invites the congregation to a feast in honour of the birth of a son." The whole House of Prayer rang with laughter. My face was flaming. But there was nothing I could do. After all, I *was* the one responsible for the circumcision honours and rituals.

Half the town came running. You couldn't wedge another soul in. Women brought peppered chick-peas, and there was a keg of beer from the tavern. I ate and drank as much as anyone, and they all congratulated me. Then there was a circumcision, and I named the boy after my father, may he rest in peace. When all were gone and I was left with my wife alone, she thrust her head through the bed-curtain and called me to her.

"Gimpel," said she, "why are you silent? Has your ship gone and sunk?"

"What shall I say?" I answered. "A fine thing you've done to me! If my mother had known of it she'd have died a second time."

She said, "Are you crazy, or what?"

"How can you make such a fool," I said, "of one who should be the lord and master?"

"What's the matter with you?" she said. "What have you taken it into your head to imagine?"

I saw that I must speak bluntly and openly. "Do you think this is the way to use an orphan?" I said. "You have borne a bastard."

She answered, "Drive this foolishness out of your head. The child is yours."

"How can he be mine?" I argued. "He was born seventeen weeks after the wedding."

She told me then that he was premature. I said, "Isn't he a little too premature?" She said, she had had a grandmother who carried just as short a time and she resembled this grandmother of hers as one drop of water does another. She swore to it with such oaths that you would have believed a peasant at the fair if he had used them. To tell the plain truth, I didn't believe her; but when I talked it over next day with the schoolmaster he told me that the very same thing had happened to Adam and Eve. Two they went up to bed, and four they descended.

"There isn't a woman in the world who is not the granddaughter of Eve," he said.

That was how it was; they argued me dumb. But then, who really knows how such things are?

I began to forget my sorrow. I loved the child madly, and he loved me too. As soon as he saw me he'd wave his little hands and want me to pick him up, and when he was colicky I was the only one who could pacify him. I bought him a little bone teething ring and a little gilded cap. He was forever catching the evil eye from someone, and then I had to run to get one of those abracadabras for him that would get him out of it. I worked like an ox. You know how expenses go up when there's an infant in the house. I don't want to lie about it; I didn't dislike Elka either, for that matter. She swore at me and cursed, and I couldn't get enough of her. What strength she had! One of her looks could rob you of the power of speech. And her orations! Pitch and sulphur, that's what they were full of, and yet somehow also full of charm. I adored her every word. She gave me bloody wounds though.

In the evening I brought her a white loaf as well as a dark one, and also poppyseed rolls I baked myself. I thieved because of her and swiped everything I could lay hands on: macaroons, raisins, almonds, cakes. I hope I may be forgiven for stealing from the Saturday pots the women left to warm in the baker's oven. I would take out scraps of meat, a chunk of pudding, a chicken leg or head, a piece of tripe, whatever I could nip quickly. She ate and became fat and handsome.

I had to sleep away from home all during the week, at the bakery. On Friday nights when I got home she always made an excuse of some sort. Either she had heartburn, or a stitch in the side, or hiccups, or headaches. You know what women's excuses are. I had a bitter time of it. It was rough. To add to it, this little brother of hers, the bastard, was growing bigger. He'd put lumps on me, and when I wanted to hit back she'd open her mouth and curse so powerfully I saw a green haze floating before my eyes. Ten times a day she threatened to divorce me. Another man in my place would have taken French leave and disappeared. But I'm the type that bears it and says nothing. What's one to do? Shoulders are from God, and burdens too.

One night there was a calamity in the bakery; the oven burst, and we almost had a fire. There was nothing to do but go home, so I went home. Let me, I thought, also taste the joy of sleeping in bed in mid-week. I didn't want to wake the sleeping mite and tiptoed into the house. Coming in, it seemed to me that I heard not the snoring of one but, as it were, a double snore, one a thin enough snore and the other like the snoring of a slaughtered ox. Oh, I didn't like that! I didn't like it at all. I went up to the bed, and things suddenly turned black. Next to Elka lay a man's form. Another in my place would have made an uproar, and enough noise to rouse the whole town, but the thought occurred to me that I might wake the child. A little thing like that—why frighten a little swallow, I thought. All right then, I went back to the bakery and stretched out on a sack of flour and till morning I never shut an eye. I shivered as if I had had malaria. "Enough of being a donkey," I said to myself. "Gimpel isn't going to be a sucker all his life. There's a limit even to the foolishness of a fool like Gimpel."

In the morning I went to the rabbi to get advice, and it made a great commotion in the town. They sent the beadle for Elka right away. She came, carrying the child. And what do you think she did? She denied it, denied everything, bone and stone! "He's out of his head," she said. "I know nothing of dreams or divinations." They yelled at her, warned her, hammered on the table, but she stuck to her guns: it was a false accusation, she said.

The butchers and the horse-traders took her part. One of the lads from the slaughterhouse came by and said to me. "We've got our eye on you, you're a marked man." Meanwhile the child started to bear down and soiled itself. In the rabbinical court there was an Ark of the covenant, and they couldn't allow that, so they sent Elka away.

I said to the rabbi, "What shall I do?"

"You must divorce her at once," said he.

"And what if she refuses?" I asked.

He said, "You must serve the divorce. That's all you'll have to do."

I said, "Well, all right, Rabbi. Let me think about it."

"There's nothing to think about," said he. "You mustn't remain under the same roof with her."

"And if I want to see the child?" I asked.

"Let her go, the harlot," said he, "and her brood of bastards with her."

The verdict he gave was that I mustn't even cross her threshold—never again, as long as I should live.

During the day it didn't bother me so much. I thought: It was bound to happen, the abscess had to burst. But at night when I stretched out upon the sacks I felt it all very bitterly. A longing took me, for her and for the child. I wanted to be angry, but that's my misfortune exactly, I don't have it in me to be really angry. In the first place—this was how my thoughts went—there's bound to be a slip sometimes. You can't live without errors. Probably that lad who was with her led her on and gave her presents and what not, and women are often long on hair and short on sense, so he got around her. And then since she denies it so, maybe I was only seeing things? Hallucinations do happen. You see a figure or a mannikin or something, but when you come up closer it's nothing, there's not a thing there. And if that's so, I'm doing her injustice. And when I got so far in my thoughts I started to weep. I sobbed so that I wet the flour where I lay. In the morning I went to the rabbi and told him that I had made a mistake. The rabbi wrote on with his quill, and he said that if that were so he would have to reconsider the whole case. Until he had finished I wasn't to go near my wife, but I might send her bread and money by messenger.

III

Nine months passed before all the rabbis could come to an agreement. Letters went back and forth. I hadn't realized that there could be so much erudition about a matter like this.

Meanwhile Elka gave birth to still another child, a girl this time. On the Sabbath I went to the synagogue and invoked a blessing on her. They called me up to the Torah, and I named the child for my mother-in-law—may she rest in peace. The louts and loudmouths of the town who came into the bakery gave me a going over. All Frampol refreshed its spirits because of my trouble and grief. However, I resolved that I would always believe what I was told. What's the good of *not* believing? Today it's your wife you don't believe; tomorrow it's God Himself you won't take stock in.

By an apprentice who was her neighbour I sent her daily a corn or a wheat loaf, or a piece of pastry, rolls or bagels, or, when I got the chance, a slab of pudding, a slice of honeycake, or wedding strudel—whatever came my way. The apprentice was a goodhearted lad, and more than once he added something on his own. He had formerly annoyed me a lot, plucking my nose and digging me in the ribs, but when he started to be a visitor to my house he became kind and friendly. "Hey, you, Gimpel," he said to me, "you have a very decent little wife and two fine kids. You don't deserve them."

"But the things people say about her," I said.

"Well, they have long tongues," he said, "and nothing to do with them but babble. Ignore it as you ignore the cold of last winter."

One day the rabbi sent for me and said, "Are you certain, Gimpel, that you were wrong about your wife?"

I said, "I'm certain."

"Why, but look here! You yourself saw it."

"It must have been a shadow," I said.

"The shadow of what?"

"Just of one of the beams, I think."

"You can go home then. You owe thanks to the Yanover rabbi. He found an obscure reference in Maimonides that favoured you."

I seized the rabbi's hand and kissed it.

I wanted to run home immediately. It's no small thing to be separated for so long a time from wife and child. Then I reflected: I'd better go back to work now, and go home in the evening. I said nothing to anyone, although as far as my heart was concerned it was like one of the Holy Days. The women teased and twitted me as they did every day, but my thought was: Go on, with your loose talk. The truth is out, like the oil upon the water. Maimonides says it's right, and therefore it is right!

At night, when I had covered the dough to let it rise, I took my share of bread and a little sack of flour and started homeward. The moon was full and the stars were glistening, something to terrify the soul. I hurried onward, and before me darted a long shadow. It was winter, and a fresh snow had fallen. I had a mind to sing, but it was growing late and I didn't want to wake the householders. Then I felt like whistling, but I remembered that you don't whistle at night because it brings the demons out. So I was silent and walked as fast as I could.

Dogs in the Christian yards barked at me when I passed, but I thought: Bark your teeth out! What are you but mere dogs? Whereas I am a man, the husband of a fine wife, the father of promising children.

As I approached the house my heart started to pound as though it were the heart of a criminal. I felt no fear, but my heart went thump! thump! Well, no drawing back. I quietly lifted the latch and went in. Elka was asleep. I looked at the infant's cradle. The shutter was closed, but the moon forced its way through the cracks. I saw the newborn child's face and loved it as soon as I saw it—immediately—each tiny bone.

Then I came nearer to the bed. And what did I see but the apprentice lying there beside Elka. The moon went out all at once. It was utterly black, and I trembled. My teeth chattered. The bread fell from my hands, and my wife waked and said, "Who is that, ah?"

I muttered, "It's me."

"Gimpel?" she asked. "How come you're here? I thought it was forbidden."

"The rabbi said," I answered and shook as with a fever.

"Listen to me, Gimpel," she said, "go out to the shed and see if the goat's all right. It seems she's been sick." I have forgotten to say that we had a goat. When I heard she was unwell I went into the yard. The nannygoat was a good little creature. I had a nearly human feeling for her.

With hesitant steps I went up to the shed and opened the door. The goat stood there on her four feet. I felt her everywhere, drew her by the horns, examined her udders, and found nothing wrong. She had probably eaten too much bark. "Good night, little goat," I said. "Keep well." And the little beast answered with a "Maa" as though to thank me for the good will.

I went back. The apprentice had vanished.

"Where," I asked, "is the lad?"

"What lad?" my wife answered.

"What do you mean?" I said. "The apprentice. You were sleeping with him."

"The things I have dreamed this night and the night before," she said, "may they come true and lay you low, body and soul! An evil spirit has taken root in you and dazzles your sight." She screamed out, "You hateful creature! You moon calf! You spook! You uncouth man! Get out, or I'll scream all Frampol out of bed!"

Before I could move, her brother sprang out from behind the

oven and struck me a blow on the back of the head. I thought he had broken my neck. I felt that something about me was deeply wrong, and I said, "Don't make a scandal. All that's needed now is that people should accuse me of raising spooks and *dybbuks*." For that was what she had meant. "No one will touch bread of my baking."

In short, I somehow calmed her.

"Well," she said, "that's enough. Lie down, and be shattered by wheels."

Next morning I called the apprentice aside. "Listen here, brother!" I said. And so on and so forth. "What do you say?" He stared at me as though I had dropped from the roof or something.

"I swear," he said, "you'd better go to an herb doctor or some healer. I'm afraid you have a screw loose, but I'll hush it up for you." And that's how the thing stood.

To make a long story short, I lived twenty years with my wife. She bore me six children, four daughters and two sons. All kinds of things happened, but I neither saw nor heard. I believed, and that's all. The rabbi recently said to me, "Belief in itself is beneficial. It is written that a good man lives by his faith."

Suddenly my wife took sick. It began with a trifle, a little growth upon the breast. But she evidently was not destined to live long; she had no years. I spent a fortune on her. I have forgotten to say that by this time I had a bakery of my own and in Frampol was considered to be something of a rich man. Daily the healer came, and every witch doctor in the neighbourhood was brought. They decided to use leeches, and after that to try cupping. They even called a doctor from Lublin, but it was too late. Before she died she called me to her bed and said, "Forgive me, Gimpel."

I said, "What is there to forgive? You have been a good and faithful wife."

"Woe, Gimpel!" she said. "It was ugly how I deceived you

all these years. I want to go clean to my Maker, and so I have to tell you that the children are not yours."

If I had been clouted on the head with a piece of wood it couldn't have bewildered me more.

"Whose are they?" I asked.

"I don't know," she said. "There were a lot . . . but they're not yours." And as she spoke she tossed her head to the side, her eyes turned glassy, and it was all up with Elka. On her whitened lips there remained a smile.

I imagined that, dead as she was, she was saying, "I deceived Gimpel. That was the meaning of my brief life."

IV

One night, when the period of mourning was done, as I lay dreaming on the flour sacks, there came the Spirit of Evil himself and said to me, "Gimpel, why do you sleep?"

I said, "What should I be doing? Eating *kreplach?*"

"The whole world deceives you," he said, "and you ought to deceive the world in your turn."

"How can I deceive all the world?" I asked him.

He answered, "You might accumulate a bucket of urine every day and at night pour it into the dough. Let the sages of Frampol eat filth."

"What about the judgment in the world to come?" I said.

"There is no world to come," he said. "They've sold you a bill of goods and talked you into believing you carried a cat in your belly. What nonsense!"

"Well then," I said, "and is there a God?"

He answered, "There is no God either."

"What," I said, "*is* there, then?"

"A thick mire."

He stood before my eyes with a goatish beard and horn, long-toothed, and with a tail. Hearing such words, I wanted to snatch him by the tail, but I tumbled from the flour sacks and nearly broke a rib. Then it happened that I had to answer the call of nature, and, passing, I saw the risen dough, which seemed to say to me, "Do it!" In brief, I let myself be persuaded.

At dawn the apprentice came. We kneaded the bread, scattered caraway seeds on it, and set it to bake. Then the apprentice went away, and I was left sitting in the little trench by the oven, on a pile of rags. Well, Gimpel, I thought, you've revenged yourself on them for all the shame they've put on you. Outside the frost glittered, but it was warm beside the oven. The flames heated my face. I bent my head and fell into a doze.

I saw in a dream, at once, Elka in her shroud. She called to me, "What have you done, Gimpel?"

I said to her, "It's all your fault," and started to cry.

"You fool!" she said. "You fool! Because I was false is everything false too? I never deceived anyone but myself. I'm paying for it all, Gimpel. They spare you nothing here."

I looked at her face. It was black; I was startled and waked, and remained sitting dumb. I sensed that everything hung in the balance. A false step now and I'd lose Eternal Life. But God gave me His help. I seized the long shovel and took out the loaves, carried them into the yard, and started to dig a hole in the frozen earth.

My apprentice came back as I was doing it. "What are you doing, boss?" he said, and grew pale as a corpse.

"I know what I'm doing," I said, and I buried it all before his very eyes.

Then I went home, took my hoard from its hiding place, and divided it among the children. "I saw your mother tonight," I said. "She's turning black, poor thing."

They were so astounded they couldn't speak a word.

"Be well," I said, "and forget that such a one as Gimpel ever existed." I put on my short coat, a pair of boots, took the bag that held my prayer shawl in one hand, my stock in the other, and kissed the *mezzuzah*. When people saw me in the street they were greatly surprised.

"Where are you going?" they said.

I answered, "Into the world." And so I departed from Frampol.

I wandered over the land, and good people did not neglect me. After many years I became old and white; I heard a great deal, many lies and falsehoods, but the longer I lived the more I understood that there were really no lies. Whatever doesn't really happen is dreamed at night. It happens to one if it doesn't happen to another, tomorrow if not today, or a century hence if not next year. What difference can it make? Often I heard tales of which I said, "Now this is a thing that cannot happen." But before a year had elapsed I heard that it actually had come to pass somewhere.

Going from place to place, eating at strange tables, it often happens that I spin yarns—improbable things that could never have happened—about devils, magicians, windmills, and the like. The children run after me, calling, "Grandfather, tell us a story." Sometimes they ask for particular stories, and I try to please them. A fat young boy once said to me, "Grandfather, it's the same story you told us before." The little rogue, he was right.

So it is with dreams too. It is many years since I left Frampol, but as soon as I shut my eyes I am there again. And whom do you think I see? Elka. She is standing by the washtub, as at our first encounter, but her face is shining and her eyes are as radiant as the eyes of a saint, and she speaks outlandish words to me, strange things. When I wake I have forgotten it all. But while the dream lasts I am comforted. She answers all my queries, and what comes out is that all is right. I weep and implore, "Let me be with you." And she consoles me and tells me to be patient. The time is nearer than it is far. Sometimes she strokes and kisses me and weeps upon my face. When I awaken I feel her lips and taste the salt of her tears.

No doubt the world is entirely an imaginary world, but it is only once removed from the true world. At the door of the hovel where I lie, there stands the plank on which the dead are taken away. The gravedigger Jew has his spade ready. The grave waits and the worms are hungry; the shrouds are prepared—I carry them in my beggar's sack. Another *shnorrer* is waiting to inherit my bed of straw. When the time comes I will go joyfully. Whatever may be there, it will be real, without complication, without ridicule, without deception. God be praised: there even Gimpel cannot be deceived.

Translated by Saul Bellow

Act of Faith

IRWIN SHAW

Irwin Shaw was born in New York, in 1913. After attending Brooklyn College he began writing for radio, and then turned to playwriting. His plays include *Bury the Dead* and *The Gentle People*. Shaw is well-known for his novels, which include *The Young Lions, The Troubled Air, Lucy Crown, Two Weeks in Another Town* and *Voices of a Summer Day*, and also for his short stories. His stories have been published in a number of magazines, among them, *The New Yorker* and *Colliers*. Shaw is married, has one son, and lives in Europe.

"Present it in a pitiful light," Olson was saying, as they picked their way through the mud toward the orderly room tent. "Three combat-scarred veterans, who fought their way from Omaha Beach to—what was the name of the town we fought our way to?"

"Konigstein," Seeger said.

"Konigstein." Olson lifted his right foot heavily out of a puddle and stared admiringly at the three pounds of mud clinging to his overshoe. "The backbone of the Army. The non-commissioned officer. We deserve better of our country. Mention our decorations in passing."

"What decorations should I mention?" Seeger asked. "The marksman's medal?"

"Never quite made it," Olson said. "I had a cross-eyed scorer at the butts. Mention the Bronze Star, the Silver Star, the Croix de Guerre, with palms, the unit citation, the Congressional Medal of Honour."

"I'll mention them all." Seeger grinned. "You don't think the C.O.'ll notice that we haven't won most of them, do you?"

"Gad, sir," Olson said with dignity, "do you think that one Southern military gentleman will dare doubt the word of another Southern military gentleman in the hour of victory?"

"I come from Ohio," Seeger said.

"Welch comes from Kansas," Olson said, coolly staring down a second lieutenant who was passing. The lieutenant made a nervous little jerk with his hand as though he expected a salute, then kept it rigid, as a slight superior smile of scorn twisted at the corner of Olson's mouth. The lieutenant dropped his eyes and splashed on through the mud. "You've heard of Kansas," Olson said. "Magnolia-scented Kansas."

"Of course," said Seeger. "I'm no fool."

"Do your duty by your men, Sergeant." Olson stopped to wipe the rain off his face and lectured him. "Highest ranking non-com present took the initiative and saved his comrades, at great personal risk, above and beyond the call of you-know-what, in the best traditions of the American Army."

"I will throw myself in the breach," Seeger said.

"Welch and I can't ask more," said Olson, approvingly.

They walked heavily through the mud on the streets between the rows of tents. The camp stretched drearily over the Rheims plain, with the rain beating on the sagging tents. The division had been there over three weeks by now, waiting to be shipped home, and all the meagre diversions of the neighbourhood had been sampled and exhausted, and there was an air of watchful suspicion and impatience with the military life hanging over the camp now, and there was even reputed to be a staff sergeant in C Company who was laying odds they would not get back to America before July Fourth.

"I'm redeployable," Olson sang. "It's so enjoyable . . ." It was a jingle he had composed to no recognizable melody in the early days after the victory in Europe, when he had added up his points and found they only came to 63. "Tokyo, wait for me . . ."

They were going to be discharged as soon as they got back to the States, but Olson persisted in singing the song, occasionally adding a mournful stanza about dengue fever and brown girls with venereal disease. He was a short, round boy who had been flunked out of air cadets' school and transferred to the infantry, but whose spirits had not been damaged in the process. He had a high, childish voice and a pretty baby face. He was very good-natured, and had a girl waiting for him at the University of California, where he intended to finish his course at Government expense when he got out of the Army, and he was just the type who is killed off early and predictably and sadly in motion pictures about the war, but he had gone through four campaigns and six major battles without a scratch.

Seeger was a large, lanky boy, with a big nose, who had been wounded at Saint Lô, but had come back to his outfit in the Siegfried Line, quite unchanged. He was cheerful and dependable, and he knew his business and had broken in five or six second lieutenants who had been killed or wounded and the C.O. had tried to get him commissioned in the field, but the war had ended while the paperwork was being fumbled over at headquarters.

They reached the door of the orderly tent and stopped. "Be brave, Sergeant," Olson said. "Welch and I are depending on you."

"O.K.," Seeger said, and went in.

The tent had the dank, Army-canvas smell that had been so much a part of Seeger's life in the past three years. The company clerk was reading a July, 1945, issue of the *Buffalo Courier-Express,* which had just reached him, and Captain Taney, the company C.O., was seated at a sawbuck table he used as a desk, writing a letter to his wife, his lips pursed with effort. He was a small, fussy man, with sandy hair that was falling out. While the fighting had been going on, he had been lean and tense and his small voice had been cold and full of authority. But now he had relaxed, and a little pot belly was creeping up under his belt and he kept the top button of his trousers open when he could do it without too public loss of dignity. During the war Seeger had thought of him as a natural soldier, tireless, fanatic about detail, aggressive, severely anxious to kill Germans. But in the past few months Seeger had seen him relapsing gradually and pleasantly into a small-town, wholesale hardware merchant, which he had been before the war, sedentary and a little shy, and, as he had once told Seeger, worried, here in the bleak champagne fields of France, about his daughter, who had just turned twelve and had a tendency to go after the boys and had been caught by her mother kissing a fifteen-year-old neighbour in the hammock after school.

"Hello, Seeger," he said, returning the salute in a mild, off-hand gesture. "What's on your mind?"

"Am I disturbing you, sir?"

"Oh, no. Just writing a letter to my wife. You married, Seeger?" He peered at the tall boy standing before him.

"No, sir."

"It's very difficult," Taney sighed, pushing dissatisfiedly at the letter before him. "My wife complains I don't tell her I love her often enough. Been married fifteen years. You'd think she'd know by now." He smiled at Seeger. "I thought you were going to Paris," he said. "I signed the passes yesterday."

"That's what I came to see you about, sir."

"I suppose something's wrong with the passes." Taney spoke resignedly, like a man who has never quite got the hang of Army regulations and has had requisitions, furloughs, requests for court-martial returned for correction in a baffling flood.

"No, sir," Seeger said. "The passes're fine. They start to-morrow. Well, it's just . . ." He looked around at the company clerk, who was on the sports page.

"This confidential?" Taney asked.

"If you don't mind, sir."

"Johnny," Taney said to the clerk, "go stand in the rain some place."

"Yes, sir," the clerk said, and slowly got up and walked out.

Taney looked shrewdly at Seeger, spoke in a secret whisper. "You pick up anything?" he asked.

Seeger grinned. "No, sir, haven't had my hands on a girl since Strasbourg."

"Ah, that's good." Taney leaned back, relieved, happy he didn't have to cope with the disapproval of the Medical Corps.

"It's—well," said Seeger, embarrassed, "it's hard to say—but it's money."

Taney shook his head sadly. "I know."

"We haven't been paid for three months, sir, and . . ."

"Damn it!" Taney stood up and shouted furiously. "I would like to take every bloody chair-warming old lady in the Finance Department and wring their necks."

The clerk stuck his head into the tent. "Anything wrong? You call for me, sir?"

"No," Taney shouted. "Get out of here."

The clerk ducked out.

Taney sat down again. "I suppose," he said, in a more normal voice, "they have their problems. Outfits being broken up, being moved all over the place. But it is rugged."

"It wouldn't be so bad," Seeger said. "But we're going to Paris to-morrow. Olson, Welch and myself. And you need money in Paris."

"Don't I know it." Taney wagged his head. "Do you know what I paid for a bottle of champagne on the Place Pigalle in September . . . ?" He paused significantly. "I won't tell you. You won't have any respect for me for the rest of your life."

Seeger laughed. "Hanging," he said, "is too good for the guy who thought up the rate of exchange."

"I don't care if I never see another franc as long as live." Taney waved his letter in the air, although it had been dry for a long time.

There was silence in the tent and Seeger swallowed a little embarrassedly, watching the C.O. wave the flimsy sheet of paper in regular sweeping movements. "Sir," he said, "the truth is, I've come to borrow some money for Welch, Olson and myself. We'll pay it back out of the first pay we get, and that can't be too long from now. If you don't want to give it to us, just tell me and I'll understand and get the hell out of here. We don't like to ask, but you might just as well be dead as be in Paris broke."

Taney stopped waving his letter and put it down thoughtfully. He peered at it, wrinkling his brow, looking like an aged bookkeeper in the single gloomy light that hung in the middle of the tent.

"Just say the word, Captain," Seeger said, "and I'll blow . . ."

"Stay where you are, son," said Taney. He dug in his shirt pocket and took out a worn, sweat-stained wallet. He looked at it for a moment. "Alligator," he said, with automatic, absent pride. "My wife sent it to me when we were in England. Pounds don't fit in it. However . . ." He opened it and took out all the contents. There was a small pile of francs on the table in front of him. He counted them. "Four hundred francs," he said. "Eight bucks."

"Excuse me," Seeger said humbly. "I shouldn't have asked."

"Delighted," Taney said vigorously. "Absolutely delighted." He started dividing the francs into two piles. "Truth is, Seeger, most of my money goes home in allotments. And the truth is, I lost eleven hundred francs in a poker game three nights ago, and I ought to be ashamed of myself. Here . . ." he shoved one pile toward Seeger. "Two hundred francs."

Seeger looked down at the frayed, meretricious paper, which always seemed to him like stage money, anyway. "No, sir," he said, "I can't take it."

"Take it," Taney said. "That's a direct order."

Seeger slowly picked up the money, not looking at Taney. "Some time, sir," he said, "after we get out, you have to come over to my house and you and my father and my brother and I'll go on a real drunk."

"I regard that," Taney said, gravely, "as a solemn commitment."

They smiled at each other and Seeger started out.

"Have a drink for me," said Taney, "at the Café de la Paix.

A small drink." He was sitting down to write to his wife he loved her when Seeger went out of the tent.

Olson fell into step with Seeger and they walked silently through the mud between the tents.

"Well, *mon vieux?*" Olson said finally.

"Two hundred francs," said Seeger.

Olson groaned. "Two hundred francs! We won't be able to pinch a whore's behind on the Boulevard des Capucines for two hundred francs. That miserable, penny-loving Yankee!"

"He only had four hundred," Seeger said.

"I revise my opinion," said Olson.

They walked disconsolately and heavily back toward their tent.

Olson spoke only once before they got there. "These raincoats," he said, patting his. "Most ingenious invention of the war. Highest saturation point of any modern fabric. Collect and hold more water per square inch than any material known to man. All hail the quartermaster!"

Welch was waiting at the entrance of their tent. He was standing there peering excitedly and short-sightedly out at the rain through his glasses, looking angry and tough, like a big-city hack-driver, individual and incorruptible even in the ten-million coloured uniform. Every time Seeger came upon Welch unexpectedly, he couldn't help smiling at the belligerent stance, the harsh stare through the steel-rimmed G.I. glasses, which had nothing at all to do with the way Welch really was. "It's a family inheritance," Welch had once explained. "My whole family stands as though we were getting ready to rap a drunk with a beer glass. Even my old lady." Welch had six brothers, all devout, according to Welch, and Seeger from time to time idly pictured them standing in a row, on Sunday mornings in church, seemingly on the verge of general violence, amid the hushed Latin and Sabbath millinery.

"How much?" Welch asked loudly.

"Don't make us laugh," Olson said, pushing past him into the tent.

"What do you think I could get from the French for my combat jacket?" Seeger said. He went into the tent and lay down on his cot.

Welch followed them in and stood between the two of them, a superior smile on his face. "Boys," he said, "on a man's errand."

"I can just see us now," Olson murmured, lying on his cot with his hands clasped behind his head, "painting Montmartre red. Please bring on the naked dancing girls. Four bucks' worth."

"I am not worried," Welch announced.

"Get out of here," Olson turned over on his stomach.

"I know where we can put our hands on sixty-five bucks." Welch looked triumphantly first at Olson, then at Seeger.

Olson turned over slowly and sat up. "I'll kill you," he said, "if you're kidding."

"While you guys are wasting your time," Welch said, "fooling around with the infantry, I used my head. I went into Reems and used my head."

"Rance," Olson said automatically. He had had two years of French in college and he felt, now that the war was over, that he had to introduce his friends to some of his culture.

"I got talking to a captain in the Air Force," Welch said eagerly. "A little fat old paddle-footed captain that never got higher off the ground than the second floor of Com Z headquarters, and he told me that what he would admire to do more than anything else is take home a nice shiny German Luger pistol with him to show to the boys back in Pacific Grove, California."

Silence fell on the tent and Welch and Olson looked tentatively at Seeger.

"Sixty-five bucks for a Luger, these days," Olson said, "is a very good figure."

"They've been sellin' for as low as thirty-five," said Welch hesitantly. "I'll bet," he said to Seeger, "you could sell yours now and buy another one back when you get some dough, and make a clear twenty-five on the deal."

Seeger didn't say anything. He had killed the owner of the Luger, an enormous S.S. major, in Coblenz, behind some paper bales in a warehouse, and the major had fired at Seeger three times with it, one knicking his helmet, before Seeger hit him in the face at twenty feet. Seeger had kept the Luger, a long, heavy, well-balanced gun, very carefully since then, lugging it with him, hiding it at the bottom of his bedroll, oiling it three times a week, avoiding all opportunities of selling it, although he had been offered as much as a hundred dollars for it and several times eighty and ninety, while the war was still on, before German weapons became a glut on the market.

"Well," said Welch, "there's no hurry. I told the captain I'd see him to-night around eight o'clock in front of the Lion D'Or Hotel. You got five hours to make up your mind. Plenty of time."

"Me," said Olson, after a pause. "I won't say anything."

Seeger looked reflectively at his feet and the other two men avoided looking at him. Welch dug in his pocket. "I forgot," he said. "I picked up a letter for you." He handed it to Seeger.

"Thanks," Seeger said. He opened it absently, thinking about the Luger.

"Me," said Olson, "I won't say a bloody word. I'm just going to lie here and think about that nice fat Air Force captain."

Seeger grinned a little at him and went to the tent opening to read the letter in the light. The letter was from his father, and even from one glance at the handwriting, scrawly and hurried and spotted, so different from his father's usual steady, handsome professional script, he knew that something was wrong.

"Dear Norman," it read, "some time in the future, you must forgive me for writing this letter. But I have been holding this in so long, and there is no one here I can talk to, and because of your brother's condition I must pretend to be cheerful and optimistic all the time at home, both with him and your mother, who has never been the same since Leonard was killed. You're the oldest now, and although I know we've never talked very seriously about anything before, you have been through a great deal by now, and I imagine you must have matured considerably, and you've seen so many different places and people. . . . Norman, I need help. While the war was on and you were fighting, I kept this to myself. It wouldn't have been fair to burden you with this. But now the war is over, and I no longer feel I can stand up under this alone. And you will have to face it some time when you get home, if you haven't faced it already, and perhaps we can help each other by facing it together. . . ."

"I'm redeployable," Olson was singing softly, on his cot. "It's so enjoyable, In the Pelilu mud, With the tropical crud . . ." He fell silent after his burst of song.

Seeger blinked his eyes, at the entrance of the tent, in the wan rainy light, and went on reading his father's letter, on the stiff white stationery with the University letterhead in polite engraving at the top of each page.

"I've been feeling this coming on for a long time," the letter continued, "but it wasn't until last Sunday morning that something happened to make me feel it in its full force. I don't know how much you've guessed about the reason for Jacob's discharge from the Army. It's true he was pretty badly wounded in the leg at Metz, but I've asked around, and I know that men with worse wounds were returned to duty after hospitalization. Jacob got a medical discharge, but I don't think it was for the shrapnel wound in his thigh. He is suffering now from what I suppose you call combat fatigue, and he is subject to fits of depression and hallucinations. Your mother and I thought that as time went by and the war and the Army receded, he would grow better. Instead, he is growing worse. Last Sunday morning when I came down into the living-room from upstairs he was crouched in his old uniform, next to the window, peering out . . ."

"What the hell," Olson was saying, "if we don't get the sixty-five bucks we can always go to the Louvre. I understand the Mona Lisa is back."

"I asked Jacob what he was doing," the letter went on. "He didn't turn round. 'I'm observing,' he said. 'V-1's and V-2's. Buzz-bombs and rockets. They're coming in by the hundreds.' I tried to reason with him and he told me to crouch and save myself from flying glass. To humour him I got down on the floor beside him and tried to tell him the war was over, that we were in Ohio, 4,000 miles away from the nearest spot where bombs had fallen, that America had never been touched. He wouldn't listen. 'These're the new rocket bombs, he said, 'for the Jews.' "

"Did you ever hear of the Pantheon?" Olson asked loudly.

"No," said Welch.

"It's free."

"I'll go," said Welch.

Seeger shook his head a little and blinked his eyes before he went back to the letter.

"After that," his father went on, "Jacob seemed to forget about the bombs from time to time, but he kept saying that the mobs were coming up the street armed with bazookas and Browning automatic rifles. He mumbled incoherently a good deal of the time and kept walking back and forth saying, 'What's the situation? Do you know what the situation is?' And he told me he wasn't worried about himself, he was a soldier and he expected to be killed, but he was worried about Mother and myself and Leonard and you. He seemed to forget that Leonard was dead. I tried to calm him and get him back to bed before your mother came down, but he refused and wanted to set out immediately to rejoin his division. It was all terribly disjointed and at one time he took the ribbon he got for winning the Bronze Star and threw it in the fireplace, then he got down on his hands and knees and picked it out of the ashes and made me pin it on him again, and he kept repeating, 'This is when they are coming for the Jews.' "

"The next war I'm in," said Olson, "they don't get me under the rank of colonel."

It had stopped raining by now and Seeger folded the unfinished letter and went outside. He walked slowly down to the end of the company street, and facing out across the empty, soaked French fields, scarred and neglected by various armies, he stopped and opened the letter again.

"I don't know what Jacob went through in the Army," his father wrote, "that has done this to him. He never talks to me about the war and he refuses to go to a psychoanalyst, and from time to time he is his own bouncing, cheerful self, playing in tennis tournaments and going around with a large group of girls. But he has devoured all the concentration camp reports, and I have found him weeping when the newspapers reported that a hundred Jews were killed in Tripoli some time ago.

"The terrible thing is, Norman, that I find myself coming to believe that it is not neurotic for a Jew to behave like this today. Perhaps Jacob is the normal one, and I, going about my business, teaching economics in a quiet classroom, pretending to understand that the world is comprehensible and orderly, am really the mad one. I ask you once more to forgive me for writing you a letter like this, so different from any letter or any conversation I've ever had with you. But it is crowding me, too. I do not see rockets and bombs, but I see other things.

"Wherever you go these days—restaurants, hotels, clubs, trains—you seem to hear talk about the Jews, mean, hateful, murderous talk. Whatever page you turn to in the newspapers you seem to find an article about Jews being killed somewhere on the face of the globe. And there are large, influential newspapers and well-known columnists who each day are growing more and more outspoken and more popular. The day that Roosevelt died I heard a drunken man yelling outside a bar,

'Finally, they got the Jew out of the White House.' And some of the people who heard him merely laughed and nobody stopped him. And on V.E. Day, in celebration, hoodlums in Los Angeles savagely beat a Jewish writer. It's difficult to know what to do, whom to fight, where to look for allies.

"Three months ago, for example, I stopped my Thursday night poker game, after playing with the same men for over ten years. John Reilly happened to say that the Jews were getting rich out of this war, and when I demanded an apology, he refused, and when I looked around at the faces of the men who had been my friends for so long, I could see they were not with me. And when I left the house no one said good night to me. I know the poison was spreading from Germany before the war and during it, but I had not realized it had come so close.

"And in my economics class, I find myself idiotically hedging in my lectures. I discover that I am loath to praise any liberal writer or any liberal act and find myself somehow annoyed and frightened to see an article of criticism of existing abuses signed by a Jewish name. And I hate to see Jewish names on important committees, and hate to read of Jews fighting for the poor, the oppressed, the cheated and hungry. Somehow, even in a country where my family has lived a hundred years, the enemy has won this subtle victory over me—he has made me disfranchise myself from honest causes by calling them foreign, Communist, using Jewish names connected with them as ammunition against them.

"And, most hateful of all, I find myself looking for Jewish names in the casualty lists and secretly being glad when I discover them there, to prove that there at least, among the dead and wounded, we belong. Three times, thanks to you and your brothers, I have found our name there, and, may God forgive me, at the expense of your blood and your brother's life, through my tears, I have felt that same twitch of satisfaction. . . .

"When I read the newspapers and see another story that Jews

are still being killed in Poland, or Jews are requesting that they be given back their homes in France, or that they be allowed to enter some country where they will not be murdered, I am annoyed with them, I feel they are boring the rest of the world with their problems, they are making demands upon the rest of the world by being killed, they are disturbing everyone by being hungry and asking for the return of their property. If we could all fall through the crust of the earth and vanish in one hour, with our heroes and poets and prophets and martyrs, perhaps we would be doing the memory of the Jewish race a service. . . .

"This is how I feel to-day, son. I need some help. You've been to the war, you've fought and killed men, you've seen the people of other countries. Maybe you understand things that I don't understand. Maybe you see some hope somewhere. Help me. Your loving father."

Seeger folded the letter slowly, not seeing what he was doing because the tears were burning his eyes. He walked slowly and aimlessly across the dead autumn grass of the empty field, away from the camp.

He tried to wipe away his tears, because with his eyes full and dark, he kept seeing his father and brother crouched in the old-fashioned living-room in Ohio and hearing his brother, dressed in the old, discarded uniform, saying, "These're the new rocket bombs. For the Jews."

He sighed, looking out over the bleak, wasted land. Now, he thought, now I have to think about it. He felt a slight, unreasonable twinge of anger at his father for presenting him with the necessity of thinking about it. The Army was good about serious problems. While you were fighting, you were too busy and frightened and weary to think about anything, and at other times you were relaxing, putting your brain on a shelf, postponing everything to that impossible time of clarity and beauty after the war. Well, now, here was the impossible, clear, beautiful time, and here was his father, demanding that he think. There are all sorts of Jews, he thought, there are the sort whose every waking moment is ridden by the knowledge of Jewishness, who see signs against the Jew in every smile on a streetcar, every whisper, who see pogroms in every newspaper article, threats in every change of the weather, scorn in every handshake, death behind each closed door. He had not been like that. He was young, he was big and healthy and easy-going and people of all kinds had seemed to like him all his life, in the Army and out. In America, especially, what was going on in Europe had seemed remote, unreal, unrelated to him. The chanting, bearded old men burning in the Nazi furnaces, and the dark-eyed women screaming prayers in Polish and Russian and German as they were pushed naked into the gas chambers had seemed as shadowy and almost as unrelated to him as he trotted out on to the Stadium field for a football game, as they must have been to the men named O'Dwyer and Wickersham and Poole who played in the line beside him.

They had seemed more related in Europe. Again and again in the towns that had been taken back from the Germans, gaunt, grey-faced men had stopped him humbly, looking searchingly at him, and had asked, peering at his long, lined, grimy face, under the anonymous helmet, "Are you a Jew?" Sometimes they asked it in English, sometimes French, or Yiddish. He didn't know French or Yiddish, but he learned to recognize the phrase. He had never understood exactly why they had asked the question, since they never demanded anything from him, rarely even could speak to him, until, one day in Strasbourg, a little bent old man and a small, shapeless woman had stopped him, and asked, in English, if he was Jewish.

"Yes," he said, smiling at them.

The two old people had smiled widely, like children. "Look," the old man had said to his wife. "A young American soldier. A Jew. And so large and strong." He had touched Seeger's arm reverently with the tips of his fingers, then had touched the Garand he was carrying. "And such a beautiful rifle . . ."

And there, for a moment, although he was not particularly sensitive, Seeger got an inkling of why he had been stopped and questioned by so many before. Here, to these bent, exhausted old people, ravaged of their families, familiar with flight and death for so many years, was a symbol of continuing life. A large young man in the uniform of the liberator, blood, as they thought, of their blood, but not in hiding, not quivering in fear and helplessness, but striding secure and victorious down the street, armed and capable of inflicting terrible destruction on his enemies.

Seeger had kissed the old lady on the cheek and she had wept and the old man had scolded her for it, while shaking Seeger's hand fervently and thankfully before saying goodbye.

And, thinking back on it, it was silly to pretend that, even before his father's letter, he had been like any other American soldier going through the war. When he had stood over the huge dead S.S. major with the face blown in by his bullets in the warehouse in Coblenz, and taken the pistol from the dead hand, he had tasted a strange little extra flavour of triumph. How many Jews, he'd thought, has this man killed; how fitting it is that I've killed him. Neither Olson nor Welch, who were like his brothers, would have felt that in picking up the Luger, its barrel still hot from the last shots its owner had fired before dying. And he had resolved that he was going to make sure to take this gun back with him to America, and plug it and keep it on his desk at home, as a kind of vague, half-understood sign to himself that justice had once been done and he had been its instrument.

Maybe, he thought, maybe I'd better take it back with me, but not as a memento. Not plugged, but loaded. America by now was a strange country for him. He had been away a long time and he wasn't sure what was waiting for him when he got home. If the mobs were coming down the street toward his house, he was not going to die singing and praying.

When he was taking basic training he'd heard a scrawny, clerklike-looking soldier from Boston talking at the other end of the PX bar, over the watered beer. "The boys at the office," the scratchy voice was saying, "gave me a party before I left. And they told me one thing. 'Charlie,' they said, 'hold on to your bayonet. We're going to be able to use it when you get back. On the Yids.' "

He hadn't said anything then, because he'd felt it was neither possible nor desirable to fight against every random overheard voice raised against the Jews from one end of the world to another. But again and again, at odd moments, lying on a barracks cot, or stretched out trying to sleep on the floor of a ruined French farmhouse, he had heard that voice, harsh, satisfied, heavy with hate and ignorance, saying above the beery grumble of apprentice soldiers at the bar, "Hold on to your bayonet. . . ."

And the other stories—Jews collected stories of hatred and injustice and inklings of doom like a special, lunatic kind of miser. The story of the naval officer, commander of a small vessel off the Aleutians, who, in the officers, wardroom, had complained that he hated the Jews because it was the Jews who had demanded that the Germans be beaten first and the forces in the Pacific had been starved in consequence. And when one of his junior officers, who had just come aboard, had objected and told the commander that he was a Jew, the commander had risen from the table and said, "Mister, the Constitution of the United States says I have to serve in the same Navy with Jews, but it doesn't say I have to eat at the same table with them." In the fogs and the cold, swelling Arctic seas off the Aleutians, in a small boat, subject to sudden, mortal attack at any moment . . .

And the two young combat engineers in an attached company on D-Day, when they were lying off the coast right before climbing down into the landing barges. "There's France," one of them had said.

"What's it like?" the second one had asked, peering out across the miles of water toward the smoking coast.

"Like every place else," the first one had answered. "The Jews've made all the dough during the war."

"Shut up!" Seeger had said, helplessly thinking of the dead, destroyed, wandering, starving Jews of France. The engineers had shut up, and they'd climbed down together into the heaving boat, and gone onto the beach together.

And the million other stories. Jews, even the most normal and best adjusted of them, became living treasuries of them, scraps of malice and bloodthirstiness, clever and confusing and cunningly twisted so that every act by every Jew became suspect and blameworthy and hateful. Seeger had heard the stories, and had made an almost conscious effort to forget them. Now, holding his father's letter in his hand, he remembered them all.

He stared unseeingly out in front of him. Maybe, he thought, maybe it would've been better to have been killed in the war, like Leonard. Simpler. Leonard would never have to face a crowd coming for his mother and father. Leonard would not have to listen and collect these hideous, fascinating little stories that made of every Jew a stranger in any town, on any field, on the face of the earth. He had come so close to being killed so many times, it would have been so easy, so neat and final.

Seeger shook his head. It was ridiculous to feel like that, and he was ashamed of himself for the weak moment. At the age of twenty-one, death was not an answer.

"Seeger!" It was Olson's voice. He and Welch had sloshed silently up behind Seeger, standing in the open field. "Seeger, *mon vieux*, what're you doing—grazing?"

Seeger turned slowly to them. "I wanted to read my letter," he said.

Olson looked closely at him. They had been together so long, through so many things, that flickers and hints of expression on each other's faces were recognized and acted upon. "Anything wrong?" Olson asked.

"No," said Seeger. "Nothing much."

"Norman," Welch said, his voice young and solemn. "Norman, we've been talking. Olson and me. We decided—you're pretty attached to that Luger, and maybe—if you—well . . ."

"What he's trying to say," said Olson, "is we withdraw the request. If you want to sell it, O.K. If you don't, don't do it for our sake. Honest."

Seeger looked at them, standing there, disreputable and tough and familiar. "I haven't made up my mind yet," he said.

"Anything you decide," Welch said oratorically, "is perfectly all right with us. Perfectly."

They walked aimlessly and silently across the field, away from camp. As they walked, their shoes making a wet, sliding sound in the damp, dead grass, Seeger thought of the time Olson had covered him in the little town outside Cherbourg, when Seeger had been caught going down the side of a street by four Germans with a machine gun on the second storey of a house on the corner and Olson had had to stand out in the middle of the street with no cover at all for more than a minute, firing continuously, so that Seeger could get away alive. And he thought of the time outside Saint Lô when he had been wounded and had lain in a minefield for three hours and Welch and Captain Taney had come looking for him in the darkness and had found him and picked him up and run for it, all of them expecting to get blown up any second.

And he thought of all the drinks they'd had together and the long marches and the cold winter together, and all the girls they'd gone out with together, and he thought of his father and brother crouching behind the window in Ohio waiting for the rockets and the crowds armed with Browning automatic rifles.

"Say." He stopped and stood facing them. "Say, what do you guys think of the Jews?"

Welch and Olson looked at each other, and Olson glanced down at the letter in Seeger's hand.

"Jews?" Olson said finally. "What're they? Welch, you ever hear of the Jews?"

Welch looked thoughtfully at the grey sky. "No," he said. "But remember, I'm an uneducated fellow."

"Sorry, Bud," Olson said, turning to Seeger. "We can't help you. Ask us another question. Maybe we'll do better."

Seeger peered at the faces of his friends. He would have to rely upon them, later on, out of uniform, on their native streets, more than he had ever relied on them on the bullet-swept street and in the dark minefield in France. Welch and Olson stared back at him, troubled, their faces candid and tough and dependable.

"What time," Seeger asked, "did you tell that captain you'd meet him?"

"Eight o'clock," Welch said. "But we don't have to go. If you have any feeling about that gun . . ."

"We'll meet him," Seeger said. "We can use that sixty-five bucks."

"Listen," Olson said, "I know how much you like that gun and I'll feel like a heel if you sell it."

"Forget it," Seeger said, starting to walk again. "What could I use it for in America?"

The Czecho-Slovakian Chandelier

GERDA CHARLES

Gerda Charles was born in Liverpool, England. She attended nine different schools up to the age of fifteen. Her novels include *The True Voice, The Crossing Point* and *A Slanting Light.* She has been a fiction reviewer on the *New Statesman* and a contributor to *Vanity Fair, Jewish Chronicle* and *The New York Times Book Review.* In 1963 she was awarded the James Tait Black Memorial Prize for the best British novel of that year. She makes her home in London.

I have forgotten now why our neighbour—the rich one—invited the Franks to dinner. Perhaps to look Mr. Franks over as a possible tutor for those of his children who were not over-bright in examinations, possibly from a rudimentary sense of respect for culture; a sense which grew stronger as he grew richer. Or maybe he just wanted to give them a good meal.

I do not know either why my parents and I were invited to that dinner. Perhaps Mr. Kringle wanted to give us a good meal too. But though I had lately 'discovered' food as a sure-fire source of romantic transformation (I had surely only to eat caviare to become an aristocrat) almost as magical as perfume (I had just discovered verbena bath salts too) it was not the dinner which roused my richest anticipations. If the occasion was momentous to me it was because I was actually going to meet a *writer*. I do not say I would not have crossed the street to see some other kind of celebrity. I would. In those days even a Zionist speaker sent down from London was a celebrity; a baronet was someone to boast of having *seen*. But at fifteen, for awe and love of the printed word, I would have crossed England to meet a cub reporter on the *Drapers Record*. To be about to meet a real author was overwhelming.

Mr. Franks was in a way already known to me; at least by

sight and repute. By sight because of his car, a dilapidated, ancient two-seater, painted bright yellow, with a very dirty, canvas top. I had often seen him bucketing through the streets in it (an odd sight at that time in our grimly provincial city) the pointed, black beard he affected jutting out above the wheel, his mouse-coloured wife clinging beside him. By repute on two counts. The first, and more important to me, was because he had actually published a *novel* which I had read with eager curiosity (the author a living man I had seen with my own eyes!) telling myself I admired it. As I recall the book now it was one of those heavily mannered allegories thick with streams of consciousness.

The second, and more important count to everybody else—since a feeling for the creative arts is not, whatever the romantic, Gentile legend may say, characteristic of Jewish nature—was the truly appalling hostility which blew up over his 'Cards.' Already suspect in our narrow little, Orthodox-Jewish lower-middle-class world for his 'writing,' the *un*-orthodox shape of his beard, his wife (who came from Antwerp) and his car, he managed to unleash enormous quantities of ill-will by circulating his Cards.

There are always, in provincial society, small pockets of people who live more or less Chinese fashion by taking in each other's washing. Our particular washing happened to be Hebrew teaching. All the young men struggling to 'make a living,' many of the older ones, even some of the young women, all attempted full or part-time tutoring. Into this delicately balanced community with its careful, suspicious etiquette, its vast capacity for grievance, crashed Mr. Franks with his advertising Cards distributed everywhere, loudly insisting that He Was a Teacher.

I AM A TEACHER proclaimed the Cards in huge, black type. Underneath they said what he taught: not only Hebrew but (with unforgiveable superiority) French, German, Russian; all individual tuition, all made easy, all cut price.

Attempting what defence I could in the teeth of the storm of animosity which those Cards aroused I was reminded with some bitterness that I was not yet old enough to be in the racket (it wasn't put quite like that) and disqualified as referee. "But he's a Writer!" I said indignantly as if that excused everything—as indeed to me, then, it did. "What does he make out of it?" they said scornfully.

Looking across Mr. Kringle's long, oval, dinner table it was admittedly hard to see what Mr. Franks had made out of either his novel or the famous Cards. His beard was neatly cut and so was his hair above his knife-thin, black-eyed face but he wore a striped collar with his not-so-white shirt, the finger nails of his small, delicate brown hands were black-rimmed and his jacket and waistcoat didn't match either. His wife who either looked or was about seventeen years older than himself, wore an extremely crushed, brown velvet dress of no shape whatsoever. A crumpled lace collar had been tacked slightly askew round the neck and she wore a string of chunky, amber beads. She was taller than her husband who was a taut, thin little man but her shoulders were so bowed that at the table they appeared the same height. When he spoke, which was not often, he would end his sentences with "Yes, Sophia?" and she would obediently corroborate: "Yes, Mordecai."

All through the hors d'oeuvres and the soup, while the adults talked and the Kringle children squirmed and giggled and Mr. Kringle laid down the law about Germany, I burned to make myself known to Mr. Franks as his equal in culture. I longed to reveal to him that I too read books, that I, only I, of all those in the room really appreciated the importance of literature. I pictured myself leaning forward during a lull in the conversation and saying encouragingly: "Do tell us your experiences as a writer, Mr. Franks. You're a lion you know and we expect to hear you roar!" But the only one who was roaring was our host and what he was roaring about was his latest acquisition from abroad which hung, glittering, right over the centre of the table round which we were sitting; his Czecho-Slovakian chandelier. (All my life since, their euphony like the terrible, Sunday bells of my raw, sad youth, those syllables, 'Czech-o-Slo-vak-ian chan-de-lier' have suddenly, painfully, at unrelated moments, chimed in my mind.)

"Four hundred pounds!" Mr. Kringle was saying or rather roaring, his belligerent, blue eyes fixed ferociously on Mr. Franks. "The best in the world. The best! You think they can make glass elsewhere? Nonsense! You listen to me. In Czecho-Slovakia," he said impressively, slowing down, "they have technicians. Technicians! They know what they're doing there. I went over the works myself. The manager insisted, *insisted* on showing me over. Wouldn't let me go. Kept me hours. Hours! 'Mr. Kringle,' he said. 'You know what's good.' Excuse me!"

He jumped up and went to fetch a second bottle from the sideboard. We had already been given some sweet, muscatel wine. He opened the bottle and passed it down the table to Mr. Franks. "Try it!" he said. "Try it. Try it. The best port on the market. That fish all right? Best middle-cut plaice. Well? What d'you think of that for a colour? Rubies! You know where they drink this? Officers clubs! The military! *Generals!* The same wine exactly!"

Mr. Franks poured some into his glass and drank it off. The bottle went round. The young Kringles, with much scuffling, poured themselves a teaspoonful each. The oldest boy, a sudden convert to sporting interests, tried to interest us in the local football team. "But what's the difference beween soccer and the other football?" asked his mother ignorantly. I seized my chance.

"Soccer," I said in loud, refined tones and looking hopefully at Mr. Franks, "is Association Football played by the hoi polloi," (a last minute uncertainty brought this out as hwa polloy), "*Rugger* is played by Public Schools."

"Oh rahlly," shrieked all the Kringle children, giggling but impressed.

Mr. Franks did not look very impressed. Perhaps he hadn't heard, he was by then concentrating on his braised chicken. Determinedly, with what I was mentally designating as 'the utmost songfrad,' I leaned towards him as our host was fetching yet another bottle from the sideboard and said with steeled aplomb: "Do tell us something about your work, Mr. Franks."

Mr. Franks looked up startled from his plate, his mind no doubt flying to his Cards. "I Am a Teacher," he said automatically.

"Oh *yes,*" I said with gracious charm, "but I meant . . . I mean . . . well, I mean your *literature.* You have written a novel. *Have you not?*" I finished deeply.

"Oh yes," he said taking a large mouthful of chicken.

A bottle of Benedictine came down the table. "Now try that," shouted Mr. Kringle. "Marvellous! I bought it at the best wine merchants in Paris. All their customers are millionaires. Millionaires! I had trouble I can tell you before they'd even serve me. But I'll tell you something. By the time I left they were begging me to buy from them."

"Well, Sophia?" said Mr. Franks holding up the bottle of Benedictine. And he gave his wife a nodding, quizzical look. "Well?"

She gave him a mild blink from behind her glasses and dipped her old, beaked nose. He poured some out for her.

With a pertinacity which I can today only admire, I tried once more to turn the conversation to higher levels. "It must be wonderful to be a writer," I said and, although I genuinely thought so, for some reason I could not help bringing it out in a highly artificial and gushing manner. "I suppose you've met lots of other writers, haven't you?"

He nodded, looking slightly bemused.

"Oh!" I said clasping my hands to my throat. "Do tell us who!"

Mr. Kringle was sitting forward holding a large chicken leg between two hands and chewing mouthfuls off it, his eyes flashing from side to side to see if all his children were eating enough.

"I've met one or two. In London."

"Oh who-o-o?" I said in ecstatic beseechment.

"Bernard Shaw," he said picking with his little finger at a bit of chicken bone in his back teeth. "Wells." He ran his tongue round the inside of his mouth.

For a moment I was completely taken aback. It was not only something in his manner which bothered me. (I think now that he never actually met either Shaw or Wells; he had seen them on a platform perhaps, addressed them possibly from the floor at some public meeting.) It was my particular conception of the word 'writer' which was suddenly shaken. I had not somehow thought of those great men as 'writers.' They were rather . . . 'figures,' historic, almost mythical personages. My picture of a 'writer' was of someone who, *because* he wrote, must therefore have tea with actresses, adventures on Fifth Avenue, talk with devastating wit, dally in studios . . . In short: "Have you," I said, my voice shaking slightly, "ever met . . . Beverly Nichols?"

I shall never know whether Mr. Franks had in fact had that privilege (though I rather think not) for at that moment Mr. Kringle put down his chicken leg and machine-gunned his way rapidly into the conversation.

"Shaw!" he said. "A great man. I don't deny it. A great man. But . . . he's an Irishman. You agree with me, Mr. Franks? An Irishman. And the Irish are a Catholic race. Excuse me! Excuse me!" as I made to interrupt. "Ireland is a Catholic country, Mr. Franks. You follow me? Catholic. Now! Where did Shaw get his ideas from?" He looked triumphantly round the table. My mother was gossiping with Mrs. Kringle. My father was still talking sport with the eldest Kringle boy. The younger ones were arguing among themselves. Only the Franks and I were listening.

"I'll tell you," said Mr. Kringle strongly, pinching the end of his nose. "I'll tell you. *One*: from the Bible," he said leaning forward and fixing Mr. Franks with his eye. "And *Two*: from the Talmud." He sat back and nodded.

Mr. Franks put his hand over his mouth and inclined his head sideways, consideringly.

"All the great literature in the world—*in the world*—is taken from *One*: the Bible; and *Two*: the Talmud," said Mr. Kringle.

This was too much! "What about Shakespeare?" I cried—and paused for Mr. Franks to respect me.

"Allow *me*," said Mr. Kringle loftily, putting out a wide, restraining arm in my direction. "Allow *me*. You don't know anything. Shaw," he said rolling out his words with sonorous effect, "Shaw, Shakespeare, anyone you like, they all got it, *One*: from the—— It's been proved! It's been proved!" he said, shouting down my contradiction which he could see coming.

Mr. Franks poured himself a glass of the cherry brandy which had just reached him. Then he poured one for his wife.

"Well? Well, Sophia?" he said.

"Yes, Mordecai," she murmured.

With a quick, furtive gesture he tipped the liqueur over the large portion of steaming, fruit pudding before him. Then he refilled his glass. She followed suit.

"Who proved it? What authority have you got for saying that?" I said hotly, the more heated because at the sight of the Franks eating their cherry-brandied pudding a discomforting, lowering chill had overcome me.

"Read the tragedies of Shakespeare," said Mr. Kringle beginning to shout again. "From the Talmud every one of them."

"Well what about the comedies? I suppose they're from the Talmud too?" I said rudely.

My mother, made aware of what was going on gave me a shushing frown from the other end of the table and I said no more.

Mr. Franks helped himself to a peach.

"I'm not an authority, Mr. Franks," said Mr. Kringle lowering his voice with an effort. "Mind you, I'm not an authority. But to me it's obvious. The biggest scholars in the world will tell you the same thing. Shakespeare got everything from our Rabbis, our philosophers, the biggest writers in the world, *in the world,* and put it together again in his own words. They all did it. Couldn't be clearer. (I'm not counting Wells . . . that unbeliever). But mark this, Mr. Franks. Mark this. The Bible, *one*; and the Talmud, *two* . . . they started it all."

Mr. Franks finished his peach and put down his knife.

"Very likely," he said wiping his mouth with his napkin. "Very likely."

I looked at him once, incredulously. Then I looked down at my plate, my head bent right over.

After dinner Mr. Kringle, darting about with boundless energy, played operatic arias to us on his large mahogany gramophone, letting out strong, tenor notes at intervals and giving Caruso a lift over the more dramatic passages. Mr. Franks and his Sophia left about ten o'clock and shortly afterwards we went also. "All that food! And the drinks!" said my parents to each other as we walked home. "Better if he'd given them the money."

About a year after that dinner party Mr. Franks died and then, almost immediately, his wife died too. There was a slight flush of shame in the town when the brute facts of their appalling poverty came out. There are of course in every Jewish community ample communal funds to draw on for charitable purposes . . . of a kind. If the Franks had applied in the right quarters they might have received a little charity in life as well as in death. But they were after something else . . . which they would never have got.

What I have never understood is why they stayed in the town. Why didn't they go to London—or Paris—or Warsaw? Somewhere where they would have found people who would have forgiven them for being what they were. What seething, obstinate inertia kept them battering at the doors of our narrow, smug society? Why did *they* want a place in it, for heaven's sake? Why? At thought of their locked lives together, their stubborn suffering, curiosity and pain still stir in me. I would not mind so much if his book had lived. But it is forgotten now —like them. It is as though the two lives and the one book had never been. And dead too, slain over Mr. Kringle's long, oval, dining-table under the shimmering crystal of the Czecho-Slovakian chandelier, were my first, fine, high illusions about the writers of books and the colour, brilliance and glamour of the literary life.

Mr. Kaplan and the Magi

LEO ROSTEN

Leo Rosten was born in Poland. He was educated at the University of Chicago and the London School of Economics. His career has been a varied one, as he has held many university appointments, he is a member of the American Academy of Political and Social Science, he has been a special consultant to the movie industry as well as in Washington, in addition to his accomplishments as a writer. Among his books are *The Education of Hyman Kaplan, The Return of Hyman Kaplan, The Movie Makers* and *A Guide to the Religions of America.* He has contributed to many journals and magazines, including *Harpers* and *The New Yorker.* Presently, he is Special Editorial Adviser to *Look* magazine. Mr. Rosten is married, and the father of three children. He lives in New York.

When Mr. Parkhill saw that Miss Mitnick, Mr. Bloom, and Mr. Hyman Kaplan were absent, and that a strange excitement pervaded the beginners' grade, he realized that it was indeed the last night before the holidays and that Christmas was only a few days off. Each Christmas the classes in the American Night Preparatory School for Adults gave presents to their respective teachers. Mr. Parkhill, a veteran of many sentimental Yuletides, had come to know the procedure. That night, before the class session had begun, there must have been a hurried collection; a Gift Committee of three had been chosen; at this moment the Committee was probably in Mickey Goldstein's Arcade, bargaining feverishly, arguing about the appropriateness of a pair of pyjamas or the colour of a dozen linen handkerchiefs, debating whether Mr. Parkhill would prefer a pair of fleece-lined slippers to a set of mother-of-pearl cufflinks.

"We shall concentrate on—er—spelling drill tonight," Mr. Parkhill announced.

The students smiled wisely, glanced at the three empty seats, exchanged knowing nods, and prepared for spelling drill. Miss Rochelle Goldberg giggled, then looked ashamed as Mrs. Rodriguez shot her a glare of reproval.

Mr. Parkhill always chose a spelling drill for the night before the Christmas vacation: it kept all the students busy simultaneously; it dampened the excitement of the occasion; above all, it kept him from the necessity of resorting to elaborate pedagogical efforts in order to hide his own embarrassment.

Mr. Parkhill called off the first words. Pens and pencils scratched, smiles died away, eyes grew serious, preoccupied, as the beginners' grade assaulted the spelling of 'Banana . . . Romance . . . Groaning.' Mr. Parkhill sighed. The class seemed incomplete without its star student, Miss Mitnick, and barren without its most remarkable one, Mr. Hyman Kaplan. Mr. Kaplan's most recent linguistic triumph had been a fervent speech extolling the D'Oyly Carte Company's performance of an operetta by two English gentlemen referred to as 'Goldberg and Solomon.'

"Charming . . . Horses . . . Float," Mr. Parkhill called off.

Mr. Parkhill's mind was not really on 'Charming . . . Horses . . . Float.' He could not help thinking of the momentous event which would take place that night. After the recess the students would come in with flushed faces and shining eyes. The Committee would be with them, and one member of the Committee, carrying an elaborately bound Christmas package, would be surrounded by several of the largest students in the class, who would try to hide the parcel from Mr. Parkhill's eyes. The class would come to order with uncommon rapidity. Then, just as Mr. Parkhill resumed the lesson, one member of the Committee would rise, apologize nervously for interrupting, place the package on Mr. Parkhill's desk, utter a few half-swallowed words, and rush back to his or her seat. Mr. Parkhill would say a few halting phrases of gratitude and surprise, everyone would smile and fidget uneasily, and the lesson would drag on, somehow, to the final and distant bell.

"*Ac*cept . . . *Ex*cept . . . Cucumber."

And as the students filed out after the final bell, they would cry 'Merry Christmas, Happy New Year!' in joyous voices. The Committee would crowd around Mr. Parkhill with tremendous smiles to say that if the present wasn't *just right* in size or colour (if it was something to wear) or in design (if it was something to use), Mr. Parkhill could exchange it. He didn't *have* to abide by the Committee's choice. He could exchange the present for *any*thing. They would have arranged all that carefully with Mr. Mickey Goldstein himself.

That was ritual, fixed and unchanging, of the last night of school before Christmas.

"Nervous . . . Goose . . . Violets."

The hand on the clock crawled around to eight. Mr. Parkhill could not keep his eyes off the three seats, so eloquent in their vacancy, which Miss Mitnick, Mr. Bloom, and Mr. Kaplan ordinarily graced with their presences. He could almost see these three in the last throes of decision in Mickey Goldstein's Arcade, harassed by the competitive attractions of gloves, neckties, an electric clock, a cane, spats, a 'lifetime' fountain pen. Mr. Parkhill grew cold as he thought of a fountain pen. Three times already he had been presented with 'lifetime' fountain pens, twice with 'lifetime' pencils to match. Mr. Parkhill had exchanged these gifts: he had a fountain pen. Once he had chosen a woollen vest instead; once a pair of mittens and a watch chain. Mr. Parkhill hoped it wouldn't be a fountain pen. Or a smoking jacket. He had never been able to understand how the Committee in '32 had decided upon a smoking jacket. Mr. Parkhill did not smoke. He had exchanged it for fur-lined gloves.

Just as Mr. Parkhill called off "Sardine . . . *Ex*quisite . . . Palace" the recess bell rang. The heads of the students bobbed up as if propelled by a single spring. There was a rush to the door, Mr. Sam Pinsky well in the lead. Then, from the corridor their voices rose. Mr. Parkhill began to print, 'Banana' on the blackboard, so that the students could correct their own papers after recess. He tried not to listen, but the voices in the corridor were like the chatter of a flock of sparrows.

"Hollo, Mitnick!"

"Bloom, Bloom, vat is it?"

"So vat did you gat, Keplen? Tell!"

Mr. Parkhill could hear Miss Mitnick's shy "We bought——" interrupted by Mr. Kaplan's stern cry, "Mitnick! Don' say! Plizz, faller-students! Come *don* mit de voices! Titcher vill awreddy hearink, you hollerink so lod! Still! Order! Plizz!" There was no question about it: Mr. Kaplan was born to command.

"Did you bought a Tsheaffer's Fontain Pan Sat, guarantee for de whole life, like *I* said?" one voice came through the door. A Sheaffer Fountain Pen Set, Guaranteed. That was Mrs. Moskowitz. Poor Mrs. Moskowitz, she showed so little imagination, even in her homework. "Moskovitz! Mein Gott!" the stentorian whisper of Mr. Kaplan soared through the air. "Vy you don' open op de door Titcher should *positivel* hear? Ha! Let's goink to odder and fromm de hall!"

The voice of the beginners' grade died away as they moved to the 'odder and' of the corridor, like the chorus of *Aida* vanishing into Egyptian wings.

Mr. Parkhill printed 'Charming' and 'Horses' on the board. For a moment he thought he heard Mrs. Moskowitz's voice repeating stubbornly, "Did—you—bought—a—Tsheaffer—Fontain—Pan—Sat—*Guarantee?*"

Mr. Parkhill began to say to himself, 'Thank you, all of you. It's *just* what I wanted,' again and again. One Christmas he hadn't said 'It's just what I wanted' and poor Mrs. Oppenheimer, chairman of the Committee that year, had been hounded by the students' recriminations for a month.

It seemed an eternity before the recess bell rang again. The class came in *en masse*, and hastened to the seats from which they would view the impending spectacle. The air hummed with silence.

Mr. Parkhill was printing 'Cucumber.' He did not turn his face from the board as he said, "Er—please begin correcting your own spelling. I have printed most of the words on the board."

There was a low and heated whispering. "Stend op, Mitnick!" he heard Mr. Kaplan hiss. "You should stend up *too!*"

"The *whole* Committee," Mr. Bloom whispered. "Stand op!"

Apparently Miss Mitnick, a gazelle choked with embarrassment, did not have the fortitude to 'stend op' with her colleagues.

"A fine raprezantitif *you'll* gonna make!" Mr. Kaplan hissed scornfully. "Isn't for *mine* sek I'm eskink, Mitnick. Plizz *stend op!*"

There was a confused, half-muted murmur, and the anguished voice of Miss Mitnick saying, "I *can't.*" Mr. Parkhill printed 'Violets' on the board. Then there was a tense silence. And then the voice of Mr. Kaplan rose, firmly, clearly, with a decision and dignity which left no doubt as to its purpose.

"Podden me, Mr. Pockheel!"

It had come.

"Er—yes?" Mr. Parkhill turned to face the class.

Messrs. Bloom and Kaplan were standing side by side in front of Miss Mitnick's chair, holding between them a large, long package, wrapped in cellophane and tied with huge red ribbons. A pair of small hands touched the bottom of the box, listlessly. The owner of the hands, seated in the front row, was hidden by the box.

"De hends is Mitnick," Mr. Kaplan said apologetically.

Mr. Parkhill gazed at the tableau. It was touching.

"Er—yes?" he said again feebly, as if he had forgotten his lines and was repeating his cue.

"Hau Kay!" Mr. Kaplan whispered to his confreres. The hands disappeared behind the package. Mr. Kaplan and Mr. Bloom strode to the platform with the box. Mr. Kaplan was beaming, his smile rapturous, exalted. They placed the package on Mr. Parkhill's desk, Mr. Bloom dropped back a few paces, and Mr. Kaplan said, "Mr. Pockheel! Is mine beeg honour, becawss I'm Chairman fromm de Buyink an' Deliverink to You a Prazent Committee, to givink to you dis fine peckitch."

Mr. Parkhill was about to stammer, "Oh, thank you," when Mr. Kaplan added hastily, "Also I'll sayink a few voids."

Mr. Kaplan took an envelope out of his pocket. He whispered loudly, "Mitnick, *you still got time to comm op mit de Committee,*" but Miss Mitnick only blushed furiously and lowered her eyes. Mr. Kaplan sighed, straightened the envelope, smiled proudly at Mr. Parkhill, and read.

"Dear Titcher—dat's de beginnink. Ve stendink on de adge fromm a beeg holiday." He cleared his throat. "Ufcawss is all kinds holidays in USA. Holidays for politic, for religious, an' *plain* holidays. In Fabrary, ve got Judge Vashington's boitday, a *fine* holiday. Also Abram Lincohen's. In May ve got Memorable Day, for dad soldiers. In July comms, netcheral, Fort July. Also ve have Labour Day, Denksgivink, for de Peelgrims, an' for de feenish fromm de Voild Var, *Armistress* Day."

Mr. Parkhill played with a piece of chalk nervously.

"But arond dis time year we have a *difference* kind holiday, a spacial, movvellous time. Dat's called—Chrissmas."

Mr. Parkhill put the chalk down.

"All hover de voild," Mr. Kaplan mused, "is pipple celebraking dis vunderful time. Becawss for som pipple is Chrissmas like for *odder* pipple is Passover. Or Chanukah, batter. De most fine, de most beauriful, de most *secret* holiday fromm de whole bunch!"

('"Sacred," Mr. Kaplan, "sacred,"' Mr. Parkhill thought, ever the pedagogue.)

"Ven we valkink don de stritt an' is snow on de floor an' all kinds tarrible cold!" Mr. Kaplan's hand leaped up dramatically, like a flame. "Ven ve see in de vindows trees mit rad an' grin laktric lights boinink! Ven is de time for tellink de fancy-tales abot Sandy Claws commink fromm Naut Pole on rain-enimals, an' climbink don de jiminies mit *stockings* for all de leetle kits! Ven we hearink abot de beauriful toughts of de Tree Vise Guys who vere follerink a star fromm de dasert! Ven pipple sayink, 'Oh, Mary Chrissmas! Oh, Heppy Noo Yiss! Oh, bast regotts!'

Den ve *all* got a varm fillink ind de heart for all humanity which should be brodders!"

Mr. Feigenbaum nodded philosophically at this profound thought; Mr. Kaplan, pleased, nodded back.

"*You* got de fillink, Mr. Pockheel. *I* got de fillink, dat's no qvastion abot! Bloom, Pinsky, Caravello, Schneiderman, even Mitnick"—Mr. Kaplan was punishing Miss Mitnick tenfold for her perfidy—"got de fillink! An' vat is it?" There was a momentous pause. "De Chrissmas Spirits!"

('"Spir*it*," Mr. Kaplan, "spir*it*,"' the voice of Mr. Parkhill's conscience said.)

"Now I'll givink de prazent," Mr. Kaplan announced subtly. Mr. Bloom shifted his weight. "Becawss you a foist-class Titcher, Mr. Pockheel, an' learn abot gremmer an' spallink an' de hoddest pots pernonciation—ve know is a planty hod jop mit soch students—so ve fill you should havink a sample fromm our —fromm our"—Mr. Kaplan turned the envelope over hastily —"aha! Fromm our santimental!"

Mr. Parkhill stared at the long package and the huge red ribbons.

"Fromm de cless, to our lovely Mr. Pockheel!"

Mr. Parkhill started. "Er——?" he asked involuntarily.

"Fromm de cless, to our lovely Mr. Pockheel!" Mr. Kaplan repeated with pride.

('"*Beloved*," Mr. Kaplan, "*beloved*."')

A hush had fallen over the room. Mr. Kaplan, his eyes bright with joy, waited for Mr. Parkhill to take up the ritual. Mr. Parkhill tried to say, "Thank you, Mr. Kaplan," but the phrase seemed meaningless, so big, so ungainly, that it could not get through his throat. Without a word Mr. Parkhill began to open the package. He slid the big red ribbons off. He broke the tissue paper inside. For some reason his vision was blurred and it took him a moment to identify the present. It was a smoking jacket. It was black and gold, and a dragon with a green tongue was embroidered on the breast pocket.

"Horyantal style," Mr. Kaplan whispered delicately.

Mr. Parkhill nodded. The air trembled with the tension. Miss Mitnick looked as if she were ready to cry. Mr. Bloom peered intently over Mr. Kaplan's shoulder. Mrs. Moskowitz sat entranced, sighing with behemothian gasps. She looked as if she were at her daughter's wedding.

"Thank you," Mr. Parkhill stammered at last. "Thank you, all of you."

Mr. Bloom said, "Hold it op everyone should see."

Mr. Kaplan turned on Mr. Bloom with an icy look. "*I'm* de chairman!" he hissed.

"I—er—I can't tell you how much I appreciate your kindness," Mr. Parkhill said without lifting his eyes.

Mr. Kaplan smiled. "So now you'll plizz told op de prazent. Plizz."

Mr. Parkhill took the smoking jacket out of the box and held it up for all to see. There were gasps—'Oh!'s' and 'Ah!'s' and Mr. Kaplan's own ecstatic "My! Is beauriful!" The green tongue on the dragon seemed alive.

"Maybe ve made a mistake," Mr. Kaplan said hastily. "Maybe you don't smoke—dat's how *Mitnick* tought." The scorn dripped. "But I said, 'Ufcawss is Titcher smokink! Not in de cless, netcheral. At home! At least a *pipe!*'"

"No, no, you didn't make a mistake. It's—it's *just* what I wanted!"

The great smile on Mr. Kaplan's face became dazzling. "Horray! Vear in de bast fromm helt!" he cried impetuously. "Mary Chrissmas! Heppy Noo Yiss! You should have a *hondert* more!"

This was the signal for a chorus of acclaim. "Mary Chrissmas!" "Wear in best of health!" "Happy New Year!" Miss Schneiderman burst into applause, followed by Mr. Scymzak and Mr. Weinstein. Miss Caravello, carried away by all the excitement, uttered some felicitations in rapid Italian. Mrs. Moskowitz sighed once more and said, "Soch a *sveet* ceremonia." Miss Mitnick smiled feebly, blushing, and twisted her handkerchief.

The ceremony was over. Mr. Parkhill began to put the smoking jacket back into the box with fumbling hands. Mr. Bloom marched back to his seat. But Mr. Kaplan stepped a little closer to the desk. The smile had congealed on Mr. Kaplan's face. It was poignant and profoundly earnest.

"Er—thank you, Mr. Kaplan," Mr. Parkhill said gently.

Mr. Kaplan shuffled his feet, looking at the floor. For the first time since Mr. Parkhill had known him, Mr. Kaplan seemed to be embarrassed. Then, just as he turned to rush back to his seat, Mr. Kaplan whispered, so softly that no ears but Mr. Parkhill's heard it, "Maybe de spitch I rad vas too *formmal.* But avery void I said—it came fromm *below mine heart!*"

Mr. Parkhill felt that, for all his weird, unorthodox English, Mr. Kaplan had spoken with the tongues of the Magi.

The Zulu and the Zeide

DAN JACOBSON

Dan Jacobson was born in South Africa in 1929. He spent his early years in Kimberley, attended the University of the Witwaterstrand, Johannesburg, and then spent some time in Israel and England before returning to South Africa to work as a journalist. His works include novels, among them *The Price of Diamonds, A Dance in the Sun, The Trap* and *The Evidence of Love;* two volumes of short stories; a book of essays and a travel book about California. He shared the Somerset Maugham Award for 1964. He is married, has three sons, and now resides in London.

Old man Grossman was worse than a nuisance. He was a source of constant anxiety and irritation; he was a menace to himself and to the passing motorists into whose path he would step, to the children in the streets whose games he would break up, sending them flying, to the householders who at night would approach him with clubs in their hands, fearing him a burglar; he was a butt and a jest to the African servants who would tease him on street corners.

It was impossible to keep him in the house. He would take any opportunity to slip out—a door left open meant that he was on the streets, a window unlatched was a challenge to his agility, a walk in the park was as much a game of hide-and-seek as a walk. The old man's health was good, physically; he was quite spry, and he could walk far, and he could jump and duck if he had to. And all his physical activity was put to only one purpose: to running away. It was a passion for freedom that the old man might have been said to have, could anyone have seen what joy there could have been for him in wandering aimlessly about the streets, in sitting footsore on pavements, in entering other people's homes, in stumbling behind advertisement hoardings across undeveloped building plots, in toiling up the stairs of fifteen-storey blocks of flats in which he had no business, in being brought home by large young policemen who winked at Harry Grossman, the old man's son, as they gently hauled his father out of their flying-squad cars.

"He's always been like this," Harry would say, when people asked him about his father. And when they smiled and said: "Always?" Harry would say, "Always. I know what I'm talking about. He's my father, and I know what he's like. He gave my mother enough grey hairs before her time. All he knew was to run away."

Harry's reward would come when the visitors would say: "Well, at least you're being as dutiful to him as anyone can be."

It was a reward that Harry always refused. "Dutiful? What can you do? There's nothing else you can do." Harry Grossman knew that there was nothing else he could do. Dutifulness had been his habit of life: it had had to be, having the sort of father he had, and the strain of duty had made him abrupt and begrudging: he even carried his thick, powerful shoulders curved inwards, to keep what he had to himself. He was a thick-set, bunch-faced man, with large bones, and short, jabbing gestures; he was in the prime of life, and he would point at the father from whom he had inherited his strength, and on whom the largeness of bone showed now only as so much extra leanness that the clothing had to cover, and say: "You see him? Do you know what he once did? My poor mother saved enough money to send him from the old country to South Africa; she bought clothes for him, and a ticket, and she sent him to her brother, who was already here. He was going to make enough money to bring me out, and my mother and my brother, all of us. But on the boat from Bremen to London he met some other Jews who were going to South America, and they said to him: 'Why are you going to South Africa? It's a wild country, the savages will eat you. Come to South America and you'll make a fortune.' So in London he exchanges his ticket. And we don't hear from him for six months. Six months later he gets a friend to write to my mother asking her please to send him enough money to pay for his ticket back to the old country—he's dying in Argentina, the Spaniards are killing him, he says, and he must come home. So my mother borrows from her brother to bring him back again. Instead of a fortune he brought her a new debt, and that was all."

But Harry was dutiful, how dutiful his friends had reason to see again when they would urge him to try sending the old man to a home for the aged. "No," Harry would reply, his features moving heavily and reluctantly to a frown, a pout, as he showed how little the suggestion appealed to him. "I don't like the idea. Maybe one day when he needs medical attention all the time I'll feel differently about it, but not now, not now. He wouldn't like it, he'd be unhappy. We'll look after him as long as we can. It's a job. It's something you've got to do."

More eagerly Harry would go back to a recital of the old man's past. "He couldn't even pay for his own passage out. I had to pay the loan back. We came out together—my mother wouldn't let him go by himself again, and I had to pay off her brother who advanced the money for us. I was a boy—what was I?—sixteen, seventeen, but I paid for his passage, and my own, and my mother's and then my brother's. It took me a long time, let me tell you. And then my troubles with him weren't over." Harry even reproached his father for his myopia; he could clearly enough remember his chagrin when shortly after their arrival in South Africa, after it had become clear that Harry would be able to make his way in the world and be a support to the whole family, the old man—who at that time had not really been so old—had suddenly, almost dramatically, grown so short-sighted that he had been almost blind without the glasses that Harry had had to buy for him. And Harry could remember too how he had then made a practice of losing the glasses or breaking them with the greatest frequency, until it had been made clear to him that he was no longer expected to do any work. "He doesn't do that any more. When he wants to run away now he sees to it that he's wearing his glasses. That's how he's always been. Sometimes he recognizes me, at other times, when he doesn't want to, he just doesn't know who I am."

What Harry said about his father sometimes failing to recognize him was true. Sometimes the old man would call out to his son, when he would see him at the end of a passage, "Who are you?" Or he would come upon Harry in a room and demand of him, "What do you want in my house?"

"Your house?" Harry would say, when he felt like teasing the old man. "Your house?"

"Out of my house!" the old man would shout back.

"Your house? Do you call this your house?" Harry would reply, smiling at the old man's fury.

Harry was the only one in the house who talked to the old man, and then he didn't so much talk to him, as talk of him to others. Harry's wife was a dim and silent woman, crowded out by her husband and the large-boned sons like himself that she had borne him, and she would gladly have seen the old man in an old-age home. But her husband had said no, so she put up with the old man, though for herself she could see no possible better end for him than a period of residence in a home for aged Jews which she had once visited, and which had impressed her most favourably with its glass and yellow brick, the noiseless rubber tiles in its corridors, its secluded grassed grounds, and the uniforms worn by the attendants to the establishment. But she put up with the old man; she did not talk to him. The grandchildren had nothing to do with their grandfather—they were busy at school, playing rugby and cricket, they could hardly speak Yiddish, and they were embarrassed by him in front of their friends; and when the grandfather did take any notice of them it was only to call them Boers and *goyim* and *shkotzim* in sudden quavering rages which did not disturb them at all.

The house itself—a big single-storied place of brick, with

a corrugated iron roof above and a wide stoep all round—Harry Grossman had bought years before, and in the continual rebuilding the suburb was undergoing it was beginning to look old-fashioned. But it was solid and prosperous, and within-doors curiously masculine in appearance, like the house of a widower. The furniture was of the heaviest African woods, dark, and built to last, the passages were lined with bare linoleum, and the few pictures on the walls, big brown and grey mezzotints in heavy frames, had not been looked at for years. The servants were both men, large ignored Zulus who did their work and kept up the brown gleam of the furniture.

It was from this house that old man Grossman tried to escape. He fled through the doors and the windows and out into the wide sunlit streets of the town in Africa, where the blocks of flats were encroaching upon the single-storied houses behind their gardens. And in these streets he wandered.

It was Johannes, one of the Zulu servants, who suggested a way of dealing with old man Grossman. He brought to the house one afternoon Paulus, whom he described as his 'brother.' Harry Grossman knew enough to know that 'brother' in this context could mean anything from the son of one's mother to a friend from a neighbouring *kraal,* but by the speech that Johannes made on Paulus' behalf he might indeed have been the latter's brother. Johannes had to speak for Paulus, for Paulus knew no English. Paulus was a 'raw boy,' as raw as a boy could possibly come. He was a muscular, moustached and bearded African, with pendulous ear-lobes showing the slits in which the tribal plugs had once hung; and on his feet he wore sandals the soles of which were cut from old motor-car tyres, the thongs from red inner tubing. He wore neither hat nor socks, but he did have a pair of khaki shorts which were too small for him, and a shirt without any buttons: buttons would in any case have been of no use for the shirt could never have closed over his chest. He swelled magnificently out of his clothing, and above there was a head carried well back, so that his beard, which had been trained to grow in two sharp points from his chin, bristled ferociously forward under his melancholy and almost mandarin-like moustache. When he smiled, as he did once or twice during Johannes' speech, he showed his white, even teeth, but for the most part he stood looking rather shyly to the side of Harry Grossman's head, with his hands behind his back and his bare knees bent a little forward, as if to show how little he was asserting himself, no matter what his 'brother' might have been saying about him.

His expression did not change when Harry said that it seemed hopeless, that Paulus was too raw, and Johannes explained what the baas had just said. He nodded agreement when Johannes explained to him that the baas said that it was a pity that he knew no English. But whenever Harry looked at him, he smiled, not ingratiatingly, but simply smiling above his beard, as though saying: "Try me." Then he looked grave again as Johannes expatiated on his virtues. Johannes pleaded for his 'brother.' He said that the baas knew that he, Johannes, was a good boy. Would he, then, recommend to the baas a boy who was not a good boy too? The baas could see for himself, Johannes said, that Paulus was not one of these town boys, these street loafers: he was a good boy, come straight from the *kraal.* He was not a thief or a drinker. He was strong, he was a hard worker, he was clean, and he could be as gentle as a woman. If he, Johannes, were not telling the truth about all these things, then he deserved to be chased away. If Paulus failed in any single respect, then he, Johannes, would voluntarily leave the service of the baas, because he had said untrue things to the baas. But if the baas believed him, and gave Paulus his chance, then he, Johannes, would teach Paulus all the things of the house and the garden, so that Paulus would be useful to the baas in ways other than the particular task for which he was asking the baas to hire him. And, rather daringly, Johannes said that it did not matter so much if

Paulus knew no English, because the old baas, the *oubaas,* knew no English either.

It was as something in the nature of a joke—almost a joke against his father—that Harry Grossman gave Paulus his chance. For Paulus was given his chance. He was given a room in the servants' quarters in the back yard, into which he brought a tin trunk painted red and black, a roll of blankets, and a guitar with a picture of a cowboy on the back. He was given a houseboy's outfit of blue denim blouse and shorts, with red piping round the edges, into which he fitted, with his beard and physique, like a king in exile in some pantomime. He was given his food three times a day, after the white people had eaten, a bar of soap every week, cast-off clothing at odd intervals, and the sum of one pound five shillings per week, five shillings of which he took, the rest being left at his request, with the baas, as savings. He had a free afternoon once a week, and he was allowed to entertain not more than two friends at any one time in his room. And in all the particulars that Johannes had enumerated, Johannes was proved reliable. Paulus was not one of these town boys, these street loafers. He did not steal or drink, he was clean and he was honest and hard-working. And he could be gentle as a woman.

It took Paulus some time to settle down to his job; he had to conquer not only his own shyness and strangeness in the new house filled with strange people—let alone the city, which, since taking occupation of his room, he had hardly dared to enter—but also the hostility of old man Grossman, who took immediate fright at Paulus and redoubled his efforts to get away from the house upon Paulus' entry into it. As it happened, the first result of this persistence on the part of the old man was that Paulus was able to get the measure of the job, for he came to it with a willingness of spirit that the old man could not vanquish, but could only teach. Paulus had been given no instructions, he had merely been told to see that the old man did not get himself into trouble, and after a few days of bewilderment Paulus found his way. He simply went along with the old man.

At first he did so cautiously, following the old man at a distance, for he knew the other had no trust in him. But later he was able to follow the old man openly; still later he was able to walk side by side with him, and the old man did not try to escape from him. When old man Grossman went out, Paulus went too, and there was no longer any need for the doors and windows to be watched, or the police to be telephoned. The young bearded Zulu and the old bearded Jew from Lithuania walked together in the streets of the town that was strange to them both; together they looked over the fences of the large gardens and into the shining foyers of the blocks of flats; together they stood on the pavements of the main arterial roads and watched the cars and trucks rush between the tall buildings; together they walked in the small, sandy parks, and when the old man was tired Paulus saw to it that he sat on a bench and rested. They could not sit on the bench together, for only whites were allowed to sit on the benches, but Paulus would squat on the ground at the old man's feet and wait until he judged the old man had rested long enough, before moving on again. Together they stared into the windows of the suburban shops, and though neither of them could read the signs outside the shops, the advertisements on billboards, the traffic signs at the side of the road, Paulus learned to wait for the traffic lights to change from red to green before crossing a street, and together they stared at the Coca-cola girls and the advertisements for beer and the cinema posters. On a piece of cardboard which Paulus carried in the pocket of his blouse Harry had had one of his sons print the old man's name and address, and whenever Paulus was uncertain of the way home, he would approach an African or a friendly-looking white man and show him the card, and try his best to follow the instructions, or at least the gesticulations which were all of the answers of the white men that meant anything to him. But there were enough

Africans to be found, usually, who were more sophisticated than himself, and though they teased him for his 'rawness' and for holding the sort of job he had, they helped him too. And neither Paulus nor old man Grossman were aware that when they crossed a street hand-in-hand, as they sometimes did when the traffic was particularly heavy, there were white men who averted their eyes from the sight of this degradation, which could come upon a white man when he was old and senile and dependent.

Paulus knew only Zulu, the old man knew only Yiddish, so there was no language in which they could talk to one another. But they talked all the same: they both explained, commented and complained to each other of the things they saw around them, and often they agreed with one another, smiling and nodding their heads and explaining again with their hands what each happened to be talking about. They both seemed to believe that they were talking about the same things, and often they undoubtedly were, when they lifted their heads sharply to see an aeroplane cross the blue sky between two buildings, or when they reached the top of a steep road and turned to look back the way they had come, and saw below them the clean impervious towers of the city thrust nakedly against the sky in brand-new piles of concrete and glass and face-brick. Then down they would go again, among the houses and the gardens where the beneficent climate encouraged both palms and oak trees to grow indiscriminately among each other—as they did in the garden of the house to which, in the evenings, Paulus and old man Grossman would eventually return.

In and about the house Paulus soon became as indispensable to the old man as he was on their expeditions out of it. Paulus dressed him and bathed him and trimmed his beard, and when the old man woke distressed in the middle of the night it would be for Paulus that he would call—"*Der schwarzer,*" he would shout (for he never learned Paulus' name), "*vo's der schwarzer*"—and Paulus would change his sheets and pyjamas and put him back to bed again. "*Baas Zeide,*" Paulus called the old man, picking up the Yiddish word for grandfather from the children of the house.

And that was something that Harry Grossman told everyone of. For Harry persisted in regarding the arrangement as a kind of joke, and the more the arrangement succeeded the more determinedly did he try to spread the joke, so that it should be a joke not only against his father but a joke against Paulus too. It had been a joke that his father should be looked after by a raw Zulu: it was going to be a joke that the Zulu was successful at it. "Baas *Zeide!* That's what *der schwarzer* calls him—have you ever heard the like of it? And you should see the two of them, walking about in the streets hand-in-hand like two schoolgirls. Two clever ones, *der schwarzer* and my father going for a promenade, and between them I tell you you wouldn't be able to find out what day of the week or what time of day it is."

And when people said, "Still that Paulus seems a very good boy," Harry would reply:

"Why shouldn't he be? With all his knowledge, are there so many better jobs that he'd be able to find? He keeps the old man happy—very good, very nice, but don't forget that that's what he's paid to do. What does he know any better to do, a simple kaffir from the *kraal?* He knows he's got a good job, and he'd be a fool if he threw it away. Do you think," Harry would say, and this too would insistently be part of the joke, "if I had nothing else to do with my time I wouldn't be able to make the old man happy?" Harry would look about his sitting-room, where the floorboards bore the weight of his furniture, or when they sat on the stoep he would measure with his glance the spacious garden aloof from the street beyond the hedge. "I've got other things to do. And I had other things to do, plenty of them, all my life, and not only for myself." What these things were that he had had to do all his life would send him back to his joke. "No, I think the old man has just found his level in *der schwarzer*—and I don't think *der schwarzer* could cope with anything else."

Harry teased the old man to his face too, about his 'black friend,' and he would ask his father what he would do if Paulus went away; once he jokingly threatened to send the Zulu away. But the old man didn't believe the threat, for Paulus was in the house when the threat was made, and the old man simply left his son and went straight to Paulus' room, and sat there with Paulus for security. Harry did not follow him: he would never have gone into any of his servants' rooms least of all that of Paulus. For though he made a joke of him to others, to Paulus himself Harry always spoke gruffly, unjokingly, with no patience. On that day he had merely shouted after the old man, "Another time he won't be there."

Yet it was strange to see how Harry Grossman would always be drawn to the room in which he knew his father and Paulus to be. Night after night he came into the old man's bedroom when Paulus was dressing or undressing the old man; almost as often Harry stood in the steamy, untidy bathroom when the old man was being bathed. At these times he hardly spoke, he offered no explanation of his presence: he stood dourly and silently in the room, in his customary powerful and begrudging stance, with one hand clasping the wrist of the other and both supporting his waist, and he watched Paulus at work. The backs of Paulus' hands were smooth and black and hairless, they were paler on the palms and at the finger-nails, and they worked deftly about the body of the old man, who was submissive under the ministrations of the other. At first Paulus had sometimes smiled at Harry while he worked, with his straightforward, even smile in which there was no invitation to a complicity in patronage, but rather an encouragement to Harry to draw forward. But after the first few evenings of this work that Harry had watched, Paulus no longer smiled at his master. And while he worked Paulus could not restrain himself, even under Harry's stare, from talking in a soft, continuous flow of Zulu, to encourage the old man and to exhort him to be helpful and to express his pleasure in how well the work was going. When Paulus would at last wipe the gleaming soap-flakes from his dark hands he would sometimes, when the old man was tired, stoop low and with a laugh pick up the old man and carry him easily down the passage to his bedroom. Harry would follow; he would stand in the passage and watch the burdened, bare-footed Zulu until the door of his father's room closed behind them both.

Only once did Harry wait on such an evening for Paulus to reappear from his father's room. Paulus had already come out, had passed him in the narrow passage, and had already subduedly said: "Good night, baas," before Harry called suddenly:

"Hey! Wait!"

"Baas," Paulus said, turning his head. Then he came quickly to Harry. "Baas," he said again, puzzled and anxious to know why his baas, who so rarely spoke to him, should suddenly have called him like this, at the end of the day, when his work was over.

Harry waited again before speaking, waited long enough for Paulus to say: Baas?" once more, and to move a little closer, and to lift his head for a moment before letting it drop respectfully down.

"The *oubaas* was tired tonight," Harry said. "Where did you take him? What did you do with him?"

"Baas?" Paulus said quickly. Harry's tone was so brusque that the smile Paulus gave asked for no more than a moment's remission of the other's anger.

But Harry went on loudly: "You heard what I said. What did you do with him that he looked so tired?"

"Baas—I——" Paulus was flustered, and his hands beat in the air for a moment, but with care, so that he would not touch his baas. "Please baas." He brought both hands to his mouth, closing it forcibly. He flung his hands away. "Johannes," he said with relief, and he had already taken the first step down the passage to call his interpreter.

"No!" Harry called. "You mean you don't understand what I say? I know you don't," Harry shouted, though in fact he had forgotten until Paulus had reminded him. The sight of Paulus' startled, puzzled, and guilty face before him filled him with a lust to see this man, this nurse with the face and the figure of a warrior, look more startled, puzzled, and guilty yet; and Harry knew that it could so easily be done, it could be done simply by talking to him in the language he could not understand. "You're a fool," Harry said. "You're like a child. You understand nothing, and it's just as well for you that you need nothing. You'll always be where you are, running to do what the white baas tells you to do. Look how you stand! Do you think I understood English when I came here?" Harry said, and then with contempt, using one of the few Zulu words he knew: "*Hamba!* Go! Do you think I want to see you?"

"*Au* baas!" Paulus exclaimed in distress. He could not remonstrate; he could only open his hands in a gesture to show that he knew neither the words Harry used, nor in what he had been remiss that Harry should have spoken in such angry tones to him. But Harry gestured him away, and had the satisfaction of seeing Paulus shuffle off like a schoolboy.

Harry was the only person who knew that he and his father had quarrelled shortly before the accident that ended the old man's life took place; this was something that Harry was to keep secret for the rest of his life.

Late in the afternoon they quarrelled, after Harry had come back from the shop out of which he made his living. Harry came back to find his father wandering about the house, shouting for *der schwarzer,* and his wife complaining that she had already told the old man at least five times that *der schwarzer* was not in the house: it was Paulus' afternoon off.

Harry went to his father, and when his father came eagerly to him, he too told the old man, "*Der schwarzer*'s not here." So the old man, with Harry following, turned away and continued going from room to room, peering in through the doors. "*Der schwarzer*'s not here," Harry said. "What do you want him for?"

Still the old man ignored him. He went down the passage towards the bedrooms. "What do you want him for?" Harry called after him.

The old man went into every bedroom, still shouting for *der schwarzer*. Only when he was in his own bare bedroom did he look at Harry. "Where's *der schwarzer?*" he asked.

"I've told you ten times I don't know where he is. What do you want him for?"

"I want *der schwarzer*."

"I know you want him. But he isn't here."

"I want *der schwarzer*."

"Do you think I haven't heard you? He isn't here."

"Bring him to me," the old man said.

"I can't bring him to you. I don't know where he is." Then Harry steadied himself against his own anger. He said quietly: "Tell me what you want. I'll do it for you. I'm here, I can do what *der schwarzer* can do for you."

"Where's *der schwarzer?*"

"I've told you he isn't here," Harry shouted, the angrier for his previous moment's patience. "Why don't you tell me what you want? What's the matter with me—can't you tell me what you want?"

"I want *der schwarzer*."

"Please," Harry said. He threw out his arms towards his father, but the gesture was abrupt, almost as though he were thrusting his father away from him. "Why can't you ask it of me? You can ask me—haven't I done enough for you already?

Do you want to go for a walk?—I'll take you for a walk. What do you want? Do you want—do you want——?" Harry could not think what his father might want. "I'll do it," he said. "You don't need *der schwarzer*."

Then Harry saw that his father was weeping. The old man was standing up and weeping, with his eyes hidden behind the thick glasses that he had to wear: his glasses and his beard made his face a mask of age, as though time had left him nothing but the frame of his body on which the clothing could hang, and this mask of his face above. But Harry knew when the old man was weeping—he had seen him crying too often before, when they had found him at the end of a street after he had wandered away, or even, years earlier, when he had lost another of the miserable jobs that seemed to be the only one he could find in a country in which his son had, later, been able to run a good business, drive a large car, own a big house.

"Father," Harry asked, "what have I done? Do you think I've sent *der schwarzer* away?" Harry saw his father turn away, between the narrow bed and the narrow wardrobe. "He's coming——" Harry said, but he could not look at his father's back, he could not look at his father's hollowed neck, on which the hairs that Paulus had clipped glistened above the pale brown discolourations of age—Harry could not look at the neck turned stiffly away from him while he had to try to promise the return of the Zulu. Harry dropped his hands and walked out of the room.

No one knew how the old man managed to get out of the house and through the front gate without having been seen. But he did manage it, and in the road he was struck down. Only a man on a bicycle struck him down, but it was enough, and he died a few days later in the hospital.

Harry's wife wept, even the grandsons wept; Paulus wept. Harry himself was stony, and his bunched, protuberant features were immovable; they seemed locked upon the bones of his face. A few days after the funeral he called Paulus and Johannes into the kitchen and said to Johannes: "Tell him he must go. His work is finished."

Johannes translated for Paulus, and then, after Paulus had spoken, he turned to Harry. "He says, yes baas." Paulus kept his eyes on the ground; he did not look up even when Harry looked directly at him, and Harry knew that this was not out of fear or shyness, but out of courtesy for his master's grief—which was what they could not but be talking of, when they talked of his work.

"Here's his pay." Harry thrust a few notes towards Paulus, who took them in his cupped hands, and retreated.

Harry waited for them to go, but Paulus stayed in the room, and consulted with Johannes in a low voice. Johannes turned to his master. "He says, baas, that the baas still has his savings."

Harry had forgotten about Paulus' savings. He told Johannes that he had forgotten, and that he did not have enough money at the moment, but would bring the money the next day. Johannes translated and Paulus nodded gratefully. Both he and Johannes were subdued by the death there had been in the house.

And Harry's dealings with Paulus were over. He took what was to have been his last look at Paulus, but this look stirred him again against the Zulu. As harshly as he told Paulus that he had to go, so now, implacably, seeing Paulus in the mockery and simplicity of his houseboy's clothing, to feed his anger to the very end Harry said: "Ask him what he's been saving for. What's he going to do with the fortune he's made?"

Johannes spoke to Paulus and came back with a reply. "He says, baas, that he is saving to bring his wife and children from Zululand to Johannesburg. He is saving, baas," Johannes said, for Harry had not seemed to understand, "to bring his family to this town also."

The two Zulus were bewildered to know why it should have

been at that moment that Harry Grossman's clenched, fist-like features should suddenly seem to have fallen from one another, nor why he should have stared with such guilt and despair at Paulus, while he cried, "What else could I have done? I did my best," before the first tears came.

The Prisoner

S. YIZHAR

S. Yizhar (**Smilansky**) was born in Palestine in 1916, the great-nephew of the writer, Moshe Smilansky. His first story was published in 1938, and his books, written originally in Hebrew, include *The Midnight Convoy, The Days of Ziklag,* and numerous volumes of short stories. Yizhar lives in Rehovot, Israel, and represents the party of Mapai in the Israeli Knesset. In 1950 he won the Brenner Prize and he has also won the Israel Award.

Since shepherds and their herds were scattered here and there on the steep ridges, in the pistachio scrub and the underbrush of wild roses, dotted among the winding valleys which foamed with light (those same rustling glints of *dura,* wild sorghum, glittering with summer green and yellow, the soil beneath crumbling in tiny clods like nuts that fall to a powder of dust at the touch of a foot)—and since the olives on the crests of the hills shaded figures here and there, it became evident that we could penetrate no farther without attracting attention, which took all the point out of the reconnaissance.

We sat down on the stone to rest a bit. Everything was turbulent with summer, like a golden beehive. Whirlpools of the gold of mountain fields, greenish *dura* yellowing, green hills, grey shrivelled olives, the burning sky and the powerful silence—they blinded one, and the heart longed for a cheerful word. Within all this the herds gazed placidly, the distant village dozed, engraved with a border of olive trees like tarnished copper, in a bas-relief of hills crowding sheeplike together. Oblivious that other purposes cut diagonally across theirs.

Our second lieutenant looked through his binoculars and puffed on his cigarette, planning. First of all, there was no sense in going any farther. And second, it was out of the question to go back empty-handed. At least one, out of all the shepherds, had to be caught, so that we could go back with something tangible, an accomplished fact. The second lieutenant was of medium height. He had deep-set eyes, fine eyebrows, and was going bald. We all followed his gaze. He saw what he saw, and we saw a world of hills fleeced with green, boulders and olives in the distance, a world crossed with golden valleys of *dura*—so much of a world that it brought a stillness into you, and a longing kindled in us for fertile, sprouting earth, a longing for something besides just being one of a squad which the lieutenant would decide how to fling into the quietude of afternoon.

And he was almost ready to take action, for in the shade of an oak, we had already discovered a shepherd resting, his flock around him in the stubble of *dura.* Instantly a circle was inscribed upon the world, everything else outside the circle; and within it one man marked to be snared alive. And the hunters already gone out. Most of the squad would hide itself among the scrub and the boulders to the right; and to the left, below, the lieutenant together with a few others would surround him, fall upon him by surprise, and pursue the prey into the arms of those in ambush above. We stole right into the pleasant gold of the *dura,* then burst out in a run towards the man who was sitting on a stone in the shade of the oak. Overcome by terror, he jumped to his feet, threw his stick from him, and ran senselessly like a pursued gazelle, disappearing over the ridge straight into the arms of the hunters.

Ah, what a laugh! And another quick suggestion by our platoon lieutenant! We'll take the herd too! He struck one hand upon the other and rubbed his palms together with satisfaction, saying: That's it!

But all this commotion had frightened the herd—some raised their heads, others prepared to flee, others looked as though they wanted to know what the others were going to do. Besides, how do you drive sheep? Our lieutenant complained that fools like us weren't good for anything but mucking up a nice job. He raised his voice and began calling B-r-r-r and G-r-r-r and Ta-ta-ta and all the other sounds that have been agreed upon since the beginning of the world between a shepherd and his flock.

In all the uproar we had completely forgotten that on the other side of a boulder on the slope above, between two rifle butts and two pairs of hobnailed boots, a prisoner was sitting, scared as a rabbit, a man of forty or thereabouts, with a moustache drooping over his mouth, a foolish nose and lips hanging a little open, and eyes . . . but these were bound with his own *kefia*—so that he wouldn't see . . . I don't know what he wouldn't see.

"Get up!" they said to him when the lieutenant came over, so that the lieutenant could see in its entirety, from top to bottom, his spoils. And they said to him: "So you thought we wouldn't catch him? Well, we did, all right! And without even one bullet——"

"Well done! What they'll say when we get back! Beautiful!" He turned his eyes on the prisoner then and saw a short man in a faded, yellowing gown, his breath trembling, the *kefia* around his eyes, torn sandals like hooves, and the fear of death in his raised shoulders.

"Undo his eyes, but tie his hands: he'll drive the sheep ahead of us!" Our lieutenant came up with another of his bright ideas.

They took the black *agal* from his head and twisted it around his hands, once, twice, three times, tightening it. Then they whisked the blindfold off his face and said to him: *"Navi el ri'nam kudmana!"* Which is: "Drive the sheep ahead of us."

Who knows what the prisoner thought to himself when his eyes saw light again, or what was in his heart, what his blood whispered, what his blood roared, what weakly turned over within him—but he began squealing and calling to his flock as though nothing had ever happened, and he leaped down from boulder to boulder between the bushes, with the frightened, astonished sheep behind him, and behind them and all around them were his throaty cries, the kicks of our feet and blows of our rifles; and we went down into the valley.

We were so absorbed in all this that we paid no attention to several figures of other shepherds who peered from the ridges of hills (crowded together in a golden stillness, a wordless melancholy), who were silently gathering and driving their sheep away and watching us from afar; nor did we notice the sun which all that same tumultuous hour was growing lower and lower, growing golden, until once, when we came around the side of a mountain, it threw upon us an enormous, blinding wave of glitter: plate-like, dusty, sparkling, until it seemed like a kind of dumb reproof, lofty, turning towards much more than this. Of course, we had no time to think of all this. The flock! The prisoner! The one scattering and bawling, and the other trying to make himself as small as possible and completely silent. A kind of darkness and confusion fell on him, a kind of collapse of the senses, everything behind him lost, everything before him already beyond despair; and he trod more and more silently, more and more sorrowfully, more and more shocked and bewildered. We went through the valleys between the hills (crowded together in goldening stillness), in this ripeness of summer, and a muteness fell upon our prisoner, the silence of an uprooted plant; he was so miserable as to be ridiculous, terrified and shaking and falling again and again on his face, the *kefia* jerked down over his eyebrows; the *dura* grew more golden, the sun more silently proud, the dirt road nibbled its way groping between the side of the field and the side of the mountain, and we approached our base.

The signs of an "outpost" became more and more evident. Our outpost—an abandoned Arab village, left yesterday: conquered, pillaged. Dust, desolation, waste. Isolated echoes. The remnants of man. The rottenness from so much desolation, from stinking, flea-and-lice-ridden existence. Poverty and stupidity of miserable villagers, revealed now, their garment suddenly pulled above their head, the shame of their nakedness uncovered. An abandoned anthill. Sudden emptiness. Sudden death. Strangeness, hatred, and orphanhood. An unimportance and something perhaps-mourning, perhaps-boredom, slant crookedly in the dust like the heat of the day.

Our walk became proud: spoils such as these! Our steps beat out a rhythm. The herd bawled and flowed in confusion, the prisoner, who had again had the *kefia* pulled over his eyes (because of the secrets of the "outpost"), scuffed his sandals and stumbled along blindly, without hope. . . . We were sweating, dusty. And such soldiers, and such men. And our lieutenant roared such laughter, with such satisfaction—like a barrel with the hoops loosened.

He was still laughing when one of the others came up to our lieutenant and pointed at the blindfolded prisoner:

"That him? Just let me finish him off!"

Our lieutenant was still laughing and swallowing water and wiping the sweat off his forehead and he said:

"You just step aside, buddy, and mind your own business."

The circle around us bawled with laughter. . . . There was one there who took pictures of the whole great event. And there was one who didn't know if their laughter was nice or not nice, and whose eyes pleaded for the opinion of others on what it was. There were those who had good jobs, and those who were climbing the ladder. And one in an undershirt, who gazed in astonishment and curiosity, one whose eternal "Well, what now, what now?" many dentists, and sleepless nights, and narrow airless rooms, and a thin quarrelsome wife, and unemployment and work in the party had laboured in vain to change. And those who were forever worthless and hopelessly unlucky, and those who ran to the films and to *Habima* and to the *Ohel* and to the *Matateh,* and who read the weekly supplements of two newspapers. And those who were not at all what people think about them, and those who were just exactly what they were. All these stood in a happy circle around one prisoner whose eyes were bound with a *kefia;* and he chose that precise opportunity to hold out one of his hardened palms, palms impossible to tell whether or not they were dirty, only that they were the palms of a villager, and said:

"*Fi cigara?*" in a loud, guttural, astonished voice—it was as though the wall of the house had opened its mouth and spoken —which raised cries of ridicule and reproving fingers.

And there may even have been someone there who considered the matter of a cigarette, but everything ended then in another way, more military, since two corporals and one sergeant came down from headquarters and took the prisoner and led him away; he, because of his blindness, unthinkingly rested his hand on the arm of one of the corporals, who just as unthinkingly held out his arm so that he might grasp it well. He also directed the prisoner's groping walk, and for a moment it was as though the two of them were struggling to overcome obstacles successfully, each helping the other, as though they were together, one—until a minute before they reached the building, when the prisoner growled again the same words: "*Fi cigara?*" which immediately ruined everything, and the corporal dropped the supported arm, which was almost linked to his, and shook himself, half-insulted, so suddenly that the man, unwarned, struck his foot against the threshold of the building and collapsed, almost falling on his face, his movement carrying him into the room in a burst; trying to save himself from falling, he struck a chair and came up against the table. Hopeless, entangled, and shocked, he dropped his hands and abandoned his confused soul to whatever would be.

On the other side of the table sat several officers, very official, waiting portentously, and his unexpected bursting into the room spoiled their prepared reception.

The one sitting in the middle was tall and muscular, with sharp features and disordered hair. To his left sat none other than our lieutenant himself, revealed now as almost completely bald, with greying sideburns and dark strands of hair at his temples, a cigarette stuck into his mouth, sweating, resting, the hero of the day. Against the wall, in demonstrative solitude, leaned a young man who looked through lowered eyelashes with the consciousness of one who knows a very specific truth, and waits to see how in the end, with no other possibility, it alone will be revealed.

"What's your name?"

The tall one began the interrogation all at once; the prisoner, still sunk in the confusion of his entrance, did not grasp the question. A wrinkle of certainty appeared around the mouth of the young man leaning against the wall, as though he had expected this from the beginning.

"What's your name?" the tall one repeated, spitting out his words.

"Who? Me?" Alarmed, he raised a hesitant hand to the *kefia* binding his eyes, and in the middle of the gesture, he let his hand fall again, as though it had been burnt.

"Your name?" the bald one repeated, in heavy, distinct syllables.

"Hassan," he grated, turning his head in an effort to make up for his blindness by application.

"Hassan what?"

"Hassan Achmed," he rolled out fluently, as though he had reached familiar ground; and nodded his head in confirmation.

"Age?"

"Ya'ani," he shrugged his shoulders and rubbed his hands together in bewilderment, with helpful intention.

"How old are you?"

"So-so. I don't know, *ya sidi,*" he grated between his thick lips, and for some reason he chuckled and his drooping moustache danced lightly. "Twenty, or perhaps also thirty," he volunteered.

"Well, and what's happening at your village?" The tall one continued with the same emphatic placidity which, more than it emphasized the calm, promised the storm to follow. The small cunning placidity of one who comes from afar, obliquely, and falls suddenly upon the main artery deep within the breast. . . .

"We're working in the village, *ya sidi.*" The prisoner drew him a picture of the life of the village, scenting evil to come from some place.

"Working, eh? Just as usual?" The interrogator drew a little nearer, like the spider, when one of the strands of its web begins to vibrate, heralding prey.

"Yes, *ya sidi.*" The fly twisted and slipped through the tangled strands.

It was so understood that here he would lie. It was his duty to lie, and we'd catch him out, the son of a bitch, and we'd show him.

"And who's in your village?" The hawk hovered over its prey.

"Ah?" The prisoner did not grasp the question, and licked his lips in a kind of innocence, like an animal.

"Jews? English? French?" The interrogator led him, like a teacher setting a trap for a small boy: Catch him, catch him!

"Yes, *ya sidi,* there aren't any Jews, only Arabs," he answered seriously, not dodging at all, and sent a thoughtless hand to the *kefia* over his eyes, as though the danger had passed. The interrogator sent a glance around the room at his companions: You see! Here it begins.

"Are you married?" He attacked from another angle. "Any children? And where's your father? How many brothers? Where does your village get its water from?" Thus the tall questioner wove his fine web, and thus the prisoner laboured and struggled to be satisfactory, waving his hands, gesturing pointlessly and exaggeratedly, nodding his head, and telling all sorts of small details, which annoyed his questioner and utterly confused him; the story of two daughters, and something that happened to a son, except he got out of it, not without blame on the part of his sisters, and got sick and died and left the world; and while he was telling all this, he stuck out a thumb and scratched his back aimlessly, back and forth, clenching his fingers when he made a special effort to produce out of his stammering the one requested word; and his listeners were thoroughly sick of him.

There was a pause. The guard by the door shifted from one foot to the other.

From the expression of the young man leaning against the wall, and from our bald lieutenant's getting up from the table, it was suddenly clear that nothing would help but blows.

"Listen, *ya Hassan,*" the interrogator said then. "Are there any Egyptians in your village?" (Now it begins. Now he'll start lying.)

"There are," said the prisoner, with disappointing simplicity.

"There are . . ." echoed the interrogator with a shadow of doubt and a shade of aggression, like someone who has been out-manoeuvred; he lit a cigarette and considered whether to open with rook or knight.

"How many?"

"*Ya'ani*—so-so, not many."

"How many?"

"Ten, and perhaps fifteen, so-so . . ."

"Listen, *ya Hassan,* it'll be better for you if you tell the truth."

"The truth, *ya sidi,* all the truth!"

"And don't tell stories."

"*Na'am, ya sidi.*" The prisoner did not know what to do with his hands, which were spread out before him in astonishment, and he dropped them.

"Fifteen, he said."

"Liar!"

The bald lieutenant turned his head towards them, his eyes smiling. That same elation was kindling within him which a man feels from an enjoyment which will come in another minute; and in the meantime there is enjoyment in the suppression of that other enjoyment, the prolonging of its existence for one more sweet moment, till afterwards, until he lights a cigarette in the smiling angle of his compressed lips. The five who were in the room exchanged the same glances of hidden exhilaration. The guard standing by the door shifted his stance from one foot to the other.

"On my life, *ya sidi,* fifteen!"

"No more?"

"*Abadan,* no more."

"How do you know there aren't any more? And if there are more?"

"There aren't any more."

The kick came then, suddenly, bursting out, loosed at last, at a slant, uncomfortably, too close for a nice, free-swinging kick, and it shook the prisoner, blindfolded and unprepared, so that he cried out in pain; it seemed more like an unfair game than a method of "getting information." Unexpected, unnatural. Something just not the thing. Not the thing.

"Now talk, and be careful you tell the truth!"

"*Ya sidi,* on my eyes, in the name of Allah: fifteen!"

The one leaning against the wall obviously suspected that someone might believe this gross lie. He held in his hands a long cane which he drew back and forth between his fingers with the same grace of a knight drawing his sword, and he rested it in silence, the silence of a word to the wise, on the table.

More questions. One after another. Without pause. Time after time there came, more and more easily and naturally, kick after kick. Cold kicks, kicks without anger, well-trained. If you want to now the truth: blows. If the man lies—hit him. If he's telling the truth, hit him so he won't lie in the future. Don't pity: hit. No one will have any pity on you. And besides: the goy is used to blows.

Now they came to the business of the machine-guns in the village. Because of this, Jewish blood may be spilled, our boys' blood, so it has to be cleared up. They went over it again and again, until he enmeshed himself in conflicting stories and it was clear only that he was lying. Afterwards the fortifications of the village. Describe them. And here the prisoner was unsatisfactory in description, concepts, geometry, mathematics; he dropped his hands, shuffled his feet, turned this way and that, tried to convince through gestures, and it was very clear that all this was the tangle of a lie.

"You're a liar," the interrogator argued despairingly. "I can see by your eyes that you're lying!" And he shook his fist before the blindfold.

They made no progress. It was boring. They were already fed up. They carried on a cold, involved cross-examination. No one was enthusiastic, no one pitying. They even hit him indifferently.

Then the cannon. He argued that there was no barrel longer than the length of his arm from his shoulder to his hand—marking out the distance with axe-like blows of his left hand on his right shoulder and on the tip of his right hand, saying—from here to here, devotedly, attentively, repeating the blows until there was no doubt, without knowing if that was enough or if he should go on; on his lips and around his mouth was the expression of a blind man who has lost his way.

The questions died out. The guard who was near the door, who was shifting from foot to foot (looking now and then into the space of the door, seeking possibly in the glints of the sky something different from what is in this dirty, darkened room here), felt his suspicion growing that here, now, something terrible was about to happen, that they would say to him: Take the bastard out and finish him off!

"So, like that." The interrogator leaned back in his chair, tired out from the whole business.

"I'll finish him off." The bald one took it upon himself.

"He's a complete fool," summed up one of the corporals.

"He's just pretending to be a fool," said the other.

"You just have to know how to talk to him," said the young man leaning against the wall, his lips twisted at truth insulted and betrayed.

The prisoner, understanding that it had stopped for a while, licked his thick lips and stretched out his horny hand, saying: *"Fi cigara, ya sidi?"*

Of course, nobody paid any attention to the fool; and he dropped his outstretched hand and stood in his place, an idiot of idiots, and only to himself he sighed and said: *Ahh, ya Rav,* which is: O, my God, my God.

And so what? Where now? To the quarry at the edge of the village? How do we get rid of him? And perhaps . . . maybe just give him a cigarette and send him home, this fool, get going and don't let us see you again!

In the end we talked with the first lieutenant of the company himself, and decided to send him to a P.O.W. camp (at least three in the room wrinkled their noses in disgust at this defective decision, so civilian, so compromising). The prisoner was given into charge of the guard who had stood by the door, and he brought the dusty jeep and the driver who was angry at being called when it wasn't his turn. And another soldier came out and sat down by the driver, one who had been given another duty which had been delayed due to lack of transportation, and who now received the extra job of accompanying the prisoner. There was no place left for the prisoner except on the floor, and there he sank, kneeling, two in front of him and behind him the guard who had stood by the door.

And already they were gone from the stinking village, the jeep speeding and jolting on all four, and it was good to sit in the presence of the fields washed with reddening light, which covered everything in an undertow of golden clouds, tiny, rosy, the light surging greater than any other thing. The driver and his companion smoked and sang "In the plains of the Negev a soldier fell" and "Your eyes are full of green light" turn about.

It was hard to know much about the one on the floor of the jeep, sightless, animal-like, silent.

A pillar of dust flew up behind them, a smoky train which scorched and reddened at it hems. Minor ditches and trivial obstacles danced the speeding jeep, and fields spread out illimitable arms and gave themselves to twilight, drunken with forgetfulness and softness, something so distant, so dreamlike—until suddenly, all at once, you realize with amazement that he who sits here at your feet, his life, welfare, house, three souls, the entire, complete web of his life—are delivered somehow into your hands: you, the little god sitting in the jeep. The escorted man, the stolen flock, certain souls in a village in the mountains, the skein of distant lives will cling, break, become inextricably tangled—because of the fact that you, suddenly, are their master. Only will it, and you stop the jeep and set him free—and everything will turn out differently. But . . . wait. Something stirred in the young man sitting on the back seat of the jeep. Wait: let the man go!

We'll stop the jeep here. By the wadi. We'll take the man off, undo his eyes, point straight ahead and say: Go home, man. Straight over there. Be careful of that hill. Jews there. Watch out you don't fall into our hands another time . . . Listen, let's let him go!

Why not? Isn't it only human? You stand naked before the obligation. Driver, stop. Let him go. Be a man, send him home. Hallelujah, the shepherd, this *fellah,* will go home to his wife.

No other way. Years will go by until, miraculously, he will be set free and will return to the mountains to seek his wife, his household, who are in the meanwhile fugitives from starvation, from fear to fear, from typhus, the dust of humanity, who knows what in this meanwhile, on condition in the meanwhile that some soldier somewhere hasn't knocked him off, just like that, or maybe even not just like that.

Why don't you stop? Say one word to the driver, tell the

driver and his friend that that's the order, tell them a story, say something—and even that's unnecessary.

(How can I? Besides: this is war. And he's from the other side, fighting against us. And something else: if everyone starts freeing prisoners—what'll happen? And maybe he really does know something, and is only pretending to be a fool?)

Is he a soldier? Was there a sword in his hand when you captured him? He's no fighter. He's only a poor, stinking civilian. You questioned him—now set him free. You won't get anything more out of him.

(I would have to do so many unpleasant things: talk to the driver, explain to the other one, face all the trouble afterwards, get into a mess because of some lousy Hassan. . . . If we were only alone here. It's too much: to explain, get mixed up in it, argue with people, prove, justify. . . .)

Miserable considerations against the life of a man. How would you look at the matter if you were sitting on the floor of the jeep, with a wife at home waiting, and everything lost, ruined, blown like chaff into nothingness. . . . What is he but a miserable zero, a beaten, scrawny creature, his face wrapped in a *kefia,* bent over, crossed out, a sack of worthlessness, frightened, dissolving, forged out of nothing, waiting for kicks and seeing them only as natural. (Kick him—he's an Arab! It's nothing to him!) And you, his master, have an obligation to free him, even if he himself will laugh at you for it, see weakness in it, even if your friends mock you, even if they send you for this to the state prosecutor, or to twenty state prosecutors.

You, one Hassan Achmed, whose wife is Halima or Fatma, who has two daughters, whose flock has been stolen, and who is being taken somewhere one bright afternoon—you are good for drawing out all the refuse in our hearts. . . .

Of course you don't set him free. Obvious. Pretty words. Not even fear, worse than that: a partner in sin.

Set him free!

Already obvious that nothing will happen. . . . And supposing nevertheless? Here. Now. In this place. Driver, stop. Get out, *ya Hassan.* Go home. Do something. Speak. Halt. Talk. Here and now. This minute. Be, finally, the hurt of many long and empty days; be a man the way you wanted to be.

The field was one huge and level fragmentation of gold, the whole of all the thousands of acres was a wondrous bowl, without wadis, without hills, without slopes or depressions, without villages or trees—everything was beaten into one mass of gold, one level stretch, with sparkling golden dusts hovering above it, tremulous, a round lump of gold, enormous, limitless; and even though behind this, perhaps (and one does not look there) in the evening mist falling on the mountains, even though there, perhaps, there is some other sorrow (a grinding sorrow, a sorrow of who knows? of a waiting woman, of who knows? of a shameful weakness, of who knows? of fate, of one very private "who knows?" and of another "who knows?" general), the sun will set, and it will remain here, among us, unfinished.

Translated by M. Benaya

My Grandmother's Hands

ALEXANDER BARON

Alexander Baron was born in London in 1917. He began his career as a free-lance journalist and then worked exclusively in political and theatrical reporting until the outbreak of war. He has written in a variety of forms, including a great many film and television scripts. Among his books are *From the City, From the Plough, There's No Home, The Golden Princess, The Lowlife* and a volume of linked short stories, *The Human Kind,* which was adapted as the epic film, *The Victors.* Baron is married and lives in Brighton, England.

My mother's parents lived in Spitalfields, my father's in Bethnal Green. My two grandmothers were the presiding figures of my childhood, demi-deities who loomed, one at each end of the halls of my mind, and to whom all others, even my parents, were subordinate.

How different these two women were, one from the other! My mother's mother was always laughing. When I turned the street corner I could see her beaming smile from a hundred yards away—my memory represents her as always sitting in a wooden kitchen chair in front of her house—and, my heart thumping with excitement, I would break away from my parents and run faster and faster until I was in her lap. To me her voice seemed to be made of laughter.

My father's mother was gaunt and anxious of face. She, too, always met me with a smile, but the smile was haunted by sadness and anxiety. She was quiet—my Spitalfields *booba* reigned over her house like a confident queen, and it was a house full of her children, wonderful uncles and aunts who threw me in the air, hugged me, deafened me with a conflict of greetings and overwhelmed me with sweets, presents, outings; but my Bethnal Green *booba* sat alone in a silent back room behind her husband's shop, hands folded in her lap, a woman who had always accepted that her place in life was to serve and say little —she was quiet, and her quiet voice was high and querulous.

The one drew me like a magnet. Every day of my child's life I wanted to be taken to her, to rush into the warmth of her lap, to laugh joyfully at her jokes and teasing, to be led indoors by her for the invariable meal of welcome—a boiled egg and a thickly buttered beigel. The other?—children are selfish—it was a duty to go to her.

I went mute and apathetic to my father's mother. I stood, unresponding and resigned, while she put her big hands one on each side of my head and kissed me. She kissed me with hunger, and she muttered Yiddish endearments that I did not understand, as if she were speaking to herself, and in a voice that even beneath its welcome always sounded heartbroken. She had to hold me so, for sometimes I squirmed and made it known that the sensation of being kissed was disagreeable.

One Sunday—I was six or seven years old—we set out from Dalston to visit her. It happened to be one of those days when, without any provocation, I had entered into a state of stubborn and persistent conflict with my parents. I was an affectionate creature, but like all small children except those uncommonly placid or timid, I passed through phases when I was visited by a blind and absolute compulsion to match my will against theirs. Poor children! How much adult anger or lamentation they draw upon themselves when they are in this state! Yet it is their normal adjustment to the condition of man. When I see a child with red and tear-smudged face, uttering those astonishing screams that can be heard at the end of the street, stamping its feet and defying the grown-up giants who confront it, I see the stubborn struggle of innocent free will against the (to it) novel and unreasonable forces of social necessity. Intermittently the child renews its struggle, but with diminishing ferocity, until it submits or comes peaceably to terms, and thus assumes the shape of the adult animal it will become.

I had made trouble at the breakfast table, the issue being whether I should eat the porridge my mother had made, or whether my mother should cook the sausages I wanted. My mother had given way. I had refused to wear my sailor suit and, purely as a caprice, a demonstration of strength, had demanded to be allowed to wear my red jersey. I had wearied my parents into surrender. Now, when the time came to start out for Bethnal Green, I began to weep and scream that I wanted to go to Spitalfields.

My father took charge. He lifted me on to a chair so that I stood more or less face to face with him and gave me to understand that we were going to Bethnal Green. The only choice open to me was whether I went smacked or unsmacked. I scrutinised his expression—I see children nowadays doing the same thing, their own countenances so fluid with calculation and decision, so transparently cunning—wondering if I was facing an unbreakable grown-up decree or if another screaming fit would bring me victory. A moment later I climbed down from the chair and asked if we could go on the top of a bus instead of in a tram.

When we reached my grandmother's, she was alone. My grandfather, something of a solitary philosopher, had gone for one of his contemplative walks to Victoria Park. I submitted to the usual embrace. When my parents urged me to "give *booba* a kiss" I dabbed a brief and graceless kiss upon her cheek and wriggled free, to sit with swinging legs on the sofa of cracked black leatherette that occupied the length of one wall of her kitchen. She and my parents talked. It would not be true to say that I became lost in my own thoughts. A child never does this. A child is a small animal whose five senses are always active. My mind must have taken in everything they said, without attention, yet raking through every sentence for new data about the adult world. My eyes examined the room so minutely that to-day, thirty-five years later, I can remember every detail. I was always fascinated as if for the first time by the photograph on the mantelpiece of my uncle Hymie in his wartime uniform. I always read, with absorption and pride in my ability, the sheets of newspaper which were spread over the oilcloth on the table. I can still remember and analyse the smell of that room—Bethnal Green air gritty with railway smoke, the smell of soup boiling on the gas stove, the smell of the chicken-run in the yard, the smell of the newsprint on the table. All the time boredom, like a living independent thing over which I had no command, grew in me, a pressure in my breast and bowels.

From time to time I would catch my grandmother's eye, and she would offer me something. "*Nemm* a sweet, little one." "*Nemm* a nice biscuit." "*Fannele*"—this to my mother—"let me give him a glass of nice warm milk." With a child's skill at snubbing I would look at her without any emotion at all, and say nothing. If my father or mother said: "Answer your *booba*," I would speak a few words in a voice of dead wood. If a sweet was offered, I would take it, without thanks unless they were forced from me by my parents, and eat it stolidly. I did not dislike my grandmother. I was not frightened by her. If I had been asked, I would have said with honesty that I loved her. But she had not the talent, poor good woman, to entertain a child. There were no excitements in her house. I dangled my legs from the sofa, I crawled under the table to stroke the old black cat, I roamed in my grandfather's cobbler's shop, diverted for a little while by the gloom, the smell of leather and iron, the marvellous, to-be-explored shapes of lasts and broken shoes, the cash box with its brass slot through which I could drop pennies to hear them clink, the pictures on enamelled tin plates that advertised Nugget and Cherry Blossom. But all the time boredom grew, and with it a tearful anger, that only ten minutes' walk away was the house of my other grandmother, that place of joy where, from the moment of my arrival, I would be bombarded with good things. A child's love goes to the highest bidder.

I went back into the kitchen. I leaned on my mother's knee and tugged at her sleeve. She took no notice. I whispered to her. She shushed me. My desperation grew. I wondered if I dared scream to be taken to Spitalfields. I had done this before successfully. But I caught a glance from my father. I was an expert reader of my father's expressions, and I held my peace.

My fidgeting could not have gone unnoticed by my grandmother. Each week (I know now) she waited for us to come. Every minute of our stay was precious to her, and of the four of us (my sister, who was then only a small bundle wrapped in a woollen shawl, was present but does not otherwise come into this story) it was her grandchildren who brought her most joy. Each time she looked at me she smiled, that timid smile with a lifetime of pain behind it, undeterred by the scowl of infant brutality that she received in return.

At last she thought of something to hold my attention, to win me over. She went out into the yard and came back with a live fish in a bowl of water. She had for many years preserved the ways of *der Heim*. And she was fanatically insistent on purity and freshness in the food she bought. She spent her days looking for the freshest eggs, the best bread, and the finest meat; and she always bought live fish.

She put the bowl down in front of me and smiled encouragement. The fish fascinated me. Lithe, its subtle, gleaming scales of dark-blue-barred-with-black appealing to my poignant child's perception of colour, it darted swiftly round and round the bowl. It had the air of giving a performance, flicking its fine tail with bravura, opening and shutting its gills, and every few seconds coming straight at me as if to outstare me with its bold, small eyes.

For seconds I sat over the fish-bowl. Then through my absorption there penetrated a thought, that I was the victim of a grown-up tactic. I got up, said "Silly old fish," and walked out through the shop into the street.

I had acted on impulse but (like many a grown-up) I now realised that I had put myself into a position which I must maintain. I must refuse to go back into the house. It was not that I wanted to behave in this way; simply, I had become the prisoner of my own gesture, of my need to be stubborn.

My parents did not worry about me at first. When I was small, we were all children of the streets, our only playgrounds. And I had plenty to interest me. The gutters were full of rubbish from the Sunday morning market—pages of print to pick up and read, crates and cardboard boxes to kick to pieces. From time to time a great shire horse, returning perhaps to the railway company's stables from some special week-end delivery, came plodding down the street, the empty cart rattling behind it, steelshod hooves crashing on the cobbles, harness jingling, the burly carter as often as not walking on foot beside his horse. Barefoot slum boys came running and whooping past—I used to envy them for being barefoot and for being allowed to wear such exciting, ragged, dirty clothes.

Then my grandfather came home. I greeted him eagerly and gave him a warm kiss. I was fond of him for his manliness and his moustache and the tales he told me. It was my chance to make peace without disgrace, to keep my little paw in his hand and trot indoors at his side. Perhaps I wanted to. But a fatal spurt of obstinacy prevailed. I stayed outside.

He must have spoken to the others about me. A few minutes later my mother came out, and invited me to come inside like a good boy. I went mute. She asked me gently what was the matter, and I whined that I wanted to go to my other *booba*. She snapped, "Wait!" and went inside.

Time passed, the afternoon grew cold, a new boredom seized me and I sat on the wooden doorstep feeling sorry for myself.

Anyone (in my child's world) who thwarted my wishes was a sinner. My grandmother, my parents, were alike the objects of my blame. They were wicked. Tears stung my eyes.

My father came out. He said: "Don't be silly. Come inside. Talk to your *booba* and *saida.*" I muttered that I wanted to go to my other *booba.* He said, "Come inside, *booba's* got some nice *pletzels* and hot milk for you." I was suddenly famished at the mention of the soft, delicious rolls strewn with poppy-seeds, but I said that I was not hungry. He asked me if I wanted a good smacking. I scowled at him. He took me by the shoulder and started to drag me in. I uttered a preliminary howl. He let me go. We faced each other.

I was well aware of his problem. He was no believer in spoiling children and did not want to let me get my own way, particularly when that way involved behaving rudely. On the other hand, if I was dragged inside crying, and screaming that I wanted to go to Spitalfields, it would hurt my grandparents—not only on their own behalf but on mine, for they could not bear to see me in tears. At last he said, "Come inside and sit for a few minutes like a good boy, and then we'll go."

I was contented. I went inside, sat politely but threateningly on the sofa for a little while, then stood up to join in the good-byes. I knew that I had won. I knew, too, that my grandmother knew what had happened. Gently, with the same, sweet shadowed smile as always, with undiminishable love, she stooped and put her hands, her big, ugly hands, one on each side of my face. She kissed the top of my head while I stood like a little block of wood, and she said: *"Nu, geh gesinterheit."*

With no response, no shame, no guilt, no backward glance, I ran straight out into the street and jumped up and down, filled entirely with the joy of release, impatient for my parents to take me where I wanted to go.

Both my grandmothers have been dead for many years. These two dear women, different from each other in so many ways, were alike in the qualities a child cannot see: goodness, devotion, simplicity of heart.

I am writing this story because I dreamed of my father's mother recently. In my dream the whole episode I have told was re-enacted. But in one respect it differed from the real event. At the end of the dream, before I ran out, I took my grandmother's hands and kissed them.

When I woke up I could still see her hands clearly. I can see them now. Her face I remember remotely, not sharply, and in the dream it made no impression on me at all. But her hands, the hands that used to hold my face between them—they were big and bony, humped with great knuckles, their skin of a transparent white, on the palms hard and smooth as varnish and scored with multitudinous fine lines, on the backs wrinkled, with fat, knotted blue veins and brown splotches. Ugly hands? The painter Constable once said, "I never saw an ugly thing in my life." They were the kind of hands that inspired Rembrandt and Rodin. They were hands that told the whole story of her life: toil, toil, toil, with no reward to hope for except a little love from her children—and their children.

A dream is a strange, miraculous phenomenon. I marvel at the powers of the human mind: that into the consciousness of a child, selfish and unfeeling as children can be, there can sink unbidden a memory like the memory of this pair of hands, which can come to the surface after thirty-five years have passed; to re-create in the deep darkness of sleep a long-vanished scene; but also to enact what was missing in real life—the kiss, the act of repentance; to teach the sleeper at last the lesson of love.

Angel Levine

BERNARD MALAMUD

To the memory of Robert Warshow

Bernard Malamud was born in New York in 1914. He was educated at City College of New York and Columbia University. His novels include *The Natural, The Assistant* and *A New Life.* He has published two collections of short stories, *The Magic Barrel* and *Idiots First.* He has contributed to *Partisan Review, Commentary, The New Yorker* and other magazines. He won the National Book Award in 1959. Malamud is married, has two children and is currently teaching at Bennington College in Vermont.

Manischewitz, a tailor, in his fifty-first year suffered many reverses and indignities. Previously a man of comfortable means, he overnight lost all he had when his establishment caught fire, and, because a metal container of cleaning fluid exploded, burned to the ground. Although Manischewitz was insured, damage suits against him by two customers who had been seriously hurt in the flames deprived him of every penny he had collected. At almost the same time, his son, of much promise, was killed in the war, and his daughter, without a word of warning, married a worthless lout and disappeared with him, as if off the face of the earth. Thereafter Manischewitz became the victim of incessant excruciating backaches that knifed him over in pain, and he found himself unable to work even as a presser—the only job available to him—for more than an hour or two daily, because after that the pain from standing became maddening. His Leah, a good wife and mother, who had taken in washing, began before his eyes to waste away. Suffering marked shortness of breath, she at last became seriously ill and took to her bed. The doctor, a former customer of Manischewitz, who out of pity treated them, at first had difficulty diagnosing her ailment but later put it down as hardening of the arteries, at an advanced stage. He took Manischewitz aside, prescribed complete rest for her, and in whispers gave him to know there was little hope.

Throughout his trials Manischewitz had remained somewhat stoic, almost unbelieving that all this had descended upon his head, as if it were happening, let us say, to an acquaintance, or to some distant relative; it was in sheer quantity of woe incomprehensible. It was also ridiculous, unjust, and because he had always been a religious man—an affront to God. This, Manischewitz fanatically believed amid all his suffering. When, however, his burden had grown too crushingly heavy to be borne alone, he eased himself into a chair and with shut hollow eyes prayed: "My dear God, my soul, sweetheart, did I deserve this to happen to me?" But recognizing the worthlessness of this thought, he compelled himself to put complaint aside and prayed humbly for assistance: "Give to Leah back her health, and give to me, for myself, that I should not feel pain in every step I make. Help now, or tomorrow we are dead. This I don't have to tell you." And Manischewitz, aching all over and grief-stricken, wept.

Manischewitz's flat, which he had moved into after the disastrous fire, was a meagre one, furnished with a few sticks of chairs, a table, and bed, in one of the poorer sections of the city. There were three rooms: a living room, small, poorly papered; an apology for a kitchen, with a wooden icebox; and the comparatively large bedroom where Leah lay in a second-hand bed, panting for breath. The bedroom was the warmest room of the house and it was here, after his outburst to God, that Manischewitz, by the light of two small bulbs overhead, sat reading his Jewish newspaper. He was not truly reading, because his thoughts were everywhere but on the print. However the print offered a convenient resting place for his eyes; and a word or two, when he permitted himself to comprehend them, indeed had the effect of aiding him momentarily to forget his troubles.

After a while he discovered, to his surprise, that he was actively scanning the news, searching for an item of great interest to him. Exactly what its contents would be he could not say—until he realized with astonishment that he was expecting to discover something regarding himself. At that moment he gazed up with the distinct impression that someone had entered the apartment, though he could not remember having heard the sound of the door. Manischewitz looked around: the room was still, Leah sleeping peacefully. Half-frightened, he observed her until he became convinced she was not dead; then, still disturbed by the thought of an unannounced visitor, he stumbled into the living room, and there had the shock of his life, for at the table sat a burly Negro reading a newspaper he had folded up to fit into one hand.

"What do you want here?" Manischewitz cried out in fright.

The Negro put down the paper and glanced up with a gentle smile. "Good evening." He seemed not to be sure of himself, as if he had happened into the wrong house. He was a large man, bonily built, with a heavy head covered by a hard derby hat, which he made no attempt to remove. His eyes seemed sad, but his lips, above which he wore a slight moustache, were on the verge of laughter; he was not otherwise prepossessing. The cuffs of his sleeves, Manischewitz noted, were frayed to the lining, and the dark suit was badly fitted. He had very large feet. Recovering from his fright, Manischewitz guessed he was being visited by a case worker from the Welfare Department—some came at night—for he had recently applied for relief. Therefore he lowered himself into a chair opposite the Negro, returning, as well as he was able, the man's somewhat troubled although pleasant smile. The former tailor sat stiffly but patiently at the table, waiting for the investigator to take out his pad and pencil and begin asking questions; but before long he became convinced the man intended to do nothing of the sort.

"Who are you?" Manischewitz asked uneasily.

"If I may, insofar as one is able to, identify myself, I bear the name of Alexander Levine."

Despite himself, a trace of smile appeared on Manischewitz's bitter lips.

"You said Levine?" he politely inquired.

The Negro nodded. "That is exactly right."

Carrying the jest a bit further, Manischewitz asked, "You are maybe Jewish?"

"All my life I was, most willingly."

Manischewitz hesitated. He had heard of black Jews, but had never met one. It gave an unusual sensation.

Recognizing in afterthought something strange about the tense of Levine's remark, he said doubtfully, "You ain't Jewish any more?"

Levine, at this point, removed his hat, but immediately replaced it. He said quietly, "I have recently been discarnated into an angel. As such I offer you my humble assistance, if to offer is within my province and ability—in the best sense." He lowered his eyes in apology. "Which calls for added explanation: I am what I am granted to be, and at present the completion is in the future."

"What kind of angel is this?" Manischewitz gravely asked.

"A bona fide angel of God, within prescribed limitations," answered Levine, "not to be confused with the members of any sect, order, or organization here on earth operating under a similar name."

Manischewitz was thoroughly disturbed. He had been expecting something but not quite this. What sort of mockery was it—provided Levine was an angel—of a faithful servant who had from childhood lived in the synagogues and houses of study, concerned with His word?

To test Levine he asked, "Then where are your wings?"

The Negro blushed as well as he was able. Manischewitz understood this from his expression. "Under certain circumstances we lose privileges and prerogatives upon returning to earth, no matter for what purpose, or endeavouring to assist whosoever."

"So tell me," Manischewitz said triumphantly, "how did you get here?"

"I was transmitted."

Still troubled, the tailor said, "If you are a Jew, say the blessing for bread."

Levine recited it in sonorous Hebrew.

Although moved by the familiar words, Manischewitz still could not believe he was dealing with an angel.

Somewhat angrily he demanded, "If you are an angel, show me proof."

Levine wet his lips. "Frankly, I cannot perform either miracles or near miracles, due to the fact that I am in a condition of probation. How long that will persist or even consist, I admit, depends on the outcome."

Manischewitz racked his brains for some means of causing Levine positively to reveal his true identity, when the Negro spoke again:

"It was given me to understand that both you and your wife require assistance of a salubrious nature?"

The tailor could not rid himself of the feeling that he was the butt of some jokester. Is this what a Jewish angel looks like? he thought. This I am not convinced.

But he asked one last question. "So if God sends to me an angel, why a black? Why not a white that there are so many of them?"

"It was my turn to go next," Levine explained.

Manischewitz could not be convinced. "I think you are a faker."

Levine slowly rose. His eyes showed disappointment and worry. "Mr. Manischewitz," he said tonelessly, "if you should desire me to be of assistance to you any time in the near future, or possibly before, I can be found"—he cast a quick glance at his fingernails—"in Harlem."

He was by then gone.

The next day Manischewitz felt some relief from his backache and was able to work four hours at pressing. The day after, he put in six; and the third day four again. Leah sat up a little and asked for some halvah to suck. But on the fourth day the stabbing, breaking ache returned to his back, and Leah once again lay supine, breathing with blue-lipped difficulty.

Manischewitz was miserably disappointed at the return of his active pain, and suffering. He had hoped for a longer interval of easement, long enough to have some thought other than of himself and his troubles. Day by day, hour by hour, minute after minute, he lived in pain, with pain as his only memory, and questioned the necessity of it, inveighed against it, and occasionally, though with affection, against God. Why so *much, Gottenyu?* If He wanted to teach His servant a lesson for some reason, some cause—the nature of His nature—to teach him, say, for reasons of his weakness, his neglect of God during his years of prosperity—give him a little lesson, why then, any one of the tragedies that had happened to him, any *one* would have sufficed to chasten him. But *all together*—the loss of his means of livelihood, of both his children, the health of Leah and himself—that was too much to ask one frail-boned man to endure. Who, after all, was Manischewitz that he had been given so much to suffer? A tailor. Certainly not a man of talent. Upon him suffering was largely wasted. It went nowhere, into nothing: into more pain. His pain did not earn him bread, nor fill the cracks in the wall, nor lift, in the middle of the night, the kitchen table; only lay upon him, sleepless, so sharply oppressively that he could many times have shrieked yet not heard himself through all the misery.

In this mood he gave no thought to Mr. Alexander Levine, but at moments when the pain wavered, momentarily slightly diminishing, he sometimes wondered if he had been mistaken to dismiss him. A black Jew and angel to boot—hard to believe, but suppose he *had* been sent to succour him, and he, Manischewitz, was in his blindness too blind to comprehend? It was this thought that set him on the knifepoint of agony.

Therefore the tailor, after much self-questioning and doubt, decided he would seek the self-styled angel in Harlem. Of course he had great difficulty, because he had not asked for specific directions, and all movement was tedious to him. The subway took him to 116th Street, and from there he wandered in a dark world. It was vast and its lights lit nothing. Everywhere were shadows, often moving. Manischewitz hobbled along painfully, with the aid of a cane; and not knowing where to seek in the blackened tenement buildings, looked fruitlessly into store windows. In the stores he saw people and *everybody* was black. It was an amazing thing to observe. When he was too tired, too unhappy to go farther, Manischewitz stopped in front of a tailor's store. Out of familiarity with the appearance of it, and with some heartbreak, he entered. The tailor, an old skinny Negro with a mop of woolly grey hair, was sitting cross-legged on his workbench, sewing a pair of full-dress pants that had a razor rent all the way down the seat.

"You'll excuse me, please, gentleman," said Manischewitz, admiring the tailor's deft, thimbled fingerwork, "but you know maybe somebody by the name of Alexander Levine?"

The tailor, who, Manischewitz thought, seemed somewhat antagonistic to him, scratched his scalp.

"Cain't say I ever heered dat name."

"Alex-ander Lev-ine," Manischewitz pronounced slowly.

"Cain't say I heered."

Discouraged, Manischewitz was about to depart when he remembered to say: "He is an angel, maybe."

"Oh *him,*" said the tailor, clucking. "He hang out in dat honky-tonk down a ways." He pointed with a skinny finger and returned to the split pants.

Manischewitz crossed the street against a red light and was almost killed by a taxi. On the block after the next, the fourth store from the corner was a cabaret, and the name in sparkling lights was Bella's. Ashamed to go in, Manischewitz gazed through the neon-lighted window, and when the dancing couples parted and drifted away, he discerned, at a table towards the rear, Levine.

He was sitting by himself, a cigarette butt dangling from the corner of his mouth, playing solitaire with a dirty pack of cards, and Manischewitz felt a touch of pity for him, for Levine had deteriorated in appearance. His derby hat was dented and had a white smudge across the top. His ill-fitting suit had grown shabbier, as if he had been sleeping in it. His shoes and the bottoms of his trousers were caked with mud, and his face covered by an impenetrable stubble the colour of licorice. Manischewitz, though dreadfully disappointed, was about to enter anyway, when a fat-breasted Negress in a purple evening gown appeared before Levine's table, and with much laughter through many white teeth, broke into a vigorous sinuous shimmy. Levine looked straight at Manischewitz with a haunted expression, but the tailor was too paralysed to move or acknowledge it. As Bella's heavy gyrations continued, Levine rose, his eyes lit in excitement. She embraced him with vigour, both his hands going around her big restless buttocks, and they tangoed together across the floor, loudly applauded by the other customers. She seemed to have lifted Levine off his feet and his large shoes hung lifeless as they danced. They slid past the window where Manischewitz, white-faced, stood staring in. Levine winked slyly and the tailor fled home.

Leah lay at death's door. Through shrunken lips she muttered concerning her girlhood, the sorrows of the marriage bed, the loss of her babies, yet wept to live. Manischewitz tried not to listen, but even without ears he would have heard her thoughts. It was not a gift. The doctor panted up the stairs, a broad but bland, unshaven man (it was Sunday) and shook his head. A day at most, or two. He left at once, not without mercy, to spare himself Manischewitz's multiplied despair; the man who never stopped hurting. He would someday get him into a public home.

Manischewitz visited a synagogue and there spoke to God, but God was strangely absent. The tailor searched his heart and found no hope. When she died he would live dead. He considered taking his life although he knew he never would. Yet it was something to consider. Considering, you existed in dregs. He railed against God—shouted his name without love. Can you love a rock, a broom, an emptiness? Baring his breast, he smote the naked bones, cursing himself for having believed.

That afternoon, asleep in a chair, he dreamed of Levine. He was standing before a faded mirror, preening small, decaying opalescent wings. "This means," mumbled Manischewitz, as he broke out of sleep, "that it is possible he could be an angel." Begging a neighbour lady to look in on Leah, occasionally wet her lips with a drop of water, he drew on his thin coat, gripped his walking stick, exchanged some pennies for a subway token, and rode to Harlem. He recognized this act as the last desperate one of woe: to go without belief, seeking a black magician to restore his wife to invalidism. Yet if there was no choice, he did at last what was chosen.

He hobbled to Bella's but the place had changed hands. It was now, as he breathed, a synagogue in a store. In the front, towards him, were several rows of empty wooden benches. In the rear stood the Ark, its portals of rough wood covered with many coloured sequins; under it a long table on which lay the sacred scroll unrolled, illuminated by the dim light of a bulb on a chain overhead. Around the table, as if frozen to it and the scroll, which they all touched with their fingers, sat four Negroes wearing black skullcaps. Now as they read the Holy Word, Manischewitz could, through the plate-glass window, hear the singsong chant of their voices. One of them was old, with a grey beard. One was bubble-eyed. One was humpbacked. The fourth was a boy, no older than thirteen. Their heads moved in rhythmic swaying. Touched by this sight from his childhood and youth, Manischewitz entered and stood silent in the rear.

"*Neshoma,*" said bubble eyes, pointing to a word with a stubby finger. "Now what dat?"

"That means soul," said the boy. He wore glasses.

"Let's git on wid de commentary," said the old man.

"Ain't necessary," said the humpback. "Souls is immaterial substance. That's all. The soul is derived in that manner. The immateriality is derived from the substance, and they both, casually and otherwise, derived from the soul. There can be no higher."

"That's the highest."

"Over de top."

"Way, way."

"Wait a minute," said bubble eyes. "I don't see what is dat immaterial substance. How come de one gits hitched to de odder? Speak up, man." He addressed the humpback.

"Ask me something hard. Because it is substanceless immateriality. It couldn't be closer together, like the organs of the body under one skin."

"Hear now," said the old man.

"All you done is switched de words."

"It is the *primum mobile,* the substanceless substance from which comes all things that were incepted in the idea—you, me, and everything and body else."

"Now how dat happen? Make it sound simple."

"It de speerit," said the old man. "On de face of de water moved de speerit. An' dat was good. It say so in de Book. From de speerit ariz de man."

"But now listen here. How come it become substance, if it all de time a spirit?"

"God alone done dat."

"Holy! Holy! Praise His Name."

"But has dis spirit got some kind of a shade or colour?" asked bubble eyes, deadpan.

"Man, of course not. It colourless."

"Then how come we is coloured?" he said, with a triumphant glare.

"Ain't got nought to do wid dat."

"I still like to know."

"God put the spirit in all things," answered the boy. "He put it in the green leaves an' the red flowers. He put it in little gold fishes in the water an' in the big blue sky. That's how come it came to us."

"Amen."

"Praise Lawd and utter loud His speechless name."

"Blow de bugle till it break de sky."

They fell silent, intent upon the next word. Manischewitz approached.

"You'll excuse me," he said. "I am looking for Alexander Levine. You know him maybe?"

"That's the angel," said the boy.

"Oh, *him*," snuffed bubble eyes.

"You'll find him at Bella's. It's the establishment right across the street," the humpback said.

Manischewitz explained that he could not stay, thanked them all, and limped across the street. It was already night. The city was dark and he could barely find his way.

But Bella's was bursting with strains of blues. Through the window Manischewitz recognized the dancing crowd and among them sought Levine. He was sitting loose-lipped at Bella's side table. They were tippling from an almost empty whiskey fifth. Levine had shed his old clothes, wore a shiny new checkered suit, pearl-grey derby, cigar, and big two-tone button shoes. To the tailor's dismay, a drunken gaze had settled upon Levine's formerly dignified face. He leaned toward Bella, tickled her ear lobe with his pinky, and whispered words that sent her into gales of raucous laughter. She fondled his knee.

Manischewitz, girding himself, pushed open the door and was not well received.

"This place reserved."

"Beat it, pale puss."

"Exit, Yankel, Semitic trash."

He gasped, but moved towards the table where Levine sat, the crowd breaking before him as he hobbled forward.

"Mr. Levine," he spoke in a trembly voice. "Is here Manischewitz."

Levine glared through bleary eyes.

"Speak yo' piece, son."

Manischewitz shivered. His back plagued him. Cold tremors tormented his crooked legs.

"You'll excuse me. I would like to talk to you in a private place." He looked around, but people were everywhere and all of them listening.

"Speak, Ah is a private pu'son."

Bella laughed piercingly. "Stop it, boy, you killin' me."

Manischewitz, no end disturbed, considered leaving, but Levine addressed him:

"What is the pu'pose of yo' communication with yo's truly?"

The tailor wet his cracked lips. "You are a Jew. This I am sure."

Levine rose, his nostrils flaring.

"Anythin' else yo' got to say?"

Manischewitz's tongue was in torment.

"Speak now, or fo'ever hold yo' peace."

Tears blinded the tailor's eyes. Was ever man so tried? Should he say he believed a half-drunken Negro to be an angel?

The silence turned to stone.

Manischewitz was recalling scenes of his youth, as a wheel in his mind whirred: believe, do not, yes, no, yes, no. The pointer pointed to yes, to between yes and no, to no, no it was yes. He sighed. One had still to make a choice.

"I believe you are also an angel—from God." He said it simply but in a broken voice. Yet he thought, If you said it it was said. If you believed it you must say it. If you believed, you believed.

The hush broke. Everybody talked but the music commenced and they went on dancing. Bella, grown bored, picked up the cards and dealt herself a hand.

Levine burst into tears.

"How you have humiliated me."

Manischewitz sincerely apologized.

"Wait'll I freshen up." Levine went to the men's room and returned in his old clothes.

No one said goodbye as they left.

They rode to the flat via subway. As they walked up the stairs Manischewitz pointed with his cane to his door.

"That's all been taken care of," Levine said. "You best go in now."

Disappointed that it was all over, yet torn by curiosity, Manischewitz followed the angel up four flights of stairs to the roof. When he got there the door was padlocked.

Luckily he could see through a small broken window. He heard a strange noise, as though a vibration of wings, and when he strained for a wider view, could have sworn he saw a dark figure borne aloft on strong-pinioned, magnificent black wings.

A feather drifted down. Manischewitz gasped as it turned white, but it was only snowing.

He rushed downstairs. In the flat, Leah wielded a dust mop under the bed and upon the cobwebs on the wall.

"A wonderful thing, Leyka," Manischewitz said. "There are Jews everywhere."

A Betting Man

BRIAN GLANVILLE

Brian Glanville was born in London in 1931. He received his education at Charterhouse, and then lived for some time in Italy where he became a sports journalist. He has been the sports columnist for some years on the *London Sunday Times,* for which he has covered two Olympics and two World Cups. His books include *Along the Arno, The Bankrupts, Diamond, The Rise of Gerry Logan* and three volumes of short stories. He was the recipient of the 1963 Berlin Prize for a television documentary. Glanville is married, has four children and lives in London.

As soon as he woke, he knew it was going to be a bad day; phlegm, a stiff neck, and that pain again in the small of his back which made him gasp as he tried to sit up in bed. When he remembered the tip, the thought went through him like a joyful electric shock. He lay back again thinking Red Robin, Plumpton, 7-1, put on twenty and chance it.

In the next bed, his wife stirred, and he shot at her a quick, anxious glance, to be punished at once with a violent spasm in his neck. But she wasn't awake yet; she had merely turned over to face the wall.

Put fifty on it, he thought, with tingling suspense, a hundred; and went on deliberately into paths of fantasy. Two hundred, two fifty, even. Or maybe look down the card and back it in crossed doubles with horses at shorter odds . . . or an accumulator. The phlegm bubbled up into his throat and he hawked and spat into his handkerchief. Again his wife stirred.

Sid Davis never gave a bad tip; when he told you a horse—which wasn't very often—you knew it was in with a chance. The last one had been beaten by a short head at Lingfield; another twenty yards and it would have won. "You want a horse, Sam?" he had said yesterday, with his great, flaccid, brooding bloodhound face. "I'll give you a horse—Red Robin. Third time out; it hasn't been trying yet. I know the owner."

His wife moved once more, and this time she was awake. "Sam," her voice said, and he thought, half guilty, half anguished, "I'd go mad if I didn't have a bet."

"Sam," her voice said again, hollow in the twilight of the room.

"Yes, dear?" he said.

"How long have you been awake?"

"How long?" he said. "A few minutes, that's all." Twenty years of London hadn't removed his Cork accent; they had merely taken off the edge, flattened it a little at the crown.

"Sam," she said, "what are we going to do about Marion?"

As she spoke it was as though the breath had suddenly been drawn out of him; he hung in a brief agony of suspense while a noiseless voice said not again, not again, not again.

"Sam!"

"Yes," he said at last. "I heard you. Well what can you do? She isn't a child any more. She's a wilful girl. I mean, whatever I say to her, she still does just what she likes."

There was a click, and pale yellow light filled the room, spreading from the pink, tasselled shade of the glass bedside lamp, showing up the thick blue carpet, the imitation Louis Quinze chairs, the dominant, mirrored dressing-table. He blinked unhappily in this light, gently shaking his head, with its hair tousled and receding, great, curved nose, full, petulant mouth. By contrast, his wife seemed already quite awake, propped up, handsome and alert on her levering arms, her hair dark against the pillow.

"Only that she'd let me know what's happening," she said. "No letter this week. Every time I want to find something out, I've got to 'phone her. How do *I* know what sort of life she's living up there? How do *I* know what sort of people she's mixing with? Is she so brilliant that all of a sudden she's got to be a doctor? I only know that all my friends' daughters are getting married, and every time I go to a wedding, there's a lump in my throat."

"Poor Esther," he said, sincerely, charged, as she spoke, with anger and pity. "Our luck, we had to have such a clever daughter." He could feel the pain in his back again.

"And when she comes home," said his wife, "she looks like Orphan Annie. The more I think about it, the sorrier I am we ever let her go."

"*I* didn't want to let her go; I let her go because of you. You said, 'Let her go if she wants to.' All that fighting and arguing. There was never any peace in the house."

"I don't know," his wife said, "other people have it so easy." She rang the bell for the maid.

"I mean to say, there's no feeling," he agreed, "no gratitude. It's not as if we ask so much."

The maid knocked gently at the door and entered, carrying the newspaper. As he saw it he thought, feeling the shock of joy again, Red Robin, Red Robin. Taking the paper, he turned at once to the sports page, with barely a glance at the headlines. "I'll have a kipper," he said.

"I never see the paper, Sam," his wife said, sitting up against the padded bed-head. "You always take it with you."

"You can *have* it!" he cried. "I only want to see just something in the racing."

"Racing!" she began, then stopped, remembering the presence of the maid. "Kippers?" she said. "Why have kippers? You know they'll only upset you."

"I'll settle for an egg."

The maid left the room and he shook off the blankets, getting off the bed with slow, dazed movements, a daylight owl without his glasses fumbling awkwardly for his slippers. "Don't forget we're going round to the Cohens tonight," his wife said.

"The Cohens?" he said struggling with his dressing-gown. "*You* go! Tell them I'm ill. I've got this lousy rheumatism, anyway."

"You knew we were going, Sam: why must you always make a fuss at the last moment?"

"A fuss?" he said, mock-surprised, "who's making a fuss? I'd forgotten all about it, that's all. They won't mind if I don't go . . ."

"I'm not going on my own, Sam."

"All right, don't go. I can't stand the bloody sight of them, anyway, him and his fat greasy neck and the way he talks about the money he's made—as if no one should have except him. And her with her teeth sticking out like this. He plays a lousy game of bridge, anyway."

"*Why* do you do this, Sam?" his wife cried, with sudden hysteria. "*Why* must you always mess my arrangements? I told you to make a note of the date in your diary."

"Sugar the Cohens," he said, leaving the room dressing-gown cord a-trail. "I'm going to watch the television tonight."

In the warm bath, plump and relaxed, he began to feel better. He closed his eyes and moved slightly, so that the water lapped gently over him, as though over some basking seal. Deliberately he let his mind go blank, banishing from it all thoughts of his daughter, illness, the Cohens and his practice. Raising the censorship ever so slightly, he admitted the words "Red Robin." Somewhere, faint and far off, they produced an echo. Red Rabbit. . . . Red Rider. . . . Red Ensign, that was it. Goodwood, twenty-five years ago, he and Charlie Morris and Buster Stein; they'd gone down in Buster's Ford Eight with sandwiches and he'd fancied the horse and the others had told him he was crazy. . . .

Behind the door, the maid said, "Breakfast is ready, sir," and the picture faded, the sun, the green Sussex grass, the galloping phalanx of horses.

From the bedroom his wife called, "Sam! Sam!" but he pretended not to hear.

When he sat down to breakfast his back began to hurt him again and he thought, nothing but trouble; trouble and aggravation, you'd think a girl as intelligent as she is would show a bit of consideration for her parents. Honest to God, sometimes you'd think we were her worst enemies.

He dressed carefully as always, well cut suit, hand made shirt with plenty of cuff showing, subdued Italian tie, good brilliantine on the hair. In the bedroom again, his wife said, "Sam, you've got to come with me."

"I'll see," he said, "I'll see how I feel this evening."

"*Don't* say that! You're a messer, Sam! Because if you're not coming and I now know, at least I can ring up and make an excuse."

"All right," he said. "As long as we leave *early*, though. I'm not staying late."

"*Why* must you do this to me every time?"

As he bent over to kiss her, she said, "What are we going to do about Marion?"

"Do about her? What do you want me to do? She's an obstinate girl, Esther, she's got a will of her own."

"Other girls study in London. I believe she only went up there so she could get away from us."

"What can you do?"

"What do you mean what can you do? Why have you always got to leave everything to me? I don't believe she's getting enough to eat. Let me have some more money and I'll send her a chicken today."

"Here you are," he said. "What do you want, a couple of pounds?"

"You're leaving the car, Sam?"

"Sure," he said, "I shan't be needing it."

As he waited for the smooth, soundless lift he thought, the trouble we get from that girl.

There wasn't a seat on the tube, and he stood holding a strap in one hand, his paper in the other, tweed-coated, breathing heavily, the grey trilby drawn down with absurd rakishness over the big and dominant nose. Little *momser,* he thought.

Honest to God, the more you do for them, the less pleasure you get. She should have had *my* parents; do what you're told or wallop, over the head. Not even a letter. Worrying her mother like that all the time. I'd have given anything to be a doctor, but with the old man it was, Doctor! You'll do something you can make a living at quick, without me having to keep you for years.

I could have done with the car today, he thought.

He walked slowly through Lincoln's Inn, under the leafless trees, a small, nostalgic, urban figure, crumpled newspaper in hand. In the outer office, he greeted the receptionist with great courtesy, and to his own secretary, he said, with sudden gaiety, "The top of the morning!"

The first sight of his office filled him, as usual, with a wave of ambivalent feeling; the broad, mahogany desk, the serried and imprisoning law books, portentous and impressive, seeming, at sudden, frightening moments of detachment, to have nothing to do with him at all. On the wall hung a bright, bookmaker's calendar, and two pencils on the desk were inscribed: GOODMAN'S: YOU WIN WHEN YOU LOSE. An upright leather frame held photographs of his wife and his daughter; his daughter's eyes were gentle, wide and staring, a doe surprised by the camera.

"Any news of Marion, Mr. Goldman?" his secretary asked.

"Marion's doing *mar*-vellous!" he said. "I told you she got through her last exam with honours? She's like her mother, when she makes up her mind to do a thing, she does it. I mean, you need a lot of initiative to go off into the provinces like that, all on your own. Not many girls of her age would do it."

"It's wonderful," the secretary said.

"Wonderful!" he said. "You ought to know the half of it. Sometimes I wish she was just an ordinary person, like her father."

"Oh, Mr. Goldman, you *know* you're really proud of her."

"*Proud* of her," he said with mock despair. "Believe me, you're better off when they're not so clever."

"You don't *mean* that, Mr. Goldman!"

The moment his secretary had left the room, he stretched out his hand for the telephone, weak with apprehension, like a boy hesitating at the door of a brothel. But before he could reach it, the telephone rang, and he picked it up almost with relief, to speak to one of his clients.

It was Silverman, the furrier. After they had talked about a superannuation scheme which was to be drafted, Goldman said, "Dave, do you know anything about a horse called Red Robin? It's running at Plumpton today."

"I only know that if you back it it's going to come in last," Silverman said. "Always betting, Sam; when are you going to grow out of it?"

"Listen," he said, "a bet now and again."

"Red Robin did you say? Never heard of it. You're *meshuggah*. The only time I bet is when I know the owner."

"The person who gave me this tip does know the owner."

"But do *you* know the owner? Take my advice and leave it alone."

Big mouth, he thought, as he rang off. They make a bit of money and they think they can tell you everything.

With gallantry he greeted the pale, hard featured Mrs. Levinson, who had come to talk to him about the lease of her hat shop.

"Younger and younger every time, dear! This is my favourite client, Miss Harrison—she's a real darling," and Mrs. Levinson's mouth opened briefly to smile, like the jaw of an automatic grab.

"You're a *schmoozer*, Sam!"

They asked about each other's families. "Next month, my daughter's getting married," she said. "The reception's at the Dorchester. I'm not so mad about the boy myself, still, he's making a good living . . . What about your girl?"

"Don't ask," he said. "You know as much about her as I do. She's up in Liverpool studying to be a doctor, she tells us her career comes first. She's got a mind of her own."

"She'll fall," said Mrs. Levinson. "They all mess around before they marry. My girl wanted to be a dress designer—we had murder at home. Then they meet someone they like, and that's the end of it."

When she had gone he thought, wedding at the Dorchester. Well, isn't Esther entitled to a bit of pleasure, too? When I think of all the wedding presents *we've* given and the lousy speeches we've had to sit through.

He picked up the 'phone again, asked for his bookmaker's number and said, "This is Mr. Goldman here. There's a horse running in the three o'clock at Plumpton today, Red Robin."

"Yes, Mr. Goldman, we can lay you eight to one on that."

"I'll put £300 on it," he said, and as soon as the words were out of his mouth, was astounded he had spoken them.

"Three *hundred,* Mr. Goldman?"

It was the moment to recant, but he found himself saying, in a voice that trembled a little "That's right, three hundred." Then he put down the 'phone and sat staring into space. A voice was saying you're mad, you're mad, you're mad.

At lunch time, he took a cab to a kosher restaurant. He felt curiously light and detached, as though he were floating, physically and morally, a little above the ground, free alike from contact and responsibility. The restaurant had one large, barn-like room, about which waiters prowled in shabby tailcoats, like men who had seen better days. On the far wall there hung three huge photographs of men with rabbinic beards. An old, bearded man in a kaftan wandered unsuccessfully and philosophically among the tables, trying to sell prayer books and the proprietor, talking in Yiddish to the guests, had the face of a kindly martyr to indigestion.

"Sam!" called one of the diners. "Sam!"

"Hal-*lo,* Harold!"

"It's Sam Goldman, knew him in the old days; come and sit here, Sam! Sam and I, we used to have a million laughs for nothing!"

Room was made at the table and he sat down among the big, well-dressed, soup-eating men. The one who had called him had a friendly, ugly face; grey hair, glasses, teeth uneven and awry, a big, red, jutting nose. "We used to go to the races together," he said, "remember, Sam?"

"Remember?" he said. "Sure, I remember."

"You haven't lost your Irish accent, I see. The old blarney. It must be ten years since we met. Remember that time at Fontwell? I'd got a winning treble, I stood to win five hundred pounds, and my horse won the race, then got disqualified?"

He was floating higher, now, not merely detached but euphoric, buoyant, noisier than all of them, shouting anecdotes at the top of his voice. "And what about that time at Lewes? I was down with Charlie Ross, and I said, 'Charlie, I just fancy a horse today: maybe I'm right and maybe I'm wrong. I just feel like having a go. . . .' "

"A terrible gambler, he was," Harold said. "A million laughs, we had, a million laughs for nothing."

Once, twice, the memory of the morning's bet returned to him like sudden pain, a dyspeptic stab in the midst of a banquet, but he shrugged it away and galloped on, rose still higher on the waves of laughter and appreciation. "Honest to God, I'm not exaggerating, a hundred to eight the field. . . ."

When they all got up to go, Harold said, "Give us a ring, Sam, don't let's lose touch; I'd like to see you, here's my card. I've got three grown-up kids. . . ." And he answered, "Sure, sure, and here's mine, come over and see us one evening," knowing that this moment was transient and unrepeatable; the golden past could be celebrated, never exhumed.

"Goodbye, goodbye," they said, parting in the rainy, dingy Soho street.

He called a taxi, and as it stopped and started its way to

Lincoln's Inn Fields, he was back to the real again, away from the happy surprise of lunchtime, closed in the cab and alone. He felt weak and enervated; his groin tingled with apprehension, as though he had gone so far beyond the boundaries of risk and caution as to derive some strange masochistic pleasure. Why did you do it? he thought. You're mad; why did you do it? Yet at the same time he was aware that he had done it before, and that he would do it again.

Returned to the office, shut in again among the encircling books, he felt a driving urge to talk to someone about it, at least to share the burden of knowledge. He picked up the 'phone and said, "Get me Dr. Goldman."

When the bell rang, he hesitated, then took the receiver again and said uncertainly, "George?"

"I'm just going out to a patient," his brother's voice said, brisk but not abrupt.

"I've put three hundred on a horse today," he said.

"Three *hundred?* You must be crackers. What did you back?"

"Red Robin, in the three o'clock at Plumpton."

"I backed that last month at Doncaster. It didn't even get a place."

His lips were dry and he mumbled with difficulty, "Sid Davis had a tip."

"Sid *Davis!* Ha! I say, that'll be the day; the day you get a decent tip from that deadbeat. Sid Davis? He couldn't give you an each-way bet in a two-horse race!"

"He said it hasn't been trying till now."

"Not trying? That's the oldest one of all! Why didn't you ring me up before you did it?"

"I don't know," he said, "something came over me."

"I hope you win; we'll all be going to Nice with you."

He looked at his watch and saw that it was half-past two. Sweat was running down his chest. He thought, this is the last time, even if it wins. Let it win, God, let it win.

When his secretary came bustling into the room, it was as

though she had aroused him from a coma. "Mr. Moss? Yes. . . . Show him in."

The client, small and round and effusive, said, "What's the matter, Sam, you look as if you're worried to death," and he answered, "It's nothing, only the rheumatism."

"You want to do what I do, go to Tring."

At quarter-past three, Goldman said, "Miss Harrison, ring up one of the newspapers and find out what won the three o'clock at Tring."

"Tring, Mr. Goldman?"

"Plumpton," he said, "I meant Plumpton."

He was trembling, his shirt was sticking to his back, cigarette butts had made a small white cairn in his ashtray, and the contract in front of him had dissolved as though he were looking at it through binoculars. *Please,* God, he was saying to himself, please.

When his secretary came into the room again, he was sitting quite motionless, staring into space, waxwork and unreal.

"I'm sorry I was so long, Mr. Goldman," she said, "I had to try three papers before they'd give it to me."

"Yes," he said, but his voice emerged as little more than a croak.

"Mr. Goldman, are you all right?"

"What horse won it?" he said, and now the words burst so suddenly from behind their dam that they emerged almost as a sob.

"It was a horse called Red Robin."

"I see," he said, without moving his eyes. "Thank you very much Miss Harrison."

When he let himself into the flat, his wife, in the hallway, said, "Sam, what are all the flowers for?" Her face, set in a familiar expression of glazed long suffering, suddenly became uncertain, confronted by a new situation.

"I won on a horse," he said, cheerfully.

"Won . . ." she said. "Much?"

"You can go and pick yourself out a new fur coat tomorrow, if you like," he said.

"Oh, Sam, that's *mar*vellous!" she said, hugging him. "Sam, let me take the flowers, I'll put them in water. . . . You've no idea what a day I've had here, I couldn't stop worrying about Marion, my head ached all afternoon. . . . I rang her, but she wasn't there. But how much did you put on, Sam? You must have put on an awful lot of money, it's very *naughty* of you."

He took off his hat and struggled wearily out of his coat. "Listen," he said, "if I didn't have a bet now and then."

The Hand That Fed Me

ISAAC ROSENFELD

Isaac Rosenfeld was born in Chicago in 1918. After attending the University of Chicago, he became an assistant editor of the *New Republic.* In 1945 he was awarded first prize in the *Partisan Review* Novelette Contest. His books include *Passage from Home*. He was married to Vasiliki Sarant. He died in 1956.

Dec. 21

Dear Ellen,

It was very sweet of you to send me a Christmas card. It was really a wonderful gesture, and so simple! When you prepared your Christmas list you included me—and that's all there was to it.

You know, in that one day of ours I never did manage to find out who your friends were (not that I wasn't eager to!). But I imagine your list went something like this: aunts; uncles; cousins; girl friends; boy friends. It amuses me to think that I must have been included in the latter group, in the company, let us say, of John, Bob, Steve, Chick, etc. I am quite willing to share the honour with them, even though the names of my colleagues must be entirely imaginary and even though you probably put my own name last on the list. But perhaps you had me in mind all along, knowing what a gesture that would be! Naturally, you must have assumed I'm not in the army. I'm not quarrelling with you, but there's something a little glib in that assumption. Why, so far as you are concerned, should I *not* be in the army? Do you follow me? Is it simply a habit of thinking so that whenever—rarely!—you do come to me, you immediately say, "Joe? Oh, he's still around." I can see no other way, unless, God save my mind, you've taken to obtaining information from my friends, whom you have sworn to secrecy. But how should you know who my friends are, since I never found out yours?

Of course, I may have mentioned Otto to you—he was very much on my mind that day. Would you believe it, while we were walking down Hoyne Avenue and I was, permit me, impressing you with all I had, I kept wondering what Otto would do in similar circumstances, and I was gloating, sure that he would never have been able to give such a fine account of himself! Furthermore, I still gloat over it, although—for all the fine impression I made—you never answered my letters and even once, when I called on you (for perhaps the tenth time) you actually hid from me. I know all about it. Your brother came to the door and he seemed to have half a mind to admit me; but behind him I could hear a commotion of shushing and whispering, and I'm sure it was you, ducking into the pantry and telling them to say you were out and on no account to let me in.

Of course, what makes all this slightly ridiculous, is the fact that it happened three years ago. But why did you wait three years before sending me a card? What was wrong with the Christmas of the very same year, or the one of the year following? Ah, I know how your mind works. On Christmas, 1939, you *suppressed* all thought of me. In 1940 you allowed yourself to think, but only to the following extent: "If I send him a Christmas card now, he'll think I've been unable to forget him. So we'll wait another year or two. By that time it'll be quite clear, when he gets my card, not that I've been *unable* to forget him, but that I have so good a memory that I can even recall the name and address of a man whom I saw only once, three years ago." Am I right?

But it's a trivial thing and why attach so much importance to it? I suppose you would have me believe that. You would have me believe that your card was only a way of acknowledging a pleasant day you had hitherto failed to acknowledge. Something brought it to mind—say, an onion you had eaten recently. And so the card, yes?

Not on your life, Ellen, not for one moment will I believe it. For if it were only a trivial matter, would you have waited three years? You would have sent me a card at once, or even phoned me on the following day, as you'd promised. Trivialities are the things women rush into, feeling they're important. The important things, however, are what they mull over, plot, deliberate, all to no end. It took you three years, Ellen, to convince yourself that a single afternoon you had spent with me was trivial!

So there you are.

But one more thing. On your card you have written, "From Ellen. Do you remember me?" A pretty little disingenuous note! I assure you, your card was sent in the deepest conviction that I had not once ceased to think of you. I'm sure of it. If you thought I'd forgotten you, you wouldn't have dared send a card. What, a man should receive a card from a certain Ellen and wonder who she is? Any time you'd leave yourself open! Or, on the other hand, was it a rather coy way of insinuating that you'd all but forgotten me? You see, if you are willing to admit that I may have forgotten you, isn't that another way of suggesting that you barely, barely manage to remember me?

Nonsense! I know perfectly well that you've never forgotten me. But who are you, Shakespeare, that the smallest scrap of your writing should be covered with commentaries? Enough of that.

Do you remember me?
Indeed!
Joseph Feigenbaum

Dec. 22

Dear Ellen,

It just occurred to me that while I wrote you at some length, yesterday, I forgot the obvious subject of our correspondence—Xmas. So I'm writing you again to wish you a merry Xmas.

Yours,
J. F.

P.S. Of course, I could just as well send a Xmas card.

Dec. 23

Dear Ellen,

Since I wrote to you twice, I might just as well have said something worth saying. After all, even if we have "forgotten" each other, we still have our three years to look back on—years, may I add, all the more interesting because we did not, in any way, spend them together.

Please understand my motive. If it seems sentimental to you, then you're a fool, and I've no fear of offending you when I say so. And besides what can you do about it? Can you threaten to break off our friendship? Can you threaten to stop writing? As if you would ever write! You see, Ellen, by avoiding me you've put yourself completely in my power. But that's hardly worth pointing out.

Our whole meeting comes back to me. I remember that summer, no work, no friends, no conversation, the realization I was meant for WPA. What a wonderful summer of self-discovery! Believe me, chaos is the mother of knowledge. It's a distinguished family: indolence, poverty, frustration, *seediness*—these are the blood relations of that little monster, Mr. Knowthyself. I shall never again be afraid of turning myself inside out, like an empty pocket—what treasures of lint and fuzz! Do you follow me, Ellen? I mean to say, it is sometimes a good thing to shake yourself out, and go around unhappy—you lose most of your delusions. A happy man takes a great risk—of believing that he is what he seems to be.

Well, I was forced to go on WPA; forced outwardly, that is, for inwardly I went as a free man. I knew what to expect. My friends ("my generation" as it became fashionable to call them) were all on one cultural project or another. I would go on the Writers' Project and fill out a time sheet as well as any one else. All such matters, which are done with only half a will, are called ways of keeping body and soul together; actually, they are ways of keeping them apart. That is, you do what you do, and you don't have to worry about undergoing any changes. WPA was a great social invention, it was refrigeration on a mass scale. It took us as we were, and froze us as we were; it preserved us, it kept us from decaying. But what's all this? I merely wanted to say a few things it was impossible to say when we walked out of the relief station together, and I find that I am overdramatizing myself.

I hadn't thought there would be such a long line at the C.R.A. office, so many Negroes, Poles, old men. Not a single applicant for the Writers' Project among them. It is so much better to be an unemployed writer than an unemployed anything-else that I felt especially sorry for them. An unemployed plumber, for example—a man who is starving because there are no toilet bowls for him to fix. There is something so pathetic in that! A writer, at least, is always writing. Whatever happens, he records it. It begins to rain—he says to himself: it is raining. He walks down the stairs—he says to himself: I am walking down the stairs. He is always writing in his head, and it does him good. But what good does it do to a man to go around fixing toilet bowls in his head? Pig misery! So there I was, looking at the men around me and recording them, putting down their coughs, their leanness, the dirt, the stubble on their faces, and meanwhile thinking: here am I, a writer, this is me, etc., etc.

Ellen, you look at yourself only in mirrors. Relying on a piece of glass the way you do, you probably have little notion of the actual figure you cut. That day, when you were not smearing on lipstick while looking into a compact-mirror, you were sucking the point of a pencil, and rolling it between your lips. That you, who refuse to write to me, should have come into my life at the point of a pencil!

Now I might almost begin to flatter you—to dwell on the image of a girl, a little above average in height, more than ordinary in appearance, a girl, though I suspect the word, quite beautiful, standing there in the basement among all the coughing old men, surrounded by steampipes, benches, notices plastered on the wooden walls: *Bekanntmachung, Avviso.* And all the while this girl rolls the point of a pencil in her mouth. Do you know, after you had caught my eye, you stuck your tongue out at me. First, the pencil, and then the tongue. Ellen, Ellen!

It would have meant very little. It would only have been a study in violent contrast, squalor and flirtation, sex and the relief office—and, as a matter of fact, I was not sure at the beginning that it meant anything more. But immediately the element of personal worth entered. Almost at once I talked to you, you will recall, as though you were more than a pretty girl with a pencil stuck in your mouth. It was you who did the flirting, made the advances. Do I wear make-up? Do I carry a purse full of compacts, powderboxes, lipstick? Understand, I accuse you of nothing. I am glad you behaved as you did. Perhaps because I am not thin and old and coughing, you saw to it that I should notice you. But it was I who saw to all the rest.

I want you to observe that you were ahead of me in the line. When your preliminary interview was over and your preliminary papers were filled out, you could have gone home. I expected you, at any moment, while you were idling around the basement, I expected you to break away, perhaps with a slight nod in my direction, and go home. But I knew you would not.

I said nothing, you will remember, I even pretended not to notice you. But how carefully I watched you, and how pleased I was! There you were, waiting for me, and it was all voluntary on your part, and even somewhat embarrassing. The pretexts you invented! First you sat down at one of the benches and stretched and yawned as though you were tired. Then you removed your shoes and rubbed your feet—such pretty feet, if I may say, and just barely dirty! By that time I thought I might dare acknowledge that I knew you were waiting for me. I smiled. I motioned to you. But you would not admit it. You wouldn't look at me. You curled up on the bench where you sat and pretended to go to sleep—a wonder no one saw you and put you out. I knew you were waiting for me, that you had already acknowledged me even more deeply than I had acknowledged you—since at the outset I was only responding to a flirtation, but what were you responding to? I don't flirt. You were therefore responding to me! It made me so happy, somewhat dizzy, it was even slightly alarming. I sang a song, I joked with the man who stood ahead of me in line, a short and chubby Negro whom I liked immensely. I offered him cigarettes. When he took only one, I slipped more into his hip pocket, so carefully, I might have been stealing his wallet. He was now my friend. Having become your friend, I was everybody's friend. I even smiled at the relief worker who interviewed me, a bitter hag who resented my happiness and detained me with unnecessary questions, as though to extract my secret. And when I was through with her and came out, startled to find you absent from the bench, only to see you standing at the door, so clearly, so obviously waiting!

That whole afternoon, Ellen, the walk to your house, your friendliness, your kindness in asking me up and inviting me to have lunch with you! Even now I can hardly believe that I should ever have received such gifts of kindness. Such absolute friendship, comradeship, trust, good will, and with it all the constant promise of intimacy: one moment you are at my shoulder, the next, to take my arm, or my hand, or you pretend a mosquito has landed and you slap my cheek. And what a lunch! Rye bread and borscht, served by your father, and with such good nature, even after he had learned my name and drawn certain unavoidable inferences. Borscht, furthermore with bits of green onion floating in it. I was so happy to learn you were Russian! I consider myself a Russian, you understand. As a Jew, I am also a German, an Italian, a Frenchman, a Pole, I am all Europe—but a Russian, foremost.

I am sure that all this did not come to naught because I am a Jew. To begin with, you are the kind of gentile who knows how to say "goy"—a word I distinctly heard you use. There is only one nation on the earth—the nation of those who call the rest of the world "goyim." We Jews use it in contempt, because of our fears, but it is capable of elevation into a world of pride and brotherhood. No, that is not the reason why we "broke up." There are only two possibilities, one very flattering to me, the other, degrading.

To take the base one first, I observed, when I entered your house and when I was eating lunch, that you avoided all reference to WPA. You presented me to your father, and later to your brother, as an old friend from school whom you bumped into downtown while looking for a job. You would not admit that you had applied for WPA, and you would not have them know that I, too, had done so. What a false and wicked pride, and—since you evidently know something about such matters —what utter disloyalty to your class! Your father, a carpenter as I recall, was obviously unemployed. He had that look about him. And your brother, who was building a model aeroplane in the middle of the day, evidently had nothing better to do. So what was there to be ashamed of? And what if your mother, as I gather from her absence, was the only one working in the family? What of it? Must you be ashamed? But perhaps you were even more ashamed of me than of yourself. Perhaps the very fact that you met me in a relief station was enough to queer me. Then why flirt with me and bring me to your home?

But apart from all that, what a fool you were not to go through with your WPA application. I scoured all the rolls, inquired at all the projects where you might conceivably have been taken on, but no one had heard of you. Ah, what you missed! Myself, I went on the Writers' Project and compiled a 100,000 word report on pigeon racing in Chicago, including a life-size biography of Josiah Breen, the pigeon fancier. And what did you do? Pickle works, belt-buckle factory, typist, stenographer, secretary? You are a traitor to your class, Ellen, to your better instincts and your better capacities, and you allowed what we call "the most crucial experience of our generation" to slip by you. But this is a digression.

As I say, you may have been ashamed to know me, or to continue seeing me because I was going on WPA. Or perhaps, even because I had caught you in the act, applying for the national dispensation. This, of course, is only a possibility; and I may be wrong. Assuming that I am, and that you had your own and better reasons, there remains another possibility, which I am very eager to entertain. It does me good.

This is mystery. It involves a whole world, of which you are the hub. At the centre, beside you, let me place a young man, of respectable, and somewhat better family than your own, a man whom we shall call Willard. Am I warm? When we met, you had already known Willard for a period of two years. He, a serious fellow, perhaps a student of law, or already a lawyer, could not help but have serious intentions. He doesn't laugh very often, your Willard; and when you do, opening your mouth wide, it disconcerts him. Furthermore, when you suck pencils in his presence, or show him your tongue, he is more than a little embarassed. But what can you do about it? You were to marry him. You were then, I should judge, twenty-four, the age when one begins observing that a woman is not growing any younger. Besides, you are *used* to him, miserable habit. He is good to you, he's solid, he looks down on WPA, he smokes cigars. What then? How else are you to act when this wistful, melancholy, timid, cynical and so appealing young writer comes along and speaks to you as a man has never spoken before, and dwells on you, and intimates, and sighs and stares? It is, after all, shocking to discover that one's fiancé is not the ultimate man on earth, and that another, a man you met in a basement, who has never kissed you or walked you through the park, is capable of pre-empting the emotions you have already consigned and wrapped and, furthermore, of providing you with new ones. *Nyet, krasavitsa moya?*

Ellen, if this be true, then your reticence is a tribute! Thank you for ignoring me, thank you for your silence. For it means you realized, in those few hours, that going with me would make irrecoverable your whole past life and its commitments. After all, women have been known to keep several men on a string. Thank you for not binding me. For it means you feared the string, and where it might lead you. And what if the string should break? The fear that the string might break is the fear of love!

But look at all these pages I have written, and where will I find an envelope large enough? Ellen, unintentionally, merely out of a desire to say a few things I had not said before, I have invoked more of the past than I had intended. It has brought me back to that helpless, pitiful state of mind—I despise it—where a man lives on promises. I have drugged myself into believing what I believed three years ago—your promise to call me, to write to me, to see me again. Now I know you will write, if only a few words. And I know you will answer me at once.

Always yours,
Joe

Dec. 29

Dear Ellen,

Christmas passed, and nearly six days have gone by. I tell myself that you have been very busy over the holidays, that you haven't found time to write. But I knew full well that if you were going to write, you would already have done so. Why do you deny me this? Is it my pride or your presumption? Have I touched too sensitive, too deep a point? Or could it be that I have merely bored you?

I tell myself I have bored her. But how can that be when I still believe in the love she seemed to have offered me? Is it possible? If the world were made up of such haphazard, ill fitting emotions, no pattern at all would exist—it just wouldn't hang together.

Excuse me if I have used the word love in vain. But the more I have thought of you, the more I have grown to believe that I have a right to use it. It is almost as though I have written these letters to make myself believe that you love me. God knows what I have written! God knows why I go on!

I suppose every man sometimes has the urge to pour himself out, release all the stops and let go. My sense of caution should tell me that few men have the right to confess; only murderers and hardened criminals, never men who are merely unhappy. Those who have really committed crimes, those who have an actual guilt lying over them—they have something to say. But the rest of us—perhaps we become liars when we open our mouths, liars or pathetic wishers, and half of what we say may be false, and the other half merely the result of a vain striving for a sense of personal history.

Then why do I go on? Why do I persist in writing to you in the face of what must surely amount to a personal humiliation? I'll tell you why—and may the telling damn you! A man feels humiliated only when he is cast down from one position to a lower one. Some men never learn their lesson. No sooner humiliated, they attempt to injure someone else in return. These are the unpleasant characters, the personalities charged with an explosive that any touch may set off. Your Willard may be of such a type—not because he is mean; he may even be sweet in his own way—but only insofar as he lacks subtlety. But our other type of man is a different sort entirely. When he is humiliated he does not bound back with a rage that destroys his perception. Instead, he learns. He sees most clearly what concerns him most closely; and he accepts it and makes it a part of himself. When he has been utterly humiliated, he observes that he has touched bottom; having reached bottom, he knows there's no lower he can fall. There's a comfort, a perpetual cushion in certain kinds of misery—you rest on it, just as a contented man rests at the top of his career. Top or bottom, either way—but no struggling in the middle!

Does this succeed in explaining myself to you? Most likely not. I feel you must learn something about the way in which I live, in order to understand why, after three years have passed, I shower you with letters, to which I expect no answer.

I live in what I consider to be a state of exile. Among the friends I have at present is a certain Zampechini, an Italian refugee, and a certain Lutzek, a German refugee. I have told them, "Boys, we are in exile together. Not from our separate countries—but from history." But why proceed in this fashion, at this level, away over your head? It is enough to state briefly the following conditions:

1. I am alone.
2. There is a war on and I am out of it on all fronts; neither losing nor profiting by it, and not even employed.
3. I live in a rooming house, on the allowance my father very grudgingly gives me.
4. The last six women I approached unconditionally turned me down.
5. Ever since WPA folded up,

but never mind the rest.

I was going to tell you more. I wanted, first, to tell you everything; then, a little; now, nothing. Ah, what's the difference? I cannot bear to tell you what I have suffered, because I am proud of it, and it would only bore you. Enough. Let this be a last effort at explanation in a letter full of abortive efforts. As a man who, quite confidently, has touched bottom, both in what he has suffered and in personal esteem, I feel nothing I do can injure me. Your rebuffs are *not, definitely not* a further humiliation. I understand myself too well. I am of the brotherhood of paupers who endure everything at their own expense. And so, if I go out of my way and out of my time to reach after a promised happiness of three years back, this, too, a deliberate delusion, is also at my own expense. And perhaps even the greatest irony is my knowing that while you refuse to answer my letters, you also fail to understand them.

But, no fear. I shall plague you no longer.

Feigenbaum

Dec. 31

Dear Ellen,

Contrary to the word I had given, I called on you yesterday. I am writing today to identify myself, to make it perfectly clear that it was I, and no one else, who called.

He said you were out. Who, I do not know. Perhaps it was "your Willard." I believed him, made no further inquiries. I left no message and no name. In a fit of humiliation I withheld my name. I am writing today to repudiate that humiliation. It was not of the bottom variety; it was of the rising sort that struggles midway between its origins and its hopes. It was not true to nature. My humiliation admits no hopes.

Now that there can be no doubt in your mind as to the identity of your caller, I may go on to the next point. By calling on you I satisfied a partial longing. Naturally, complete satisfaction would have come only with my seeing you. But as it is I saw your house, the door which opened, the stairs that led up, the door that closed in my face. Willard does not count. I am indifferent to him. My point is that with yesterday's closing of the door I accepted as closed our whole relationship. I shall no longer plague you with letters, no longer make any attempt to see you. And this is the truth. You may rely on it, not because I have promised you—my promises are evidently as little to be trusted as yours. But it is so because I have at last accepted it, and have willed it to be so. I find that this decision, against which I have been fighting ever since your Xmas card came, has, surprisingly, liberated me.

For what I have to say actually has nothing to do with humiliation. Very simply, Ellen, I love you. It is so easy to say, and one can say it as well as another. Why did I have to torture myself?

I love you. And why do I love you? Because you came to me. Because, in the basement of the relief station you noticed me before I noticed you, and because your flirting was not in response to an act of mine, but an overture, an opening entirely of your own. For this, all my gratitude. Because, at a moment when you did not yet exist for me, I already existed for you. Isn't this reason enough?

No, it needs further explaining. I feel that the more I love you, the less you understand me. You must know that a man like myself, so deeply displeased, dissatisfied with himself as I am, can only be saved by an act of graciousness. A blessing, external and gratuitous must come to him. For he will destroy whatever is internal, whatever comes out of himself. The lower he falls, the more he will demand and the louder he will clamour for salvation. An absolute beggar demands the entire world.

This is why I love you. But if I love you because you flirted with me, I am, at the same time, inclined to disapprove your flirtatiousness. I could understand flirtatiousness in a nun. But in a woman like yourself, Ellen! A nun, let us assume, is repressed. But you! Not repression but *bonheur,* bliss at every pore. Now that I no longer need withhold anything, now that I am free, I may tell you what I felt when I first saw you. Believe me, and here enters another irony, my first sight of you was intuitive proof that I would have you! That is what is called spontaneous love. Love pre-exists in the heart, and when it finds its object, it leaps out and enters it and does its business, establishing a conviction, while the timid soul still tells itself it has no more than an "interest." But I do not delude myself. I saw and at once believed, and I knew what I saw and what I believed, and so strong was my conviction that even the three years that passed, and the frustrations of the last week have not deprived me of it. Yes, I was sure. Furthermore, I still am. For it will not go away. I still see you as I saw you then, excited, plump, in a tight black dress, your arms bare, your hair loose, your feet in sandal-shoes. I have torn that dress from you a thousand times, but I have done it reverently, in my mind observing that same delicacy, that attention to detail I would observe in fact. Thus I have seen you naked, and I do not revile myself with the thought that what is only imaginary for me must be actual for one or many a man. It is my possession. The nakedness with which I have endowed you is solid and unique, both in the actuality it has for me, and in its expression, which is entirely its own and not compounded of other women. Nor is the look of your body a wish fulfilment, for I do not assemble you out of separate female perfections—that art of day-dreaming! No, for your breasts, as I imagine them, are even too large for my preference and your thighs could do with a little less hair. I have, furthermore, distilled a set of odours to go with your hair and your arm pits, and these, again, are distinctive; and I have supplied your skin with textures, and have given you appropriate sounds—laughter for love play, a sharp intaking of the breath for passion, and a wildness of hissing and moaning devoid of all language. This is that solemn nakedness to which we bring not only our passion, but our capacity for sensual revenge. But it is not brutal; it is tender. And above all it is persistent in the face of a thousand complications I can never make out.

And then the pencil in your mouth, the tongue stuck at me, and the conversation and your waiting for me and the walk and the invitation to your house, the lunch, and your promise and the happiness almost, almost reached, and the conviction established beyond overthrowing! Was it from this that I was to expect denial?

We lean toward the imperfect—it was too good to be true. But this is no explanation. It will satisfy only a shallow, a sceptical intelligence. The perfect must be true! What else is perfection, and why do we demand it? But however I explain it, I still do not understand. I refuse to believe my own reasons.

What then? I love you enough to think evil of you. I am angry enough to know that what I saw and believed, you, too, saw—but did not believe. You acknowledged a conviction without sharing it. And nothing human can be colder!

Look how similarities endanger us. You, with the pencil in your mouth, knew me well enough, from your own traits, to destroy me. I am of the same erotic type as you. I, too, must be fed. My whole life can be explained by hunger. You knew you would have to offer, give, yield. If only you had not known! If only your perception had been clouded with that animal stupidity for which we are, occasionally, so grateful in women! Or, if only I had known better! I should have known that a woman will make a concession on one point only when she has prepared some reservation on another. As it was, you managed to concede everything, yet withheld everything. The evil in your flirtatiousness was that it went beyond flirtation: it offered love, real love, in order to snatch it away. It was the old game played to its fullest, criminal in its intelligence, the *absolute* cheat.

Well, it's over and done with. Of course, in outdoing me you also had to deny yourself. But a woman will count her self-denial at a small cost when the game is so large and she masters it. But it's over, it's over. Yet it persists. Certain patterns are dangerous. We form them once and follow them always. And if a man will attach, as I have done, a whole morality to a single incident, he will always be at the mercy of "incidents." The insight he will gain will give him no peace. He will be forced to employ it everywhere, with all the subtle damage it can do him. And at a time like the present when there is no place for unhappy men, no understanding they can count on, no mood they can share, what good will their insight do them?

But, Ellen, I release you. I go back to my own cares, reluctantly, I admit, but with a certain confidence. My place in the world—see how quickly one can spring from his place in bed to his place in the world! Can a woman do as much?—my place in the world is assured, no matter how difficult it be, for I am my own assurance. I am that man—and there are many like me—whose place is entirely contained in his own being. So long as I exist, that is my place, my function. I do not justify myself. I merely point this out: I have so little, so little pride, so little belief, so little outward appetite, I am so pared down to my own core, that I cannot help believing I am an essential man. And besides, WPA will come back, have no fear. Do you think I wrote my report on pigeon racing for nothing? It stands there in the files, waiting, ready to be taken up again. Some day, when the war is over, and the machines have been removed from the old buildings, after the dust has settled and the activity has died down, the steel vaults will be unlocked and the steel files will be brought out, and the pigeons will flutter again. Once again the world will take account of us—we bare, pared, essential men. The earth will once again acknowledge loneliness, as real as her own mountains. What else can be done? We may be a generation—we may, as well, be an eternity. But perhaps a new wrinkle in disasters? Perhaps the night and the wolves and the waves we howled about back in the 'thirties—when there was still a little twilight—will really come down to blot out, swallow, and wash us away? What will be will be.

One only looks to his own accountable and natural future. But here, I shan't write much longer. The New Year is coming. Ellen, Ellen, at last I am free. One moment you were my great bitterness, and now I am in the clear, rid of you. My life will find another bitterness, perhaps of a higher fresher quality, perhaps even a bitterness in some successful thing. What does it matter? I am cushioned at the bottom and only look forward to what I may expect. For after all, what is humiliation? It does not endure forever. And when it has led us underground to our last comfort, look, it has served its purpose and it is gone. Who knows when new heights may not appear? A man has only so much in common with his experience. The rest he derives from God knows where.

I believe some men are capable of rising out of their own lives. They stand on the same ground as their brothers, but they are, somehow, transcendental, while their brothers are underground. Their only secret is a tremendous willingness—they do not struggle with themselves!

Ellen, all I mean to say is this: I still believe in human happiness, and in my own to boot. If I cannot make my claim on you, I will make it on life, demand that existence satisfy the longings it arouses. It must, it must! For that is happiness: the conviction that something is necessary.

But how dare I speak of happiness? After all, I was once convinced that you were necessary. And what is necessity without fulfilment? Is it possible? I shall say it is. Be gentle to the unfulfilled, be good to it. We are accustomed to sing the joys of the happy, the fulfilled men. Let us also sing the joys of the desolate, the empty men. Theirs is the necessity without fulfilment, but it is possible that even to them—who knows?—some joy many come.

I forgive you and release you, Ellen. You are beautiful—go. But God, if you only knew, if you knew how willing I am—always—to take the risk of my happiness!

A Happy New Year!

Love,
Joseph

Pools

ARNOLD WESKER

Arnold Wesker was born in London in 1932. He was educated at Upton House School, Hackney. Primarily a playwright, his plays include *The Kitchen;* the trilogy, *Chicken Soup with Barley, Roots* and *I'm Talking about Jerusalem;* and *Chips with Everything.* In 1964 he won the Premio Mazzatto Prize for *Their Very Own and Golden City.* Wesker is married, has three children and resides in London.

Very slowly Mrs. Hyams took her card, number eight, from its slot, handed it to the timekeeper, and stepped out of the clothing factory into Brick Lane. As she walked home the evening smells of the East End met in her nostrils and mingled with the damp foggy air peculiar only to London at that time of the year.

Winter is a long time going, she thought, and so engrossed was she that it was some seconds before she realized she had turned into Flower and Dean Street instead of Fashion Street. She paused just past Katie's greengrocer shop and was, for the moment, lost. It was many months since she had come into this street despite its being the one next to her own. Just like a backyard, she thought.

She was about to retrace her steps when the idea occurred to her to pay a visit to Mrs. Levy. It would be only for a few minutes, for tonight was Wednesday night and she had many things to do at home. But she must see the old lady, especially as the Passover was so near.

Mrs. Hyams continued, then, down Flower and Dean Street nodding along the way at people she knew, and stopped by at one of the shops. There she bought a box of matzos, a quarter-pound of soft cheese, some chopped liver, butter, a loaf of bread, and a box of fancy biscuits. With these she crossed the road and walked to the last block but one of Nathaniel Buildings. It was dark now, and with caution, for the lamp was not very bright, she picked her way down the uneven steps to the cellar room where Mrs. Levy lived. She knocked and called out: "Mrs. Levy?" There was no reply. The second time she knocked and called out she placed her ear near the door. "Mrs. Levy?" There was a sound of a bed creaking and soon some feet rubbed their way towards her.

"Who is there?" a little voice asked.

"Me, Mrs. Levy, me—Mrs. Hyams." She heard the rattle of the latch and the door opened.

A very small woman, with blue watery eyes, poked her head round the corner. Behind her the room was in darkness. She blinked for a few seconds and then, recognizing who it was, switched on the light and opened the door wider. Once in, with the door closed, Mrs. Levy stepped back, drew her fingers to her mouth and in Yiddish said, as though speaking to somebody beside her: "Ooh, look!" and grinned, showing her few decayed teeth. With childlike excitement she offered a seat to Mrs. Hyams.

Mrs. Hyams sat down and Mrs. Levy placed herself on the edge of the bed, which was strewn with odds and ends of covering. The furniture was almost indiscernible in the dim light of the naked electric bulb. Behind Mrs. Hyams, further back into some dark corner, was an old deal table littered with an assortment of unopened tins of soup, jars, cardboard boxes, and papers. A sideboard stood on three legs, littered with dirty pans; on the mantelpiece was a glass case containing a stuffed bird and, curiously, a pile of pipe cases. Nothing had changed.

Mrs. Levy was about sixty now, four feet ten in height, plump, with large eyes that seemed to express amazement at what was going on around her, staring as does a baby who cannot quite get over the shock of being born. Her lips were wet and sagged and her tongue slithered about her gums. She was still pale. They spoke in Yiddish.

"Nu?" Mrs. Levy opened up her hands. "How are you? Why haven't you been to see us? It's a year now, you haven't been. Such a long time." She put her hand to her face and rocked it from side to side. "Such a long time."

"My daughter had a baby," Mrs. Hyams said.

"A baby?" Mrs. Levy gave herself a pleased little hug; she always felt honoured that Mrs. Hyams came to see her. "A boy she had or a girl?"

"A boy, Mrs. Levy, a boy."

"And she's all right, the daughter; and the boy, he's all right?"

"The boy," Mrs. Hyams said, leaning forward intimately and touching her hair, "has blond hair." Mrs. Levy leaned forward with her. "And his eyes, Mrs. Levy, are blue," and she leaned back as if to emphasize the fact, and Mrs. Levy copied her movements and leaned back as well. They both smiled.

"It's so long since you have been," said Mrs. Levy again. Mrs. Hyams lifted her shoulders and looked away; this meant —there has been no time. They were silent a few seconds. Then:

"Look," said Mrs. Hyams, bringing out the few things she had bought. "I've brought you some food, it will be Passover soon." One by one she placed the foodstuffs on the table and opened them up that Mrs. Levy might see.

"For me? For me you brought this? Ah, chopped liver. Now that *is* good. I thank you, I thank you. Really good. *You* made it? You yourself? Is it dear? You should not. You cannot afford it. I'll give you some money. Is there any borsht? A good drop of borsht?"

"No borsht, Mrs. Levy."

"Ah, never mind, I'm not short, you know." She grinned all the time, every now and then adjusting the shawl on her head or pushing away a lock of hair. She was almost purring.

For some half an hour longer the two women continued talking.

Mrs. Hyams told her friend that she too now lived alone, for her daughter had gone to Bermuda, where her husband had a post as a scientist in a factory; and her son lived outside London and could only come to see her once a week. Mrs. Levy nodded her head in commiseration. She nodded most of the time for one reason or another, but mostly it was by way of indicating that this, this was the way the world is. "And your husband . . ." she nodded slowly to acknowledge the terrible fact that he was killed in the war. "And my husband . . ." said Mrs. Hyams, and she nodded once or twice, thereby finishing the sentence.

"So now at least come down to us more often," Mrs. Levy said. "We're always in, you know."

"Why don't you go out a little," Mrs. Hyams asked her. "In the fresh air go. You are down here all the time."

"Wouldn't we like to," Mrs. Levy replied. "But now it's cold and we have nothing warm. We cannot go out like this." She spread her arms wide to reveal the same old rags she had been wearing for many years. Mrs. Hyams nodded.

Soon the atmosphere began to depress her; she could stay in the room no longer.

"I thank you, thank you," Mrs. Levy said at the door.

"Look after yourself," said Mrs. Hyams.

"We shall be well," replied the old lady.

II

Mrs. Hyams thought only of making her way home, for it was cold. At the bottom of the stairs of No. 43 Fashion Street, she paused for breath. Downstairs in the basement the furrier was still working, and so too were the buttonmakers in the shop in front.

As she started to climb the steps a sound of feet jumping two stairs at a time came towards her. Before she knew what had happened a young boy jumped to her side, snatched her bag from out of her hands, and ran up to the top landing where she lived. "You'll break your little neck one day," she cried as she proceeded to follow him. "Won't!" he cried back. He was on his way down again, but this time he slid along the banister and stopped on the landing below outside his own flat, where his mother was waiting.

"I saw you coming," said Mrs. Hickory, "so I waited till I heard you start and then——"

"So that's no good," Mrs. Hyams smiled. "I've got your chicken in the bag."

"Mervin," said Mrs. Hickory, and Mervin ran upstairs again to bring back the bag. Mrs. Hyams handed her friend the chicken. "Such a lovely chicken," she said.

"Cup of tea?" Mrs. Hickory asked.

"No thank you, no. There is so much I must do." She pinched Mervin's nose and made her way up to the top landing. She was puffing now. As she took out the key to her door, Mrs. Hickory called up: "Mrs. Hyams, thank you!" She did not wait for a reply. Some seconds later, just as Mrs. Hyams was about to hang up her coat, her neighbour called again. "Mrs. Hyams?" This time she added nothing, for Mervin appeared with something in his hand. "Letter!" he said and ran off. That family, Mrs. Hyams thought, has not said a whole sentence between them since they've been here.

She looked at the envelope; the foreign stamp on it told her that it was from her daughter. She did not hasten to open it but laid it behind one of the brass candlesticks on the mantelpiece until she was ready to read it. The first thing she did was to light the fire she had laid before leaving for work in the morning. This done she changed into some slippers, went out to the landing to put some water on to boil, and then set about making herself some eggs and chips. While the chips were frying she laid the table for herself and turned on the radio to hear the news headlines and then turned to attend to the fire, which needed more coal.

It was while she was doing this that Mrs. Hyams' thoughts returned to Mrs. Levy, for she suddenly recollected that Mrs. Levy had no fire. *That* was why the old lady had been in bed with all those clothes on.

Her memory suddenly awoke, and she recalled for the first time in many years how Mrs. Levy looked when she first saw her. Almost thirty-five years ago, when Mrs. Hyams was a girl of twenty and her husband, who lived in Flower and Dean Street, was courting her, she had seen this beautiful young woman of twenty-five. What was outstanding was her carriage and the proud way she walked. The young woman, daughter of a poor family in Bessarabia, was brought over to England by her rich, elderly uncle who married her. She was so lovely then, Mrs. Hyams thought, with some horror, but so green. Her husband, she recollected, used to make cigarettes; he had treated her as a princess; he did the shopping, the cooking, the housework. When she was thirty, he died. Then what happened, Mrs. Hyams wondered. She could remember the beginning and knew the ending, but the years between, these she had lost. It was this sharp contrast that gave her such an odd feeling. For the memory of the young Mrs. Levy was a memory of the young Mrs. Hyams, and she suddenly felt very, very lonely.

It was some minutes before she could move from the fireplace to attend to the chips. At last she did move and muttered to herself—I will. I *will* put Mrs. Levy on my list. Why she had not done so before she could not think and felt rather ashamed and guilty. This evening I will place her before my own holiday. And thus decided Mrs. Hyams sat down to eat her eggs and chips.

She chewed her food without interest. Odd thoughts passed through her mind; such as Mrs. Levy asking for borsht; Mervin sliding down the banister; her son would be along to supper in two evenings' time—as on all Friday nights; what had her daughter written. She was conscious of the silence. She could think with a lot of noise around her, read too, but the silence always disturbed her. Sometimes she moved simply that something should happen in the room.

Toward the end of her meal she began to hurry, eager now to read the letter from Bermuda; or was it that she could not bear to be doing the same thing for so long? She collected the dirty dishes, having drunk the remainder of her tea standing up, and took them outside to the little table on the landing. She would wash up when the letter was read. Then she returned, cleared away the rest of the table that had been so carefully set out, and sat in an armchair by the fire to read.

It was a letter like any other letter, but the mother heard the words she read and saw each scene. Occasionally she would laugh to herself or give a low, long hum, showing how well she understood her daughter's feelings. When she came to the paragraph concerning her grandchildren she cooed and hugged herself and murmured—bless them, bless them. Soon the heat from the fire began to affect her and slowly, after a few sad, sudden starts, her head sank to her left shoulder and was still.

After some minutes Mrs. Hyams awoke. Her first thought was to get up from the chair and attend to her very important task, but she went no further than laying her hands on the arms of the chair. Instead she sat back and lifted the letter once more to read. One thing she could not understand. What foolishness had taken her daughter away from her mother's care and advice? Mrs. Hyams spoke aloud to herself. "So what has she gained?" She turned to the fire and asked with her hands. "So what, tell me!" Then she caught herself talking to herself and smiled. "Such madness!" She rose, feeling oddly pleased with her own humour, and placed the letter behind the candlestick laughing and muttering: "Oi yoi, Mrs. Hyams you, what a you, Mrs. Hyams!" But in bringing her hand down from replacing the letter, she accidentally knocked a glass ashtray to the floor.

She jumped, stared at the broken pieces for a few seconds as though not certain what had happened and then, after trying very hard to swallow down lumps in her throat, gave in and wept.

It was a long time since Mrs. Hyams had cried. She hated tears; tears for her were weakness. Now she moved into the bedroom as though to hide from the presence of life which the fire in the front room suggested. There she sat on the edge of the bed with her eyes closed and choked with the effort not to cry. It was a battle soon won.

It was because I saw Mrs. Levy today, she told herself as she blew her nose. I really must do something for her. What kind of people are we to let a woman like that go down? Before returning to the other room she looked at herself in the mirror to make sure her face would not betray her. For some odd reason she poked her tongue out at herself and then, suddenly embarrassed at her own foolishness, she grinned shyly, and impatiently returned to the front room.

With a brisk, renewed vigour the broken pieces of glass were collected, the dishes washed up, and order restored to the room. This done, she stood on a chair by the window and closed the curtains; her movements were mechanical. From a small glass cabinet she took a pen and a bottle of ink; from behind one of the candlesticks withdrew an orange envelope; and from inside a white, bulbous china vase pulled out a folded sheet of lined foolscap. These things she laid in order on the table. Satisfied that she had forgotten nothing, she moved to the door and locked it. It was Wednesday night.

From the moment that Mrs. Hyams locked the door everything she did was done in complete earnestness. There was no doubt in her movements, nor did her mind for one moment question her actions. Mrs. Hyams was about to fill in her weekly football coupon and she believed that, sooner or later, but undoubtedly, she would win £75,000.

She took her place in the same chair and first of all opened out the folded sheet of paper. It was headed:

Things I must do with my £75,000

1. Buy a house large enough for my daughter, my son, their families and me to live in so that we are all together.
2. Present them with the money they need to live their lives.
3. Give my brothers Hymie, Stanley, and Martin £3,000 each.
4. Give my friend Lottie £1,000. And also Maurice, Jackie, Gertie.
5. Spend £20 on a holiday in a little seaside village.
6. Buy myself a pair of fur-lined boots for winter.
7. Pay back £10 to Steve Isaacs.

And so on. A long list of numbered items with each detail carefully written out, and changes seriously made as to the relative importance of certain articles of clothing.

Now she carefully scrutinized her list and made one more correction. In between items four and five, that is to say after giving £1,000 to Lottie, Maurice, Jackie, and Gertie and before allotting £20 for her holiday, she wrote:

5. Put aside £5,000 to help Mrs. Levy.

Then she folded up her list and laid it aside.

Filling out the coupon was reasonably easy, but Mrs. Hyams spent a great deal of time on it, starting first with her copy coupon. She staked her money only on the Treble Chance column, and on this she gambled two shillings and sixpence each week. Meticulously she described her "O's" in the little squares and carefully wrote out her name and address—not forgetting to place an "X" in the right place, for she wished no publicity when she won. The thing she was most careful about was not to make a blot or an erasure; her one horror was that they would disqualify her winnings no matter where that blot lay or despite that the erasure was obviously explicable. The pattern of her forecast was the same each week. She backed the same numbers regardless of which team played which, and these very numbers were the ones her husband and son before her had used.

When her husband was alive nothing used to irritate Mrs. Hyams more than Wednesday night, pools' night. Every week he would ask her to write it out for him because he was afraid of making a mistake; every week he asked her whether or not he should change the numbers he used. "Will Stockport and Wolves draw, do you know?" he would ask. "If I knew," she replied, "I'd tell you, fool!" When her husband died her boy took to doing the pools, but he married at nineteen and spent his first five married years abroad in the army. Soon afterwards her daughter married. In a short, perplexing period of time her whole family, the point of her existence, had broken up. It was some years before she regained her self-possession. Time and routine hardened her; life moved in her despite herself. She forced pleasures in trivialities, making do with the remains. Soon the sense of loyalty with which she took up the pools gave way to a sense of imperativeness. She *must* win the pools, because with this money she would piece together the ruins of her family. This gave to her a calm such as a wonderful secret can give; a calm disturbed only by loneliness, when she would hurry to her brothers or a friend.

That night Mrs. Hyams spent a longer time than usual filling out her coupon. She became another woman, even to look at. The intense concentration she used showed in her eyes and the way her skin curled above them; her tongue protruded and was held still by her lips, her glasses fell halfway down her nose.

But this evening the effort was too much. When she finished Mrs. Hyams was very, very tired. Visiting Mrs. Levy, receiving the letter, breaking an ashtray, and then crying was a great deal to go through in an evening after work. Fortunately, tomorrow she was not working. At the age of sixty, three days a week was all she managed. Tomorrow she could lie in, which meant that the coupon had to be posted tonight in order to catch the first post Thursday morning. Liverpool was a long way, and it had to be there in time. But there were all those stairs to walk down and climb up again. She could not face it that evening. Instead, she did something she had never done before. She called down to Mrs. Hickory and asked if she minded sending her boy out to post a letter, please.

In the past anything that had to do with Mrs. Hyams' football coupon she saw to herself, from filling to checking. Now she regretted breaking her rules the moment the boy had run off. Would he ever get there? she wondered. Might he not lose it or put it in the wrong box? He was only a boy after all. Mervin was away for a few minutes, which to her seemed hours; as soon as he returned she questioned him. Where had he taken it? Why was he so long? Had anybody stopped him? And not only on that evening but every other evening she catechized him until Sunday morning, when she was able to check up and discover that it did not matter because that had not been her lucky week.

She did not check her coupon on Saturday nights. To her mind the results were too haphazardly arranged and one could not be certain if they were all correct. The order and certainty of a Sunday paper alone satisfied her.

III

This coming Friday she felt she had something interesting to say to her son about Mrs. Levy. She spent all day in preparing the evening meal, which that week consisted of a barley soup and a sweet-smelling *Chulant*, to be followed by a trifle, and thought how best she could make her announcement so that her son would at once be interested.

Each week Mrs. Hyams planned a sort of climax to her son's weekly visit, for she felt, vaguely, that her boy was not always pleased to spend Friday night with her. Friday night was after all the night before Shabbat, a night when all good Jewish families were together, and she surely had a right to ask of him that she see her children for one day of the week. True, she had not brought him up religiously—still, Friday night was Friday night. So she looked for topics of conversation or made an issue of trivial occurrences, sometimes bought a present for him or his wife and always some chocolate for the grandchild.

At precisely six o'clock she could hear right from the bottom of the stairs a tiny voice calling: "Grandma, boba, grandma, boba," and it continued up until the time the little boy crept round the one but last flight and stood grinning at her. "Lobus!" she cried and hurried down the remaining flight to pick him up in her arms. She kissed her son and her daughter-in-law and asked: "Nu? How are you?"

Stephen was a great deal taller than she, with a small head on his shoulders and a large nose in his head as though to balance him. His disproportion would not have mattered had he been a gay person. As it was, his heavy features were worsened by a bored, guttural look which so many young Jewish men have upon their faces. Stephen was bored with his job, his family, and himself. He and his generation had not the stamina of their parents. He bent low and kissed her and replied with a slight impatience as though the question were asked too many times: "*Azoi!* Like so! What else?" and they all made their way into the little room which was laid out for supper.

As always happened, little Jeremy occupied most of the conversation, jabbering away about what he had done that week, what he had told God and what God had said to him; how he had seen a shooting star one night and if Jesus was a Jew, grandma, why didn't he look like daddy and have a black beard instead of a light one, and isn't this a lovely supper. Until he talked himself to sleep and they laid him softly on the couch while they themselves sat on till about ten in the evening.

Before sitting down Mrs. Hyams took out a bowl of fruit and nuts and sweets and asked if they had had enough to eat. "A nice supper," said Stephen without looking up from the paper. "You always did like *Chulant*," said Mrs. Hyams. Then they were silent for some minutes. Miriam dozed in her chair.

Stephen cracked nuts with his teeth and continued to read the paper. Mrs. Hyams was wondering whether to mention her topic yet. She decided not to and instead went out to the kitchen to put on some water for tea. Then she was back in her chair looking at the fire. Stephen cracked nuts and Miriam dozed on her other side. Mrs. Hyams was up again and from the mantelpiece handed her son the letter from his sister.

"From Aida?" Stephen read the letter, shrugged his shoulders and handed it back.

"A good letter, yes?" Mrs. Hyams said. "Have some sweets."

"A good letter! A good letter!" he replied somewhat testily. "It's a letter, so?"

"You think she's doing all right out there?"

"Why not?"

"She seems happy."

"Look, she wants to live in Bermuda so let her live in Bermuda. I wouldn't, but it's her life. If she'd listened to me——" Stephen wagged his finger and then cracked another nut.

"You're right, you're right," his mother cooed. "Why don't you eat some fruit?" Again they were silent. Outside a low fog hung in the narrow streets; a few doors away the moan of a row was audible; the last cries of stubborn children echoed in the air and a barrow from the market was wheeled over the uneven stones, a weary, bored rattle.

They drank two cups of tea each and the conversation slugged with not much enthusiasm. About half an hour before the guests were to leave, Mrs. Hyams made them their last cup of tea to be drunk with some apple strudel she had baked, and then said to Stephen:

"You know what, Stevee, I'm going to add something to my list."

"Oh, mum, not again. That silly list of yours. As if you were going to win £75,000."

"I saw Mrs. Levy on Wednesday." Mrs. Hyams ignored his outburst.

"So."

"So nothing. So I'm just telling you. She makes me feel ashamed, Stevee. Such a place to live in."

"Everyone she feels pity for, everyone. Have you seen a woman like her, have you? So now I suppose you're going to give Mrs. Levy a couple of thousand pounds?" And here he smiled sweetly at his mother, feeling that he had to indulge her sometimes.

"Five thousand pounds," she said, "after giving £1,000 to Lottie, Maurice, Jackie and Gertie, and before I take £20 for my holiday."

"Isn't that rather a lot?" said Miriam. "She can't have so much longer to live."

"No matter. £5,000."

They gently picked Jeremy up in their arms and said their farewells. Mrs. Hyams kissed the sleeping child and when they were halfway down the stairs she outed the light of the room that she might the better see them from her window and wave. As she gazed she decided never again to mention her list or her pools to her children. Then she cleared up the last cups and went straight to bed, for the following day she had promised to look after Mrs. Broom's two children while Mrs. Broom attended the funeral of her sister-in-law. Mrs. Broom was one of her neighbours two doors away in Fashion Street.

IV

That following week was a depressing week. It rained almost every day. Returning from work on Wednesday night after the slow hours at the machine the little woman seemed reluctant to go home. At such times the East End impressed its slum upon her more than usual; the smells, which at moments were friendly, made her sick. The dirty sky fell over the buildings and seemed only an arm's length away. Brick Lane in particular was a gutter. People rushed past, and cars splashed her. Not even the market seemed to cry to her. And so, in this inhuman street, on this inhuman day, Mrs. Hyams lost, with good nature, her good nature.

Feeling that she ought to see Mrs. Levy once more, she stopped at the top of Flower and Dean Street. But she changed her mind. "No, I won't go. Can I help it if Mrs. Levy is unhappy? I'm unhappy. So what! So who cares? So Mrs. Levy can wait, she can. I'm no angel!" And with this ill temper she returned to her rooms.

It was pools' night tonight, but she was in an odd mood. Having eaten her supper and spread her coupon before her, Mrs. Hyams felt suddenly hopeless. "Why," she asked herself, "should Mrs. Hyams win £75,000? What is so special about this Mrs. Hyams and her family that is not so special about another Mrs. Hyams and her family?" She laid down her pen. "Finished! Not another penny." Then she stood up and moved to the fireplace, which she poked irritably. Confronting herself in the mirror she waved the poker at her image. "You, Mrs. Hyams, you! You *mishiginah,* you! Every time you post your coupon, five other people post it in just that second. And how many seconds are there?" She nodded to herself. "And how many boxes are there?" Again she nodded. "And everybody thinks that for their little penny they're going to get £75,000. You know that, Mrs. Hyams?" She sank into the armchair still holding the poker. "It's such a big world. Who's going to give you all that money? You break your heart every week. You want meat pies in the skies." This time it was a very sagacious nod, and she paused as though to fully digest what she told herself; then she whispered, moving her head so slowly that it almost nodded her to sleep: "We got no real dreams any more." She shrugged her shoulders at the fire. "Nu?" she asked herself in Yiddish, "so what shall I do else?"

She turned back to the table and was about to sit down when a sudden answer came. "Tear it up I can do, that's what!" She lifted the coupon as if to throw it on the fire. But the moment of rebellion died too soon. Again she said in Yiddish: "Indeed, what shall I do else!" Methodically, with great concern, her tongue protruding a little between her lips, Mrs. Hyams completed her pools' coupon not forgetting to put an "X" in the place to indicate she wanted no publicity when she won.

V

But the winter does pass; even in the East End the sun on any building imprints its spring; and Itchy Park, that small cemetery between the high church in Commercial Street and Christ Church School in Brick Lane, where the tramp sits and the child plays, has trees that leaf and a green smell.

And with spring came a little surprise to Mrs. Hyams. For helping them through the hardships of last winter and many winters before, the neighbours in Fashion Street rewarded the obliging old lady by collecting among themselves some £20. This they presented to her and hoped it would be enough to pay for a holiday that summer. Mrs. Hyams was embarrassed at first and refused: "I've done nothing. I've never heard of such a thing. I don't need the money!" But eventually she succumbed. "For me? Twenty pounds? Such a lot of money."

When they left her Mrs. Hyams returned to her room and laid the twenty pounds in neat piles of five on the table before her. "Such a lot of money," she repeated. She sat for a long time feeling a great love for humanity and herself, then she rose, went to the mantelpiece and withdrew from behind the candlestick her precious list. Between the item giving £5,000 to help Mrs. Levy and that allotting herself a pair of fur-lined boots for winter was the reminder that she should spend twenty pounds for a holiday in a little seaside village. This she now crossed out. "Why not?" she said to herself.

For many days she gossiped excitedly to her good neighbours about her holiday.

"Going on your own?" they asked.

"Why not?" she replied proudly. "I'm old enough!" They asked her where she planned to go. "I'm not sure," she answered. "Not yet. I'm not sure. But I'll tell you where I'm not going," she added in a whisper as though it were blasphemy. "I'm not going to Southend and I'm not going to Bournemouth and I'm not going to Brighton!"

The only person who offered any advice where in fact she could go was the young, bespectacled, arty-looking man in the post office where she bought her postal order. He knew just the place to suit her.

"A little guest house near to the seaside village of Burnham Deepdale on the north coast of East Anglia, and you can get there straight from Liverpool Street Station. Beautiful, Mrs. Hyams; some friends of mine, you see. Far from the madding crowd——"

"The which crowd?"

"—peace, rest, the smell of the salt air. Come and go as you please. Sands nearby, cliffs and the North Sea stretching like eternity before you."

"Like who?"

"Only five guineas a week and excellent food."

"Kosher?"

"Hardly," the young man smiled.

"Still, perhaps it doesn't matter," Mrs. Hyams said. "Now is modern times, we must do like the Romes do, eh? It sounds very nice," she added. It sounded so nice, in fact, that Mrs. Hyams eventually decided that there was where she would spend her vacation, in late September, so as to miss the main holiday rush.

The young man in the post office, with the utmost good nature, undertook to write to his friends and make all the necessary arrangements, while Mrs. Hyams, adopting a carefree attitude, insisted on nothing in the terms except the appearance of a Sunday newspaper. It can all take care of itself, she decided, and when she handed the young man ten guineas to pay for a two-week sojourn, she said: "Na!" and placed complete trust in him.

VI

The seaside village of Burnham Deepdale turned out to be just as Mrs. Hyams wanted it to be. Each house was a different shape; the streets were narrow and most were cobbled. Here and there was a thatched roof, and despite the appearance of about three boarding houses in what was presumably the main street, yet there was no sign of commercialization.

For some minutes Mrs. Hyams stood outside the station and wondered what it was that was missing. She felt something should happen. There she stood, a case at her side, in the white air with her head cocked to one side. Soon the hiss of the sea, slowly and rhythmically rolled into her ears. She had left behind the noise of London, that was it. She felt very happy.

The hosts at the guest house, which was two miles away from the village, proved, however, to be a little queer. Mr. and Mrs. Mortimer were a young couple. They had three children who managed to be in so many different places at once that they seemed to multiply themselves each minute. Mr. Mortimer was partly bald, wore a white T shirt, a red scarf, blue jeans and sandals, and smoked a pipe. Mrs. Mortimer wore a blue T shirt, a white scarf, red jeans and sandals, and smoked a cigarette. The two youngest children, boys aged three and four, were naked; the third, a girl aged six, wore only knickers. Mrs. Hyams was not what they had expected, and the young couple were not what Mrs. Hyams expected. After saying: "How do you do, I'm Mrs. Hyams," she pointed to the children, who were staring at her, and raising her hand to her mouth asked with concern: "They won't catch cold?" This brought a bellow of laughter from Mr. Mortimer, in which everyone soon joined and the first awkward moment was passed and forgotten. Mrs. Mortimer cuddled her guest and gaily showed her to her room, while the guest, determined to remain carefree, took in the Bohemian atmosphere which was as new as the fresh air and so part of it.

It was Friday. Mrs. Mortimer told her that there had been no other guests for the past week, but more were expected on the following Monday. Mrs. Hyams had a whole week end in which to find her way around. She would be an old inhabitant by the time the others came, and that position just suited her.

"Now this really is summer," said Mrs. Hyams on being led into her room. It was a corner room that had windows on two walls of the house. The sun spent all but the evening in it, and just now was bandying its full light from wall to wall. Here it was at home and she felt that the city amounted to not very much after all.

Perhaps more than anything this occupied Mrs. Hyams' excited mind: that four hours ago, maybe more, she was in London and now she was in a strange bedroom looking at the sea a mile away. She said the name "Fashion Street" to herself, then murmured "Burnham Deepdale." She smiled. She thought and spoke the name "Mrs. Rosenberg," then "Mrs. Mortimer." The different images that these two names conjured up amused her and she continued, muttering to herself: "Beigels—shrimps. Shmultz herring—Mr. Mortimer. Gefülter fish—bacon. Toochas—Mrs. Mortimer. Petticoat Lane—Burnham Deepdale." And all the time she giggled to herself and worked herself into the most delighted of humours. Why she could hardly remember what Mrs. Levy looked like. Rising, she looked into the mirror and grinned sheepishly. "Ah you, Mrs. Hyams, you!" she said, then turned to look at her room. It was a nice room. Nothing had gone wrong.

Mrs. Hyams washed herself and, despite that she was tired, surprised Mr. Mortimer by asking if there was a café nearby where she could have some tea and cake. There was none, but a bus was due within ten minutes which would take her to the village.

"Such a long time you wait for the bus?"

"Run every hour," Mr. Mortimer replied.

"Oh, my Gawd!" exclaimed the astonished Londoner. "And you don't complain to the company or something?"

Mr. Mortimer, not knowing whether to take the last suggestion seriously or not, managed to smile and pointed out where the bus would stop.

The Mortimers considered their guest quite strange, but "Nice, darling, and amusing rather." It was, they supposed, understandable to want to wander out as soon as you came to a guest house on holiday. A little odd, however, not to change or even unpack. They spent some time discussing her. She had not even left word as to whether she would be in for supper or not, though no doubt she would—it was part of the fee—and accordingly Mrs. Mortimer prepared the food.

It was a cold supper, but even had it been hot it would have become cold, for Mrs. Hyams had not returned at the hour when it was time to eat. She had left at four o'clock, and by nine o'clock the Mortimers had become concerned. They decided to wait until 10:30, when the last bus came from the village, and then if she was not on that they would contact the police.

There was no need to have worried, however, Mrs. Hyams was on the last bus. She was very much alive and greeted her running hosts as though she had known them for a long time. But she was extremely tired and told them: "Wait till we get in the house; such a time! I'll tell you."

Once settled, Mrs. Hyams closed her eyes. "It's so-oo lovely." Without opening them, she continued: "Such sand and stones. The air—you feel you want to rub your face on it." Her eyes opened. "I walked twenty miles from the village to the lighthouse along the sands——"

"Two miles," corrected Mr. Mortimer.

"—and I looked in all the shops. Oh, pretty shops! And I lay underneath the sun and—guess what! I bought a sixpenny cornet and I sucked it all!" The couple laughed. Mrs. Hyams lay back again and closed her eyes once more. "Then I went and had a meal and then I went to the pictures."

"To the pictures!" they exclaimed.

"Sure, why not. Nothing else to do."

Mrs. Hyams drank the cup of tea that was made for her and with a tired, aged ecstasy reiterated her pleasure at being there, and retired to her room. She would leave unpacking till the morning; all she did was open her bag, make sure the copy of her pools' coupon was there and with it the entry form for the following week, undressed and delved slowly into a deep, comfortable sleep.

The following morning the long arm of a tender sun touched open her eyes. A sensation that was too sweet to contain made her hide her head under the blankets. When eventually she emerged she could see through the window on her right side half the sun and a clear, blue sky. She had never seen it so blue before. She did not move, but stared till her eyes could hold the colour no longer, then she slid once more beneath the blankets and sighed so deeply that she coughed.

For the rest of the day the sky remained blue. Being the first impression her mind received in the morning, it affected all she saw. Even the mad lanes and the crazy cottages were a sweet, ethereal, dreamy blue.

She lay on the sands under a newspaper, eating sandwiches prepared for her by Mrs. Mortimer, leaning against the hard walls which looked like a village street placed on its side. A stray dog came up to her as she ate and settled at her side as though she had mastered it for years. But what enhanced the friendly atmosphere of the little village even more was when a small, muddy-faced boy, who had been standing watching her for some minutes with his shy hands behind his back, suddenly approached, as though having finally decided she was capable, threw a ball to her, which she missed, and waited for her to throw it back. Of course she bought him an ice cream, and in return he took her along the sands in the opposite direction she had gone the day before and showed her a real cave, one that harboured nothing more than some washed-up pieces of green wood. To her great consternation the child then began clambering over the rocks and returned with a nest of eggs. "You'll take them back?" she asked him. "Now, how would you like it if I took you away from your mother, eh? But what lovely eggs!" The child laughed, tiny laughter in all that blue sea.

Mrs. Hyams returned for supper in the evening and spent two slow hours writing to her son and her friend Mrs. Cohen. To Mrs. Cohen she wrote simply:

> It's much more than I expected here. Everything seems like blue, and I am very grateful to you and Mrs. Rosenbaum and Mrs. Jeremiah and all of you for the happiness you have caused me. I wish you was with me in the sea. Such sea is here is like somebody moved it there and could call for it tomorrow. I can't tell you how it's so nice, but maybe all being well in two weeks I shall tell you.
>
> Your very good friend,
> *Mrs. Hyams*

To her son she wrote a long letter telling him not to worry, she would soon be back and, by the way, she fancied some pickled cucumber.

Mrs. Hyams was awakened on Sunday morning by Mrs. Mortimer, who entered carrying a tray of breakfast.

"Ah, hello and good morning, Mrs. Hyams. *This* is not usual." She smiled and laid the tray by the bed. "But," she added, helping Mrs. Hyams to sit up, "as you are our only guest at the moment and as we think a special lot of you, we are making an exception."

"You shouldn't," said Mrs. Hyams. "I haven't had breakfast inside my bed for nearly ten years now." She looked at the tray and noticed there was no Sunday paper as she had ordered. "I suppose," she asked, "the papers I ordered are downstairs?"

"Papers, Mrs Hyams?" exclaimed Mrs. Mortimer. "We don't read them in this house. Only the *Statesman* at week ends."

"Has that got the football results?" Mrs. Hyams asked. The young woman laughed. "But I asked the Post Office man specially to order them."

"Oh, Clinton? *He* said nothing. Papers are such a waste of money today. Lies, gossip, sports, etc. We just don't bother."

"But I must have a paper," Mrs. Hyams said, as though it were surely obvious to everyone why she must have one.

"Perhaps you can get one in the village later on," replied Mrs. Mortimer. "Now drink up, dear, and eat well." And with that she went from the room, leaving Mrs. Hyams dazed by this most unexpected blow. It was so silly not to have a newspaper in a house. How could she check her pools? The city had never let her down.

As though working out what had happened she sat, unmoving, propped up in bed. The sky was clear. A gull flew very close to the window. Somewhere one of the Mortimer children was crying "Mummy, Mummy."

How could she check her pools without a Sunday paper?

The sun felt very warm on her arm. A slight breeze blew the curtain towards her. It was very quiet now. Only the sea brushed its hair with long, feminine arms, humming ecstatically to itself.

Confused between Fashion Street and Burnham Deepdale, wondering now how she came here, Mrs. Hyams lost her way and could only close her eyes. She saw her coupon spread before her on the table at home, a Sunday paper at its side. "I must have a paper," she muttered, and so saying moved clumsily and hurriedly out of bed and dressed. She left the house, taking only her purse with her.

"I'm going to the village for a paper," she told the surprised Mortimers on her way out. Mr. Mortimer looked at his wife.

"White's may have some still, or Hoy's, eh, darling? But," turning to Mrs. Hyams and smiling, "it's a small place. Can't chance many extras, can they? Still——"

"Oh, Mrs. Hyams," Mrs. Mortimer spoke. "Jonathan and I are taking advantage of the fact that we only have one guest. I know you won't mind. We're taking the children out for a picnic. Back about fourish, won't we, dear?" She turned to her husband, who nodded. "But there's plenty to eat, cold salads and the like. You can find your way around, can't you?"

Mrs. Hyams thanked them and walked very quickly to the bus stop, rolling slightly, like a sailor, though a bus was not due for many minutes. It was ten o'clock and the day was in its lovely innocence. But not the day's innocence nor the sky nor the scented air did Mrs. Hyams notice. She must only hurry and try to find a newspaper. For how, she asked herself again, can I see if I have won my pools? And if I've won, how can I tell them when I don't know? If I don't tell them, she reasoned, I shall not get my money.

The bus drew up all too slowly and with a teasing gurgle continued, in holiday mood, to dribble happily along the road to the village.

The two shops, White's and Hoy's, had no papers left. "You don't keep any back?" she asked. "So if visitors come they can't have? They must go without?" She left the shops in disgust.

The streets were deserted. Sunday hung empty and pure over the village. Not knowing what else to do she walked towards the beach. Her steps took her to one of the boarding houses. She stopped outside and looked through the windows like a hungry, envious pauper, at the residents sitting in the lounge inside. They were all of them reading newspapers. Her first impulse was to walk in and ask to look at one. Shyness overcame her. How could she ask to look at a newspaper simply to check her pools? She felt ashamed and sheepishly moved away.

As she approached the other boarding house a young man came out reading a paper. At the gate he paused to digest more intently something that interested him. Mrs. Hyams moved quickly.

"Excuse me, forgive me," she said. The young man lowered his paper and smiled at her.

"Yes?" he asked.

She hesitated. "Can you tell me the way to the beach?" she said instead.

In the indolence of the country she had been too free, intoxicated with the freshness of her change. At home she could rely on life, here nothing mattered.

Just as she was regretting ever having come on holiday she saw a boy on a bicycle delivering newspapers. It all happened very quickly. He had a spare paper and gave it to her. She gave him a shilling and told him to keep the change. As a child who laughs through its tears on being given the toy it had been forbidden to play with, Mrs. Hyams hugged the newspaper and hurried, laughing, noticing the blue sky, smelling the air again, to a café that seemed to have opened only out of habit. She could now check her pools.

But her coupon was not with her. She had left it in her handbag in the bedroom. Or was it out of her bag on the floor? And had Mrs. Mortimer swept it up? She must return at once. Slowly obsession followed upon urgency like the next man in the queue.

She waited twenty minutes for a bus to crawl up to her like a guilty dog. The conductor was the same who had brought her into the village. She fumbled with her money and gave him a farthing instead of a sixpence. The twopence change dropped to the floor. She lay the paper on the seat and bent to pick them up, but the conductor reached there before her and handed them back, saying what fine weather it was.

Was the coupon on the table or in her bag? She was so taken up with this thought that she noticed too late the bus go past the guest house. Awkwardly she jumped up and asked for the bus to be stopped. Her thoughts and her actions betrayed her at each point for, in hurrying from the bus she forgot the paper and realized this only when she discovered that in fact her coupon was quite safe in her handbag.

Exhausted and frustrated, Mrs. Hyams sank on the bed and moaned like an old woman lamenting a death. Defeated at every turn, her holiday collapsed about her. She lost confidence. There remained only one thing to do—return to London.

To Mrs. Hyams this seemed not only obvious, but simple, for surely Fashion Street was not far away, and there in London she could get a newspaper and check her pools. Hastily she packed her bags, scribbled a note to the kind Mortimers, and waited for a bus to take her to the station. The conductor was the same as had accompanied her on her previous two journeys.

So complete is the satisfaction of a final decision that one does not consider alternatives; that is, why Mrs. Hyams did not think to ask the conductor if he had picked up her paper which was lying in his case at that moment; nor did she feel annoyed that people in the carriage of her train were the proud possessors of five different Sunday journals. Liverpool Street Station would be filled with news vendors. It was not that she was calm now, but that a subdued hysterical smugness came over her. It was the child again, happy with her promise of the toy, yet waiting to burst into tears should anyone frustrate her more.

Mrs. Hyams began thinking of her list and how lovely it will be to fulfil all the items. Seventy-five thousand pounds was a lot of money. But why had she not been able to find a newspaper? It was such a common thing. Perhaps it was a good sign. Of course. This is the way all luck stories turn out. For ten years she had received her papers regularly, but apart from an odd pound or so nothing big had ever come of her weekly gamble. And now, now she had not been able to find one she had won. She would reach London, buy her paper, and then send the telegram. Then she would go to her son's house and discuss it all with him. She could not go back to Fashion Street, the neighbours might be offended at her quick return. That was life for you.

The train arrived later than she anticipated. It was beginning to get dark. The smell of the station fitted sweetly into place, but Mrs. Hyams did not stop to savour her homecoming. Had she done so she might have collected her wits and made order out of the confused movement of traffic. As it was the station loomed large and busy. People rushed and the noise grew and subsided, rocking and heaving like a large woman breathing in a nightmare. In and out of the crowds, having left her case at the luggage office, she made her way to where the papers were usually sold. But the first stall was emptied and the second was deserted, and the third sold lascivious magazines, and the fourth had only soiled copies of last night's papers, a fifth had flowers, and a sixth was packing up having just sold a last copy.

Where were the papers? Had London gone mad not to have news? I must send a telegram she thought.

She wandered back to the station, too dazed to remember the little sweet shop at the corner of Artillery Row. It was so late and Liverpool was such a long way away. She muttered to herself: "I must let them know I've won."

Under the stairs near to the entrance stood a row of telephone kiosks with their doors open like sentries at ease. Trembling now, she dialed "O" and waited for a long time till the operator answered.

"Number please?"

"This is Mrs. Hyams of 43 Fashion Street, London, E.1. Send a telegram and tell them I've won before it's too late."

"You want telegrams, madam," a soft voice at the other end said. "Hold the line, please, I'll put you through."

"Send a telegram to pools, please," she cried to the new voice, and told them again her name and address.

"Which pool are you claiming, caller?" asked the operator.

"Penny Points—no, Treble Chance," for a moment she was not certain. "I've won £75,000, haven't I?" she asked, hoping that the man at the other end had in some way a connection with such a vast organization.

"Please place 3s. 9d. in the box, caller, and then press button A," was all he replied.

This done, she tumbled out of the hot kiosk and stood for a second trying to control her excitement. It was all so much for an old woman. She was wondering what to do next when she noticed, fluttering on the floor, dirty and forgotten, the front and back page of a Sunday newspaper. She was disturbed. The reality at last of a newspaper emerged from another world and vaguely threatened her. As if not content merely to remind her of reality the paper fluttered again, demanding to be picked up. Looking shyly around to make sure she was not being watched, she bent down suddenly and retrieved it. It was today's. But where would she go now to check her pools?

Nearby was the women's toilet. She entered. But she could not check up there before the attendant and a long line of hostile mirrors. There remained only one place. Once inside the small cubicle, though alone and unseen, Mrs. Hyams felt embarrassed as she pulled down the seat cover upon which to rest her copy. Carefully she folded the newspaper leaving in sight in the smallest space possible all the results she wanted. Then, withdrawing a yellow pencil from her handbag she checked, one by one, her entries on her coupon.

Now that the excitement was over she could not recollect why it had ever been. Her feelings were bruised, but she and the world were quite normal now. "Why," she said to herself, "should Mrs. Hyams win £75,000 anyway?" She walked out of the toilet into the huge dome of the station. "Who is Mrs. Hyams?" she asked, walking toward the luggage office. Idly she bumped into someone and said: "I beg your pardon," then continued among the crowds and answered herself: "She's no one. She's nothing. So? Nu?"

(Winter 1958-59)

Acknowledgments

Acknowledgments and thanks are due to the following authors and publishers for permission to reprint stories: to Philip Roth and Houghton Mifflin Company for *The Conversion of the Jews*; to Yehuda Yaari and Karni Publishers Ltd., for *The Judgment of Solomon*; to Nadine Gordimer and Victor Gollancz Ltd., for *Face from Atlantis* from *Six Feet of the Country*; to Methuen & Co. Ltd. and Criterion Books, Inc., for *First Love,* reprinted by permission of S. G. Phillips Inc., from the *Collected Stories of Isaac Babel,* copyright 1955 S. G. Phillips, Inc.; to Leo Rosten, Constable & Co., and Harcourt Brace & World Inc., copyright 1937 and reprinted with their permission for *Mr. Kaplan and the Magi* from *The Education of Hyman Kaplan;* to Dan Jacobson, Weidenfeld & Nicolson Ltd. and Little Brown Inc., copyright 1956 and reprinted with their permission for *The Zulu and the Zeide* from *A Long Way from London;* to Alexander Baron and *The Jewish Chronicle* for *My Grandmother's Hands;* to Brian Glanville and Secker & Warburg Ltd., for *A Betting Man* from *A Bad Streak*; to Mrs. Isaac Rosenfeld and *Partisan Review* (1945) for *The Hand that Fed Me*; to S. Yizhar for *The Prisoner*; to Arnold Wesker and *The Jewish Quarterly* for *Pools.*

Gimpel the Fool by Isaac Bashevis Singer is reprinted by permission of Farrar, Straus & Giroux, Inc. Copyright 1953 by The Viking Press, Inc., Copyright © 1957 by Isaac Bashevis Singer.

Angel Levine is reprinted from *The Magic Barrel* by Bernard Malamud, by permission of Farrar, Straus & Giroux, Inc. Copyright 1955, 1958 by Bernard Malamud.

Act of Faith, copyright 1946 by Irwin Shaw. Reprinted from *Mixed Company,* by Irwin Shaw, by permission of Random House, Inc. Originally appeared in *The New Yorker.*